PATH OF JUSTICE

A Mara Brent Legal Thriller Novel

ROBIN JAMES

I

Neveah Ward stared at me from a pair of stunning, amber eyes that held far more wisdom than her twenty-one years should.

She was beautiful. Tall with a reedy frame that belonged on a fashion week runway. Lustrous dark curls that today she tied back in a ponytail thicker than my right arm.

"I've told this story a hundred times," she said, flicking her gaze out the window. It was raining today. Thick, crooked streaks glistened down the pane.

"You have," I said.

"Are you trying to trip me up?" she asked. "See if I'll change it?"

I set my coffee cup down on the table between us. I didn't usually drink it this late in the afternoon, but when Neveah offered it, I didn't want to say no. She brewed it strong, with a robust flavor. Like her. It was the thing I counted on. The only thing that might give her what we both wanted.

"In a word?" I said. "Yes."

"Well, I won't," she said. "I haven't. I'll tell you a hundred more times. A thousand. I know what that man did to me. They can call me a liar. A slut. Worse. It's nothing I haven't heard before."

"They might do worse than call you names, Neveah," I said. "You have to be prepared for that. Simon Pettis is known for brutal cross-examinations. He has been around forever. He was trying cases before you were born. Before I was born."

"You afraid?" she asked me, those amber eyes fixing on me once more.

I folded my hands on the table. "No. I'm not afraid. Not for me."

She waved a dismissive hand. "Then you don't really know these people."

I looked around the room. Neveah rented a house in College Village. They were hard to come by. Three blocks from campus, students could avoid the hefty price tag of a parking pass and the hunt for an elusive spot in the student lot. I knew the rent reflected that perk.

The jury would wonder how Neveah afforded this place. They might assume. She was right about the picture the defense would paint of her. I could protect her from some, but not all.

"I need you to tell me again," I said. "From the beginning. I need to know the details as well as you do."

"I didn't know who he was," she said. "That's the first thing people don't want to believe. But I'm not from here, Mara. I grew up with my mom in Detroit. I'd never heard the man's name before."

"All right," I said.

"Mr. Sizemore came to guest lecture in my political science course on municipal government. Professor Perry's class."

"Were you attracted to him?" I asked. I had a notepad in front of me. I kept my pen poised above it as Neveah told me her story again.

"I thought he was decent-looking," she said. "I've always gone for older guys. My shrink thinks I've got daddy issues. I think that's crap. Anyway, he gave a talk. To be honest, I zoned out for most of it. The guy seemed nervous in front of the class. More than anything, that's what drew me to him. Disarmed me, if you want to know the truth. There were a lot of students in the class fawning over him. Kissing his butt. I did not get that at all. I'm telling you. I was not on the make. I wasn't stalking this guy."

"Then what happened?" I asked.

"Class was over. I had plans to meet my friend Renee. Mr. Sizemore was standing up at the front of the room answering questions from other people. I was just minding my own business, gathering my things. I got a text from Renee. She said she had a change of plans. The bar we were planning to go to had a power outage so she wanted to meet at Lilly's on the other side of town. I was getting kind of tired so I decided to just head home. I put my phone in my bag and that's when I looked up. He was standing there, smiling at me."

"Was anyone else around?" I asked.

"No," she said. "The other students cleared out by then. It was just me and Mr. Sizemore."

"Who spoke first?"

"He did," she said. I checked my notes against the statement Neveah had given to the police. So far, her story was consistent.

"He asked me how he did," she continued. "That's the first thing that got me. He wasn't cocky. Most of these people who come into these classes, they're full of themselves. They don't even really plan what they're going to say. They just think their war stories or personalities are going to be enough for all of us. He wasn't like that. He had notes he read from. He was thoughtful in the way he answered questions. There was something in his eyes. Like a need. I could tell he was honestly worried if he'd done a good job for us. I found it interesting. Charming even."

"That's when he asked you out?" I asked. It was a test. To see if Neveah would take the bait and alter the story.

"No." She shook her head. "Not then. You know, he never really did ask me out. Not in those words."

Again, she passed the test.

"It was a six o'clock class," she said. "So it was close to nine when the lecture was over. The custodians like to close the building by nine thirty. We'd been talking for almost a half hour. He offered to walk me to my car. I told him mine was on the fritz and how close I lived and that I was just going to walk. But it was so late by then. Everyone else had left. There are usually other people walking that same route so I'm not alone. He offered to drive me home. I said yes. I shouldn't have. But I did."

"So you kept talking? About what?"

"I was curious about the campaign process. That's always been where I wanted to land. I volunteered for the governor's campaign when I was eighteen. It was just passing out flyers and yard signs but that's what got me thinking about poli sci in high school. Anyway, I told Mr. Sizemore all of that. He listened. That's the other thing I thought was different about him. He wasn't talking about himself. He was asking *me* what I thought about things."

"And this was all on the way to his car?" I asked.

"Yes. I mean it was April so it was kind of warm out. We stood there for a while, just talking. You know. In the parking lot."

"Neveah, what happened next?" I asked. On the stand, I would take her through it, just like this.

"He said he liked talking to me. He said he knew what this was going to sound like, but that he was looking for a new intern. He said that was one of his ulterior motives in agreeing to guest lecture for Professor Perry. He wanted me to apply for it."

"Was that something that interested you?"

"No," she said. "I told him I couldn't afford an unpaid internship. Between classes and working at the bar. Anyway, he said it wasn't like that. This was a paid gig. Well, that interested me. I couldn't believe it."

"Then what happened?" I asked.

Neveah's expression darkened just as it always did when she got to this point in her story.

"I was such an idiot. I should have known what was going to come next. It's just he was who he was. And it wasn't like we were in some seedy bar and he was a random guy."

"But you said you didn't realize who he was before that night," I challenged her, knowing full well Simon Pettis, the legendary defense attorney, would do the same.

"I said I didn't know who he was when he showed up to give his lecture," she said. "Of course I googled him while he was speaking. I'd listened to him for almost three hours by then. I'm saying it wasn't like I was sitting at a bar listening to some line by a sleazeball."

"I see," I said.

"He said he had more questions for me. He said he had meetings all the next day and was leaving for a three-day conference after that. He said he knew it was last minute, but would I mind doing an informal interview with him that night?"

"He asked you out," I said.

"No! He was just going to take me home. We were going to talk in the car."

"But your apartment at the time was only a few blocks from campus."

"I wasn't thinking about geography," she said. "I was thinking about maybe I'd get a break. I wanted to hear more about the internship."

"Okay," I said. "Then what happened?"

"Then," she said, her bottom lip quivering. "Then I got in his car."

"And he drove you home."

She shook her head. "No. Like you said. It was just a few blocks. That would have taken, what, a few minutes? We were talking. He was asking me about my family. My background. What got me interested in politics. Then he started telling me what his vision and ambitions were and all the roadblocks to getting there. We kept circling the block. I didn't mind. He was listening to me. Ms. Brent, people don't always listen to me. Not like that."

"I see."

"You don't," she said. "Nobody does. They think I'm lying because nobody can be that dumb."

"I don't think that at all, Neveah. If I did, I wouldn't be here."

"Well, somehow, we ended up in the parking lot of McCauley Park. One of the street lamps was out. I remember thinking, why did he park right under that one? I was going to ask him. But he was telling me what he wanted from me. As an intern. His expectations. He said it's all hands on deck in his office as he was gearing up to run again. That I wouldn't just be making copies or answering phones. That he'd want me in meetings. He would expect me to become familiar with his position on things. God. It all sounded so good. I was so excited."

"Neveah, what happened next?" I asked.

Her eyes brimmed with tears. "Then, he put his arms around me and tried to kiss me."

"What did you do?"

"I pushed back. I told him no. I told him I wasn't okay with that."

"Then what happened?"

"He laughed," she said. "In a heartbeat, he became someone else. Like a mask he'd been wearing just slipped. He reached under my seat and hit the lever that reclined it. He was on top of me. He's a big guy, Ms. Brent. And I just ... I couldn't believe it was happening. I shut down for a second. That's the thing I go over and over in my head. I froze. If I hadn't. Maybe if I'd have slapped him. Would he have snapped out of it? Would it have made a difference?"

I stayed silent, needing Neveah to get her story out in her words. But the answer was no. It very likely would have made no difference at all.

"He pinned me down," she said. "With his whole body on top of me. I pulled his hair. Or tried to. He covered my mouth with his hand. I couldn't breathe. There was no room to fight. He ... he pulled my shirt up. Pinched my breasts. Hard. My eyes watered. I had no room to kick. To push him off. He had me wedged against the car door. He ... he bit me. On my breasts."

She reached for her own cup of coffee. Though her voice shook, her hands were steady as she took a sip.

"What did he do to you then, Neveah?" I asked.

"He raped me," she said, her voice gone cold. "I'd been wearing a skirt. That's another thing. Maybe if I hadn't. If I'd worn jeans or something. But you don't wear jeans to class. At least, I don't. It made it easier for him to do what he did."

"Neveah," I said. "It's not your fault."

"I know," she said. "I didn't ask for it. I know that. I'm just saying there were things that made it easier for him. If I'd made different choices, it would have made it a little harder. Made it take an extra second or two. Maybe enough time for me to do something."

"He outweighed you by seventy pounds," I said. "He was stronger, Neveah. And he hurt you."

"Yeah," she said. "He hurt me."

"He raped you," I said.

She nodded. "Then it was over. It was just ... over. I was still so numb. I just lay there on that seat. He drove out of the parking lot and went around the block. He ordered me to get out of his car. Like he was done with me. So now I was just a piece of trash. Garbage you'd throw out your car window."

"What did you do?"

"I was shaking so badly, I couldn't work the door handle. I started to cry. That set him off. He yelled. Screamed at me. Get out. Get the hell out! I was on autopilot. I actually asked him what I was supposed to do next."

"Then what?"

"When I couldn't get the door open, he reached for me. My God. I turned to stone. For a second, I thought he would start again. But he reached over me, opened the car door and pushed me out."

"He pushed you out?"

She nodded. "I fell to the pavement on my hands and knees. My clothes were torn. I was bleeding. That's when ... it's like he finally realized I was actually hurt. He rolled down the window and asked me if I could walk. I managed to get to my feet. His eyes were kind of wide. I think ... I think maybe he was a little shocked too. He looked scared. He asked me if I could make it home. I nodded. The thought of him, what, offering to give me a ride? I just wanted him to go away. He smiled then. It was ghoulish. He said something like, he knew the name of a good mechanic, or that he could call me a mechanic. As if my car was what I was worried about. Like I needed him to do me a favor."

"I'm so sorry, Neveah," I said.

"After that, he rolled up his window and drove off. He left me there. I tried to start walking but it was like my legs wouldn't work. Like I was stuck in cement. I couldn't get my heart to stop pounding. He circled back. God, I was terrified. He opened the window and threw my bag out on the sidewalk next to me. His tires squealed as he drove away."

She'd stopped crying. Her eyes went cold. She closed them against the memory. When she opened them, they lit with new strength.

"I'm ready, Mara," she said. "I know what his lawyer will do. I know what they'll try to say about me. And I know you can't promise me we'll win. But you have to let me up there so I can testify. So I can look that bastard in the eyes and call him out for what he is. For what he did."

I slid my notepad into my briefcase. "That, I can promise," I said. "You'll have your chance to confront him. I'll do everything I can to make sure he pays, Neveah. I can promise that much."

"I gave up everything I thought I wanted because of him," she said, brushing a tear away. "I dropped out of school. I was lost. I've had to restart my entire life."

"You've been strong," I said. "So strong."

"I'm thinking about starting class again this fall. Did I tell you that?"

"No! That's great."

"I'm meeting with an academic advisor."

In the months after the rape, Neveah had indeed restarted her life. She'd taken a job as a teacher's aide at a private school on the other side of town. It was still Waynetown, but felt worlds away from the life she'd had before.

For the first time since we sat down, Neveah Ward smiled. She let me hug her as we said our goodbyes. I wanted to tell her the hard part was over. We both knew it wasn't. In six weeks, I would put the former mayor of Waynetown on trial for rape.

2

I made my way through the gauntlet of reporters camped outside the entrance to the city-county building. Behind them stood a group of supporters holding Re-Elect Dennis Sizemore signs. They waved them at me like weapons as I stated my tenth "no comment" of the day.

Inside, my team waited for me. We were few, but mighty. Howard Jordan, my Maumee County Assistant Prosecutor counterpart, bounced on his heels in the door of the conference room. Our boss, Kenya Spaulding, sat at the table behind him, her brow furrowed as she stared at the whiteboard set up in the corner.

There wasn't much on the board. The evidence in this case was simple, damning, and very likely not enough.

"How was she?" Kenya asked as I set down my briefcase.

"I ordered in," Hojo said right after. "You good with pizza?"

"I'm good with the tail end of a dead rhinoceros at this point," I said. "It's been a long day."

"Pettis just served us with another discovery request," Kenya said. She slid a stapled stack of papers at me.

"We're six weeks out from trial," I said. "He can't do that."

"You want to tell him that?" she asked.

"Yes," I said. I glanced at the paperwork. It was bull. Another ream of documents from Neveah's doctor that we'd already provided. Twice.

"This is a ploy," I said. "He's trying to rattle Neveah and set up grounds for appeal if they lose, and we don't comply."

"We need an intern," Kenya said. "You can't keep dealing with this stuff yourself, Mara."

This was a point of contention between us. Our last few interns had done more harm to the office than good. I wasn't willing to take another chance on one until after the Sizemore trial was over. It meant our already thinly spread office had to stretch even thinner.

"I don't have a choice," I said. "Plus, we're too far into this for me to train somebody new. I can handle it."

Kenya shook her head, but she knew me well enough to understand there was no changing my mind. It was us. Our small, ragged, but fierce band of three against a foe that might end all of our careers.

"So how was she?" Kenya asked me for a second time.

"Determined," I said. "Solid. She hadn't changed so much as a beat of her story. She'll get through it fine on the stand."

"Until Pettis rips her apart," Hojo said.

"She's ready," I said.

Kenya looked at me, her stoic expression hiding what I knew was a swirl of emotions behind it. It was Kenya's neck on the line. She'd signed off on this case. If we lost ... if I lost, she'd pay at the ballot box next year. I had no doubt whoever came in to take her place would clean house. Hojo might survive, but I wouldn't. We'd be the two bitches who tried to mess with Mayor Sizemore.

"She understands that her testimony is the only thing that can sway this thing," Hojo said. "If she cracks. I mean at all ... they'll acquit this bastard."

"She knows," I said. "And so do I."

"He raped her," Hojo said, pounding his fist against the table. "We've got him on DNA. On her medical exam. This girl was beaten. Held down. Forced to ... I mean the physical evidence is there. He can't actually get up there and say it didn't happen."

"He can say it wasn't rape," I said.

"If he takes the stand," Kenya said. "Right now, I have no idea if Pettis will call him."

"He has to," I said. "Besides, Denny Sizemore won't be able to resist the limelight. He'll get up there and try to charm the jurors. He's an imperfect man. Neveah was a moment of weakness. But it wasn't rape. We can have all the physical evidence in the world, but it'll still boil down to which story they believe. Neveah's or Sizemore's."

"Who are you calling first?" Hojo asked.

I sat down beside him and stared up at the board. Neveah's picture stared down at me. It was one taken in the hospital a few hours after she reported what happened to her. She stared at the camera with vacant eyes, her bottom lip swollen where Sizemore had hit her.

"Her father called me today," Kenya said. "He still wants me to try to talk her out of taking the stand."

"He's scared for his daughter," Hojo said.

"He's scared for his pocketbook," I answered. "He's losing business at his body shop from the negative attention this case is bringing. Neveah hadn't had much to do with him in the last couple of years. He wasn't a factor in her life growing up. She says he's only coming around now because he thinks there might be a payday for him at the end of all of this."

"I'll talk to him," Kenya said. "I'll impress upon him how important it is that he stays away from the press. If they get one whiff that he's questioning Neveah's story. If he tries to discredit her in any way ..."

"He will," I said. "Count on it. No one's met his price yet, that's all. Neveah warned me. She's barely spoken to the man in years. He left the family when Neveah was maybe eight or nine. He resurfaces every once in a while when he needs money."

"I'll talk to him," Kenya insisted.

"Be careful," I said. "We have to assume Sizemore's people have already approached him. He's a weak link. He's on Pettis's witness list."

"This guy is a world-class sleazeball," Hojo said.

"Which one?" I asked. "Pettis or Sizemore?"

"Both!" Howard stood up. He walked over to the whiteboard and ripped the picture of Dennis Sizemore down. It was his official government photo. He sat smiling against the backdrop of an American flag. It appeared on all his campaign literature along with one of him and his devoted blonde, blue-eyed wife and trusty cocker spaniel.

"He's not made of Teflon," Hojo said. "Don't forget. He was a one-term mayor. He lost his first bid for re-election four years ago."

"And since then, we've been under the helm of one of the weakest mayors Waynetown has ever seen," Kenya said. "Until this case broke, Sizemore had hero status around here. Every political operative I know thinks the election loss was the best thing that ever happened to the guy. He was poised to ride in like some kind of savior. People have short memories. And plenty of them think this whole trial has been orchestrated just to damage him. By me."

"We have Neveah's testimony," I said. "I told you. She's solid. I've got a positive rape kit. I've got a girl with severe injuries consistent with rape. I've got security footage showing his car parked in a darkened part of McCauley Park just like she said it was. Kenya, if I didn't like my chances, I would have said something. I know it's your call in the end, but you made the right one. This girl was raped. Sizemore did it. She deserves her chance at justice, no matter what happens in that courtroom. I'm ready for that. Are you?"

She met my gaze. "I thought it was my job to give you the pep talks, Mara."

"You have. And I'm sure I'll need one again before this is all over. But this one? Neveah Ward? Even if we lose. Even if we're all out of jobs because of it. It's worth it. It has to be worth it. Neveah is worth it."

Kenya smiled. "As pep talks go, that's a pretty good one. Okay. So deep breaths for all of us. We do what we do. If we lose, we lose. Plus, I for one can't wait to see you go up against the likes of Simon Pettis."

That part, I knew, was personal. Kenya's most notable trial loss was against Pettis a decade ago. A murder case lost on a bad search warrant. The defendant went on to kill again two years after he was acquitted. We all had cases like that. Some stung more than others. A victory over Pettis in this case wouldn't bring those victims back, but sometimes we had to take our satisfaction where we could find it.

"What do you need from me?" she asked. The Kenya I knew and loved was back.

"Right now? If you *do* think you can help manage the dad, Gary Mosely, that's great. Be careful though. Like I said, there's no doubt Pettis's team is sitting on him. He's going to fight dirty."

"I wish we could," Hojo said through gritted teeth.

"We don't need to," I said. "We just need to do our jobs. On that note, do you think you could handle this for me?"

I slid the newest discovery paperwork over to Hojo. He saluted me as he took it. "I'll bury the idiot with boxes of paperwork."

"Just give him what he asked for."

Hojo rolled his eyes, but he agreed and went off to do as I asked. I felt bad. Kenya was right that this was an intern's job. Hojo was far too valuable for it. I started to gather my things.

"The pizza isn't here yet," Kenya reminded me.

"I know. I just want to go home if you don't mind."

"To an empty house? Isn't it Jason's week with Will?"

I'd left her the opening. Kenya slid right in.

"Yes." I smiled.

"You okay on that score? Where does the custody trial stand?"

For the past few months, I'd been fighting off my ex on a custody motion he filed. He wanted to move my eleven-year-old son, Will, to D.C. with him permanently.

"We go to mediation in a few weeks," I said.

"Great," Kenya said. "It's not like you have anything else going on. He did that on purpose, didn't he? He's baiting you, trying to see if you'll ask for a continuance due to your work schedule."

"Pretty much," I said. "But I can handle it. I promise."

"Oh, I know you can," Kenya said. "I just hate that you have to. Is there anything I can do?"

I put a hand on her shoulder as I made my way to the door. "Just be you. Be my friend."

"You know I'll do more than that. If they call me as a witness ..."

"I know," I said. "And I'll take you up on it."

"What does your lawyer say?" she asked.

I adjusted my briefcase on my shoulder. "I'm meeting with her tomorrow morning," I said. "That's actually the thing you can do for me. I might be an hour late coming in ..."

"Take the morning," she said. "We'll cover things here."

"You don't have the manpower to—"

"We'll cover things here," she said, more forcefully. "Do what you have to do. Don't let that jerk take your kid from you, Mara. I've got your back. You know that."

I did. I loved her for it. I tried to swallow past a lump in my throat. The words wouldn't come. There were none adequate to express how much Kenya meant to me.

But she knew. She quickly wiped a tear and tried to cover. I squared my shoulders and left the room.

3

I drove an hour outside of town, across the Michigan border to a little town most people just drove past on their way to Ann Arbor. But when I asked around for the best family law attorney I could find, nobody said anything about a big firm in Toledo or Columbus. I was told to come here to Delphi, Michigan and talk Jeanie Mills into crossing the border for me.

Thankfully, she agreed.

Jeanie worked out of the Leary Law Group in a century-old converted farmhouse. It was quaint. Out of the way. Unassuming. But the woman occupying the first floor office impressed me from the first moment I met her. She looked me straight in the eye and told me I could exhale. It took everything in me not to break down into tears on the spot.

"You're late," Jeanie said as she swung her office door open for me. Her office took up half of the building's first floor. She had a huge mahogany desk she preferred not to use. Instead, she favored the cozier leather couches she kept around a fireplace that, as far as I knew, didn't work.

I joined her on one of the couches.

"Sorry about that," I said. "I had a hearing that ran late this morning."

"Did you eat?" she asked. "You don't look like you ate. Miranda!"

"I'm fine," I said, my ears still ringing from her booming voice. Her office manager, Miranda, buzzed the intercom.

"You bellowed?" she asked.

"Do we still have some donuts back there? Mara looks hungry."

"I'm fine." I smiled. "Really. I'll eat a big lunch."

"Cream filled or regular?"

Jeanie stared me down. The woman wasn't kidding.

"Just a glazed if you've got them."

"You hear that, Miranda?" Jeanie yelled.

"Do your legs still work?" Miranda shot back over the intercom.

"Oh, my gosh, really, I'm fine," I said.

Jeanie wouldn't hear of it. She hoisted herself off the couch and charged out into the lobby. I heard a muffled exchange between the two women. Then Jeanie came back with a tray of donuts, a carafe of coffee, and two mugs. She poured my coffee and plated a big, fat, glazed donut for me. I couldn't hide my growling stomach. The thing melted in my mouth.

"See?" she said. "First lesson.. I know what's good for you."

Jeanie Mills was a bit of a courtroom legend in southeast Michigan and northwest Ohio. In her mid-seventies, she'd practiced for half a century, starting at a time women lawyers were still a rarity.

She was also physically hard to forget. In heels, she maybe topped four eleven at best. She had short, spiky black hair with very little gray and favored pant suits with a tightly knotted scarf. Today, the scarf was patterned in black and white polka dots. "Noted," I said as I sipped my coffee. "And I really am sorry for keeping you waiting."

"You've got your hands full down there, I hear," she said. "You really planning on trying to prosecute Denny Sizemore?"

"I am."

She whistled low. "Brass balls on you, then."

"How well do you know him?" I asked.

Jeanie sipped her own coffee. "The kid? Not a lot. I knew his old man, Donald. Real son of a bitch, that one. He taught a con law course when I was a first year law student. Back in the olden days. That was before he ran for the Ohio legislature. The kid, though, I gotta say, I heard he was actually fairly effective as a politician."

"He is," I said. "Conventional wisdom before all this was that he had a lock on taking back his mayor's seat in Waynetown this election."

"So you're not too popular with the party these days, I take it," Jeanie said.

"Oh, I'm never too popular with the party," I said.

"That why you never run for office in your own right?" she asked. "You could, you know. With your family backing. Your name. Either one of them, I mean."

I squirmed in my seat. There weren't that many people who knew about my mother's family's political influence. Not here. That influence didn't carry much further than New Hampshire, where I was born.

"I think whatever political capital my family had we cashed in getting my ex elected to Congress," I said.

"Bastard's doing a decent job of it too, isn't he?" she asked, though I knew she already knew the answer.

"He is," I said. "Jason is a lousy husband. But he's good at his job. And ... he's been a good father to Will."

Jeanie nodded. "Yeah. I understand that. But you're going to have to put that opinion aside. You get that, right?"

"I won't bash Jason as a dad, if that's what you're driving at."

Jeanie put up a hand in protest. "I didn't say bash him. Lord. That's the last thing I want you to do."

Something cracked inside of me. Something I'd been holding together for all these weeks since Jason served me with custody papers.

"Jeanie," I said. "Tell me the truth. What are the chances Jason's going to win this? Am I going to lose my son?"

She put her coffee cup down. "We're both lawyers here, Mara."

"Don't," I said. "Don't give me the ethically required spiel about how we don't guarantee outcomes."

"I won't," she said. "What this is going to come down to is how well we convince the mediator what's in Will's best interests. It's not about what you want or what Jason wants."

This was hard. Excruciating.

"You don't like giving up control," Jeanie said. "I get that. What weighs in your favor is Will's school, among other things. He's doing well at Grantham overall?"

"He is," I said.

Jeanie had a file in front of her. She flipped through some pages. "There was an incident last year where he got into a fight? And another where someone plastered news articles about your personal life in his locker? He's been bullied there."

"The locker thing was about Jason," I said. "He was having an affair and it hit the internet."

She nodded, but didn't unfurrow her brow.

"Jason's going to argue that Will's not protected there. Both you and he have public jobs. Granted his more so than yours, but his lawyer says Jason's got security concerns."

"Will has friends at Grantham. He has teachers, counselors, and specialists he trusts. You've seen the report from his psychologist. She's recommending Will not switch schools."

"Right," Jeanie said. "And you know Jason's going to produce a report from another shrink saying the opposite."

"Someone he's paying," I snapped. "Someone who's never treated Will."

"And that's my argument to make," she said. "It's a strong one. With Will's special needs ..."

"Jeanie," I said, trying to keep the desperation out of my voice. "I can't lose him. Will has come so far. Jason and I moved to Waynetown in the first place for Will. I had a job offer at a big firm in New York. But we both decided Will would do better in a small town setting. Waynetown is Jason's hometown originally, not mine."

"And he flitted off to D.C. and you stayed for the kid," she said.

"Partly. I mean primarily, yes. Only now, Waynetown is our home. Jason agreed. Now he's done a one-eighty. This isn't about Will. This is about him trying to punish me. Or it's about some focus group he's got who says the image of him as a family man will help him in some future senate race."

"This won't be easy," she said. "And I won't sugar-coat anything. Jason is trying to make a case that your job is impacting Will's mental health. He's become fixated on some of the people you've prosecuted in the last couple of years."

I looked out the window. "We're past that," I said. "But yes. There was one case of mine that Will started reading about online. It scared him. But we worked through it. Helped him find some balance."

"Good," she said. "And I have the reports from his therapist backing you up on that. All in all, I like our chances better than I do Jason's. That's the God's honest truth, Mara."

"How much more?" I asked.

Jeanie sat back. "You're his mother. Jason can bluster all he likes, but you're the one who's been there for that kid day to day. He's the one who left the family home."

"He didn't just leave," I said. "He lied to me for years. Cheated on me."

"And that's what he did to you. Not Will."

"The heck he didn't!" I yelled. "He did it to our family. Will is that family. And I have never once told him about it. I have never once said anything negative about Jason to him. I never will."

"Good," she said. "But as much as I'd love to make an issue of Congressman Jason Brent's infidelities, they don't have a bearing on what's in Will's best interests. If I go after that, it could backfire. That doesn't mean I won't do it. I just mean I need to be careful. And you need to trust me to know when something's a non-starter."

"I do trust you."

She closed the file and leaned back. "I need to ask you about Kathleen, Jason's sister."

"Kat? She lives here. That's another thing in our favor. She's one of Will's primary caregivers when I'm not at home. Even after the divorce, I still consider her my sister. And one of my best friends."

"But she's Jason's sister," Jeanie said. "His only blood family, am I right?"

"Other than Will, yes," I said. "But I told you ..."

"I heard you," Jeanie cut me off. "The thing is, when push comes to shove, and it will, we have to assume Kat is going to ultimately side with Jason. They're going to want to hear from her. They're going to put her on the spot and ask her to tell the court who she thinks Will is better off living with. And if Jason convinces her to move to D.C. and be his live-in nanny, that's going to hold some sway."

"He wouldn't," she said. "And Kat wouldn't go. He's asked her before. She has a life here. She has a significant other here."

"Sabrina Wharton," Jeanie said.

"Bree, yes."

"Were you aware this Bree has been offered a job at a research facility near Georgetown?"

I felt the blood drain from my face. "Jason did this. He pulled some strings. He's trying to manipulate Kat."

"Yes," Jeanie said bluntly. "So you need to fully understand what we're dealing with. He knows how valuable Kat's opinion will be. He knows how important she is to Will's stability. As close as you are, do you really think she'll go to bat for you over her own brother?"

I hated this. I hated Jason. Would he really try to poison my relationship with Kat? At that moment, I realized what he was doing.

"He's trying to force me to back down," I said. "He's playing chicken, using Kat against me. She probably isn't even aware of it."

"Odds are."

"That son of a ..."

"This is going to get tougher before it gets easier. And it's never really going to get easy," Jeanie said. "I have my work cut out for me. But like I said, I still like our chances better than Jason's. Because you're right. Waynetown is Will's home. He has a deep support system here. But this thing? It's going to get messy. You need to be prepared for that. It may require more of your attention than you're accustomed to giving."

"What do you mean?" I asked, then I knew.

"We can ask for a continuance," Jeanie said. "Until after the Sizemore trial is over."

"If we do that, it'll play into Jason's hands. That's what he's counting on. He wants the court to think my job interferes with my ability to fully parent Will. It's crap, Jeanie. It's misogynistic crap. Jason's job is just as demanding as mine is and no one makes an issue of it. No, it's fodder for his campaign literature."

"Okay then," she said. "No continuance. I think you're right. The hardest part about this is going to be you letting me do what I do. Giving up control."

"I trust you," I said. "And I know you're going out on a limb for me. You don't normally practice in Ohio."

"No. I do not. But I'm paying my bar dues down there. Might as well use it."

"Thank you," I said.

"Will comes back next week?" she asked.

I nodded.

"Good. I strongly recommend you don't talk about this with him."

"He's going to ask," I said.

"Then you tell him something basic. You tell him you and his dad are trying to work out what's best for him. That he shouldn't worry. And I would not talk to Kat about anything substantive, either. Resist the urge to pry anything out of her."

"Okay," I said, though I wouldn't have dreamt of it.

"We'll talk in a few days," she said.

"Sounds good," I said.

"You got time for lunch?" she asked. "Cass is due back from court any minute. I know she'd love to see you."

I'd had occasion to work with Cass Leary, Jeanie's law partner, a couple of years ago. I respected her as much as I did Jeanie.

"I wish I could," I said. "I've got to get back. Tell her I said hello and put me down for a rain check."

"Will do. Speaking of checks ..."

Jeanie shook my hand. I reached into my briefcase to hand her a check for the rest of her sizable retainer. A knife twisted in my gut as I stared down at it. It wasn't the amount, though Jeanie didn't come cheap. It was the source of the funds. The check was written on behalf of the Natalie Montleroy Trust.

My mother was footing my legal bills. As rewarding as my job as a prosecutor was, lucrative, it was not.

"She called me, you know. Your mother," Jeanie said as she took the check.

"Ugh. I'm sorry about that. I told her the ground rules."

"So did I. Feel free to remind her. I'll cash her checks, but I talk to you and you only."

"Thank you. And I'm sorry. I'll try to rein her in."

"Glad she's on our side anyway." Jeanie chuckled. "God help whoever crosses her."

"Believe me," I said, smiling. "You don't know the half of it."

"Keep your chin up, kiddo," Jeanie said. Coming from her, it didn't even feel patronizing. Jeanie Mills was another person the world would be careful not to cross. For Will's sake and mine, I was grateful.

4

Detective Gus Ritter hated everyone. Unless he loved you. Then he'd mow down anyone or anything that tried to do you harm. An endearing quality, to be sure. Today, though, if we weren't careful, he'd end up in a viral video.

"Gus," I said, putting a gentle hand on his arms. A handful of Denny Sizemore sign-holders blocked our path into the Sheriff's Department side entrance. They didn't usually camp out here, preferring the higher profile of the front lobby.

"Gus," I said again. Gus had gone nonverbal, growling at the skinny kid nearest him. Then, Gus actually barked. The kid's eyes went wide beneath his glasses and he wisely got out of Gus's path.

"Come on," I said. From the corner of my eye, I saw two of the Sizemore supporters had their phones out, ready to record anything interesting that happened. It was my job to make sure nothing did.

Mercifully, Gus came along more or less willingly. Though he slammed the door behind us.

"Idiots," he said. "Nutless pencil heads."

"Well put," I said as we made our way through the bullpen of Maumee County's sparse detective bureau. Handling homicides and other crimes against persons were Gus, Brody Lance, and Leslie Poehler. Lieutenant Sam Cruz held the corner office, overseeing them. The county assigned four other detectives to property crimes and one and a half people made up the sex crime unit on account of the fact that Detective Ritter did double duty.

Gus cleared off a swivel chair in his cubicle and offered it to me. He took the desk seat and dug for a file under a pile of other files. Though you'd be a fool to think Gus was disorganized. I'd known him to have a near eidetic memory. He could recall the tiniest details from decades-old cases. He could, as they say, tell you where all the bodies were buried and when.

"That's gonna get worse," he said, pointing over his shoulder in the direction of the door we'd entered.

"The protestors?" I asked. "I'm not worried about them. I'm worried about you. You can't lose your temper out there. I can't have my lead detective going viral while tramping on their civil rights."

"Hmmph," he said, then threw off a few colorful words that would blow your hair back.

"I mean it, Gus. Sizemore's people have your number. They're looking for a reason to discredit you on the stand. If they can't find it, they'll manufacture it. Don't give them the chance."

This time, he growled at me. "I already got this lecture from Cruz."

I looked past Gus. Lieutenant Cruz caught my eye through the glass wall of his office and waved. He had his phone to his ear but made a gesture, indicating he wanted me to stop and see him. I waved and turned my attention back to Gus.

"You should listen to him," I said. "Sam's a smart guy. He's also got your best interests in mind, just like I do."

"I want to get this guy," he said. "Sizemore's as sleazy as they come."

"Me too," I said. "But that's the last time you get to say that out loud."

"You think I don't trust the people in this room? Or you?"

"Gus," I said. He was baiting me a little, I knew. Still, I couldn't let Gus's temper torpedo the case before we even got to jury selection.

"Is Neveah still talking to you?" he asked.

"She is. And she's solid." I spent a few minutes having the same conversation with Gus that I'd had back at the office. My star witness knew what she was getting into.

"Her past is your problem," he said, pulling a stack of stapled papers out of his file. "And I gotta be honest, it's the reason I almost didn't write an arrest warrant on this one."

"I know," I said. Gus held the forensic report on Neveah's laptop. "But she isn't the same girl she was three years ago. She's turned her life around."

"I think she's trying," he said. "But you know Pettis is going to dig into this."

This was Neveah's activity on a dating website. Dating was a loose term for it, actually.

"She had a sugar daddy," Gus said. "A couple of them."

"She wasn't a prostitute," I said. "She met these men online. They helped her out. That isn't against the law."

"Right," he said. "Only you know what it looks like just as well as I do."

"If I get my way, none of that will come in," I said. "Pettis is smart enough to know that could backfire. This is the twenty-first century. We're beyond believing a woman is asking for it."

"Hmmph," Gus said. "I just don't want to see that girl dragged."

"I don't either. But she's going to get dragged. We knew that going in. I'll do what I can to protect her."

"Well, I'm glad it's you," Gus said. It was the highest compliment he could give. I smiled.

"And I'm glad it's you."

There was a moment as my heart swelled for Gus Ritter.

"We supposed to hug now?" he grumbled. The moment was gone. I laughed.

"You should be so lucky," I said.

Then, Gus grew serious again. There was something on his mind. "Mara," he said. "This guy. Sizemore. It's not just

Neveah Ward. He's protected. There's a reason he lives out in Chatham Township, the farthest corner of the county. They've got their own Podunk police force out there. They protect him. That's the thing that's never tracked about this case. Sizemore's an idiot, but he's not stupid."

"What do you mean?"

"I mean, why take her to McCauley Park? He knew that was our jurisdiction. Why not take her closer to his own backyard?"

"So what if he had?" I asked. "For one thing, that's what, fifteen, twenty minutes in the other direction of Neveah's apartment where he was supposed to be driving her. Maybe he worried she was going to put up a fight sooner."

"If he'd taken her to Chatham Township, I think this thing never would have gone further," Gus said.

"You really think the Chatham cops would have looked the other way? On an alleged rape? With a victim who had clear injuries and a positive rape kit?"

Gus curled his fist. "I'm saying it wouldn't surprise me if they've done it before. I know they have."

"Is there any way you can prove it though?" I said. "If I can show a pattern of behavior ..."

"I told you," he said. "Sizemore's an idiot, but he's not stupid. Mara, he's been getting away with this crap for years. It's an open secret that he likes to take his frustrations out on his wife Claire's face. She won't admit it. They live in that Falling Waters gated subdivision. She calls the Chatham Township boys and they go out and get him to sober up. Give her first aid. Keep their mouths shut."

My stomach churned. "But you can't prove it. You know this how?"

"Because I know. People talk under the table. But none of those glorified rent-a-cops out there would ever have the balls to admit it where it counts. And Sizemore knows if he pulled that crap here, under county jurisdiction? We'd kill him."

I put a hand up. "I don't want to hear that last bit. But I take your point. Gus, if there's anything. Anyone who's willing to come forward and go on the record with your suspicions ..."

"I know," he said. "Believe me, I'm trying. But they've closed ranks. You've got them running scared. They'll protect their boy."

"Still, keep an ear out. I may try talking to the wife."

"She won't say a word," Gus said. "I'm not sure spooking her wouldn't do more harm than good. But follow your gut. I'll do what I can."

"I'm counting on you," I said. "Your testimony and Neveah's is my whole case. That and the DNA evidence. And that's why I need you to walk on eggshells for the next few weeks. I mean it. Squeaky-clean behavior."

He saluted me. Laughing, I realized I would have preferred the hug.

"I'll let you get back to work. Sam looks like he wanted to see me about something." When I looked back toward his office, Sam wasn't in it anymore.

"Looks like you missed him," Gus said. "You want me to hunt him down?"

"No," I said, still staring at Sam's empty desk. "I've got to get back to the office. Just tell him to give me a call on my cell if it's something that can't wait."

"Sure thing," Gus said. When I looked back at him, there was something about his expression that gave me pause.

"You okay?" I asked.

"Yeah. It's just ... Mara, you know you're going to lose this one, right?"

I gathered my briefcase. "Thanks for the vote of confidence, Gus."

"No," he said, touching my sleeve. "You know I think you're one of the few lawyers worth a damn around here. It's not that. It's Sizemore. Who he is. What he does. I don't care how strong that girl is. How believable. This town isn't going to put Denny Sizemore in jail. They just aren't."

"Well," I said. "Then at least we'll go down fighting on the good side. Sometimes that's all there is, isn't there?"

Gus pursed his lips. "Yeah. Damn few of us left."

We left it at that. I headed down the hall toward the front lobby. I didn't get too far before I remembered what might be waiting for me out there. I knew a service exit so headed that way.

I looked down to rummage for my phone in the outer pocket of my bag. Before I made it to the stairs, I ran smack into David Pham, Maumee County's medical examiner.

"Ooof!" I said as David and I collided. David caught me by the arms. For a man with his profession, David had one of the happiest faces I'd ever seen, owing to his set of deep dimples and expressive eyes.

"You okay?" he asked, genuine concern in his tone.

"I'll live. Not sure your shirt will."

David looked down. The collision had dislodged a pen from his breast pocket. Blue ink stained the fabric.

"Perfect," he said. "That'll look great on the stand."

"You're testifying today?" I asked.

"Yeah. Civil trial over in Judge Flander's court."

I grabbed the lapels of his suit jacket to see how well they'd cover the stain. It took a beat before I realized it was an overfamiliar gesture. My mom instincts kicked in before I knew what I was doing.

David's smile deepened. I blushed.

"Sorry," I said. "Let's just say I've spent one too many years as a parent volunteer on school picture day. Seems like they always serve spaghetti in the cafeteria those days."

"Noted," David said. "It's okay. I keep a spare shirt at the office. I'll have one of my lab techs run one over."

"Better have them hurry," I said. "What time are you due in court?"

"Twenty minutes," he answered. "Actually, I'm glad I ran into you. I mean, not *ran* into you. But uh ... I'd been meaning to give you a call."

"Oh?"

"Yeah. I'm ... uh ... well ... shoot. Forgive me. I'm a little out of practice with this. But I was wondering if you might be free for dinner sometime next week."

I ran through a quick mental check of all the cases I had pending where David might have to testify. Neveah Ward's case had monopolized my time lately.

Then I stopped cold, realizing what David was really asking me. Apparently, I was worse at this than he just claimed he was.

"Oh," I said. "You mean ... are you ..."

David's smile disarmed me. "I'm trying to," he said. "I think. But it's just dinner. You know. Outside of work. You do know what that's like?"

"Uh. Yes. Vaguely. I remember."

"Good. How about Thursday? If you're working late, I could pick you up at the office."

I ran through a dozen reasons why going out on a date with David Pham, or anyone, might be a terrible idea. But at that moment, I don't know what happened to me. It was as if something else took over and worked my voice for me before my brain could catch up.

"Sure!" I said. "Um ... yes. I think meeting after work would make the most sense."

"Great," David said, still smiling. The man knew how to quit while he was ahead. "I'll pick you up at the office around six. It's a date."

He was shouting the last bit across the hall as he bounded toward the front door.

What had I done? What had I just said?

Then David was gone. I stood there slack-jawed in his wake. It was then I noticed Sam Cruz standing at the duty station across the hall. He'd seen the whole thing. Heard the whole thing. I felt color rush to my cheeks.

"Hey ... Sam," I said, feeling awkward. Feeling guilty of ... something. "Um, you wanted to see me?"

He tilted his head ever so slightly, considering his next words. "It can wait," he said. "I'll catch you tomorrow."

Before I could answer, Sam waved and disappeared further down the hall.

5

Later that week, Simon Pettis came to Waynetown. Caro spotted him from our office window.

"Ho-lee Moses," she exclaimed, leaning over the radiator. "He's huge!"

Kenya came out of her office. Hojo poked his head out of his. I stood at the copier watching as Hojo went to Caro's side, jaw on the floor.

"How tall is he?" Hojo asked. "I mean, he's gotta be six eight. Sizemore's six feet. He only comes up to his shoulder."

"You sure he's not standing on the step?" Caro asked.

"I don't think so," Hojo answered.

"Oh, for Pete's sake," Kenya said. "Who cares how tall he is?"

"Mara," Caro called back. "You better get to a browser or a television. He's got an audience."

Caro's computer was the closest. I tapped the screen and went to the local news website. Sure enough, under a big, red, blinking, breaking news banner, they were live streaming from the courthouse steps.

I clicked it to full screen and sat in Caro's chair. The others crowded around me. Though I shared Kenya's opinion on the irrelevance of the man's physical stature, I had to admit. Simon Pettis was a giant.

"Thank you all for coming," he said. Simon wore a finely tailored black suit and red tie, an American flag pinned dead center in the middle over his left lapel. Right over his heart.

"Mr. Pettis," one reporter shouted. "Is there any truth to the rumor your client is in negotiations to accept a plea deal?"

"A what?" Kenya and I said it in unison.

"What rumor?" Hojo said. "Where's he coming up with that? Who asked the question?"

"Shh," Kenya said.

"While I cannot comment on legal strategies, of course, I can tell you that should a plea deal be offered, my client wouldn't consider it."

"Hmm," I said. "Which would be a legal strategy, Mr. Pettis. I mean, as long as you're not commenting on those."

"Shh!" Kenya said, louder this time.

"If you'll permit me," Simon said, raising and lowering his hands as if he were Moses parting the Red Sea of reporters. "I've prepared a brief statement. Then I'll entertain a few quick questions. Let me be crystal clear. My client is innocent of the grievously false charges against him. He emphatically denies any criminal behavior where Ms Ward was concerned. We're confident that the truth will come out at trial. In fact,

Mr. Sizemore is very much looking forward to Ms. Ward's opportunity to have her day in court. As we said, we know the truth will come out and Mr. Sizemore will be exonerated once and for all. Mr. Sizemore also wishes to convey his concern and sympathy for Ms. Ward. As you can imagine, this has been an extremely difficult time for Mr. Sizemore and his family. He is deeply humbled and grateful for the support he's received both from the public at large and, of course, his family."

Pettis brought Denny Sizemore forward a bit.

It was at that point I noticed his wife, Claire Sizemore, shrinking against his side. Sizemore put his arm around her. She found a smile.

"I think I'm going to throw up," Caro said. "She looks scared to death."

She did. For a moment. Then Claire found a genuine smile. She beamed up at her husband.

"Mr. Sizemore! Denny! Are you maintaining your relationship with Neveah Ward was consensual?"

The barrage of questions continued. Claire's smile faded. It was subtle. Had I not been watching her face, I might not have seen it. But Simon Pettis jerked his chin. It was a signal. Claire stepped out of Denny's grasp and came to the forefront.

"Thank you," she said, smoothing an errant blonde hair away from her face. "Thank you for respecting our family's privacy up until now. I know you have questions. Believe me, we'd love to answer them all right here and now. But we need to let our fine justice system play out. I promise, we'll have plenty more to say after the verdict. A verdict which I'm confident will exonerate my husband completely. Thank you."

Denny Sizemore wisely said nothing.

"What a creep," Caro said. "She's got to know he's guilty as sin. This has to be killing her. And yet there they are. Those two sleazeballs, trotting her out and making her clean up Denny's mess."

"It's slick all right," I said. "Judge Saul has us under a gag order. But it only applies to Pettis and me. Claire Sizemore's free to say whatever she likes."

"You sure about that?" Hojo said. "Seems to me Pettis is the one putting those words in her mouth. I'd wager she would rather have gotten dragged over actual hot coals than stand out there today."

Kenya reached over and clicked off the monitor. "I've seen enough. This is what Pettis does. He's part of the political machine. I'm sure the party bosses in Columbus are paying his legal fees."

"I'm sure you're right," I said. "I'm surprised Pettis doesn't run for office himself. Or maybe this trial is part of that strategy down the road. He'll get plenty of attention."

"He wouldn't have taken it unless he was sure of a win," Hojo added, less than helpfully.

"All right," Kenya said. "Show's over. Back to work, everybody. Let's not give that windbag out there any more of our air. Mara? You got a second for me?"

"Always," I said, though I looked at the clock. It was ten minutes to five. I was never one to run out of the office right on the dot at five, but I promised Will we'd FaceTime at five thirty. I wanted to be home for that, not here at the office.

"I'll be quick," Kenya promised, reading something on my face.

I joined her in her office. She closed the door. "Hojo isn't wrong, you know," she said.

"About this case being a loser?" I said. "Yeah. I'm not sure he is."

"I didn't say I thought it was a loser. I said Hojo isn't wrong. Pettis thinks he's going to win. Doesn't mean he will. But ...I got a phone call today from a Web Margolis. He's on Pettis's witness list, if I recall."

She handed me a pink message sheet.

"Did you talk to him?" I asked. "Margolis has been dodging my calls."

"I didn't," she said. "That he's calling me tells me he thinks going over your head will get him something. Do you know what he's going to say?"

"Ritter interviewed him," I said. "Margolis was a friend of Neveah's. They had a relationship. They met through a dating app and Margolis is going to claim he paid a portion of Neveah's college tuition and her rent while they were involved."

"A sugar daddy," Kenya said.

"That's the argument Pettis will probably make. But he'll color it that he was paying her for sex. If Saul lets him testify at all. I'll argue hard that it's inadmissible. Neveah's past sexual history shouldn't come in."

"Good," Kenya said. "I cannot believe that in this day and age we are still having this argument in court. But here we are."

"Here we are," I agreed. "Thank you for this. And thanks for not taking the call. I have a feeling if I return it, he's just going to hang up on me."

"You can use my landline if you'd like," she said. "Let him think it's me calling back on his caller ID?"

"That won't keep him from hanging up," I said. "I want to talk to him in person. The guy runs Mar-Bradley Logistics. Gus gave me a tip. He takes lunch every Wednesday at Highland Hills Golf Club. I'll pay him a visit tomorrow morning."

"You want to take Hojo with you?" she asked.

"I'm not afraid of the guy," I said. "I think he's more scared of me. I just want to make sure he doesn't change his story ahead of trial. I want to see how hard Pettis has been leaning on him. If he's successful getting that testimony in, I plan to impeach him with it."

"You think Pettis is that sloppy?" she asked.

"I think he's that cocky," I said. "And I think he thinks I'm some backwater county prosecutor he's going to wipe the floor with. I'm not inclined to disabuse him of that idea just yet."

"Go get 'em, Mara," Kenya said. "Whatever you need. Just let me know."

"Thanks, I'll be in after ten in case anyone's looking for me."

"Got it," Kenya said. It was five o'clock. I had just enough time to get home before my call with Will. I said my goodbyes to the office and headed for the parking lot.

"Mara!" Sam Cruz's voice reached me from the sidewalk. I tapped the lock button on my car key and waved Sam's way.

"Hey, Sam," I said. "Sorry I missed you the other day. Was there something you needed to talk to me about?"

He smiled. "Nothing pressing," he said. "Besides, you had your hands full with Gus. Then you and Pham looked deep in conversation."

Sam smiled. He had a mischievous twinkle in his eye. David. My accidental date with David. Lord. It was supposed to be tomorrow night. What had I been thinking?

"David and I are just friends," I blurted. I had no idea why. I didn't owe Sam an explanation. He was a friend. A good one. We'd shared a moment or two here and there that might have been something more but ...

"Relax," he said. "David's a great guy. You need a life outside of work."

Sam's smile had faded. He seemed as awkward as I felt now.

"It's just dinner," I said, still fumbling for the right thing to say. Still fumbling for why I felt the need to say anything at all. Except I did need to. Sam's opinion mattered. Though I hadn't been ready to process why it did.

"Sam ... I ... things have been. And we ... you and me ..."

He was smiling again. "Mara," he said. "You don't need my permission to live your life."

"I wasn't asking for it," I said and it came out more harshly than I meant. Ugh. I was bungling this.

"I'm sorry," I said. "I mean ... dammit, Sam. I'm not sorry. You're teasing me. And you seem to be enjoying it."

He laughed. "I am a little. I don't know. I kind of like keeping you off guard."

"I'm not off guard," I said, though we both knew I was lying. Covering. Fumbling, still. "It's just you and me. We've had some, um, moments. But we've been unclear."

He nodded. He took a step toward me. It got darn hard to breathe. "Then let me be clear," he said, his voice lowering. "I like you, Mara. A lot. I'm pretty sure you like me too. Someday, I'm probably going to act on it. But you're not ready for that yet. Because of Jason. Because of Will. Because of you. Again, so we're clear. When I *do* act on it, I'm not looking to be some rebound guy for you. So for now, this is good, you and me. For now ... David's a good guy."

"A good rebound guy," I said with an edge to my tone.

Sam smiled. "Yeah."

"And you think you get to decide when you're going to act on this," I said, swirling my hand in the space between us. "That's your call? I don't get a say?"

"Maybe." He kept on smiling. "But don't worry. When it's time, you'll know."

"Oh, really?"

"Yeah," he said. He was walking backward, still smiling. I had the urge to smack it right off. "You'll definitely know."

I opened my mouth but no sound would come out. My heart flipped. Sam's smile widened. He shot me a wink, then turned, leaving me breathless in his wake.

6

I got lucky the next day. Margolis was eating brunch alone in a darkened back corner booth at the Highland Hills Country Club just outside of Toledo. My mother's name carried enough clout to get me past the hostess.

I walked in as his server brought him a martini. He sipped it as I approached the table. It was eleven o'clock on Wednesday. He didn't act surprised to see me and I had to assume someone tipped him off when I walked in. I suppose I should have given Margolis credit for not dodging me again.

"Mrs. Brent," he said, putting his drink down long enough to stand up and extend a hand to mine to shake. "I suppose it's time we talked, one way or another."

I didn't want to touch him. I didn't want to appear rude or judgmental. I shook his hand.

He wore a thousand-dollar Gucci suit. The jacket hung over one of the empty chairs. He had his crisply pressed white dress shirt rolled up, revealing deeply tanned, veined, hairless forearms. The shirt fit tightly over biceps that seemed overly defined. Neveah said he wouldn't admit to steroid use, but it seemed obvious the man was unnaturally enhanced.

"Thanks for meeting me," I said. I ordered nothing more exciting than ice water as the server came back.

The dining room was relatively full. It surprised me that Margolis hadn't insisted we walk outside. This was as public as it could be for a private club. The other patrons knew him. He waved at several people as they walked past the table. It was as if he wanted to show off to them, having me sitting here with him. But the thing was, everyone knew who I was. Or if they didn't, a quickly whispered inquiry and they'd soon find out.

"Do you feel like a sandwich yet? They've kicked over to lunch, but I can have the chef make you something off the breakfast menu if you'd prefer."

"No," I said, waving off the offer of menus. "I've ambushed you. I'll keep this brief so you can get back to your day."

Margolis's face fell. His disappointment quickly replaced with the hard jaw of irritation.

"You know I have questions about your relationship with Neveah Ward," I said.

"Is she really going to go through with it?" he asked.

"Do you mean is she still willing to testify against Denny Sizemore? Yes. She's ready. I know you're aware the trial starts the week after next."

"She's so strong," he said. "And naïve."

"She knows what happened to her."

He said nothing. Instead, he studied my face. It made me uncomfortable.

"Mr. Margolis ..."

"Call me Web," he said. "In fact, I insist. And I want you to know if I can help Neveah, I would have. I offered to get her her own lawyer."

"Neveah isn't charged with a crime," I said. "She's the victim here."

"I suppose," he said. "But if this thing goes south, I worry about her. I don't know if she's emotionally equipped for what's about to happen."

"Mr. Margolis ... Web. You've been subpoenaed by the defense. I know you've spoken to Simon Pettis. You took a meeting with him?"

"Just like I'm now taking a meeting with you," he said. "I'm neutral in this, Mrs. Brent. I care a lot about what happens to Neveah, but as I told Simon Pettis, I have no information about her relationship with Denny Sizemore or any other man she might have had ... encounters with."

"Web, the encounter in question was a violent rape. Do you have any information or belief that things happened some other way?"

"No," he said abruptly. "I'm not saying that."

"Okay, then let's start from the beginning." I pulled a thin file folder out of my briefcase. I had transcripts of Neveah's texts and her cell phone records.

"Tell me how you and Neveah met," I said. Though I fully knew the answer, I needed to hear how Web Margolis would characterize it.

"I travel a lot for my business," he said. "I'm never in one place for more than a few days at a time. It makes it difficult for me to meet people and form connections. I live alone. I've never had children. So on occasion, I've found it worthwhile to avail myself of certain social websites."

"Dating apps," I said. "You're talking about dating apps."

"I am," he said.

"And that's how you met Neveah?"

"It's how I meet a lot of people," he said.

"Did you seek her out? Did she seek you out?"

"You know, I think I messaged her first."

I looked at my files. "This was through MOCA? An app called MOCA?"

"Yes."

"Men of a Certain Age," I said.

He smiled. "I'm not responsible for the naming convention of the app."

"Who initiated the contact?"

"I believe I clicked on Neveah's profile."

"You messaged her first?"

"I believe I did, yes. It was two years ago or so."

"Mr. ... Web. You're aware how Mr. Sizemore's defense team is going to likely characterize your relationship, aren't you?"

"They're welcome to say anything they like," he said. "Neveah and I know what we were to each other."

"Which was what?" I asked, not liking his answer here one bit. He was too flippant. Too cavalier.

"We were friends. I considered myself a mentor to Neveah. She was ... she is ... unsophisticated about the world. She grew up in poverty. Her education was lacking. She was looking for someone to talk to who was more worldly. She needed advice. I was happy to give it. That's really what MOCA caters to. I never had children, I told you. I don't have a family that I'm close to. I live this fairly big life and I know things. There are younger people like Neveah who seek people like me out. We connected. I consider her a friend."

"I see. She confided in you?"

"Oh, of course," he said. "Neveah's very impressionable. She's never had positive role models in her life until she met me. I'm the one who encouraged her to apply for college."

"You did more than encourage her," I said. "She says you paid for her tuition."

"That's true, yes," he said. "I told you, she's a dear friend."

"Web, the defense, if they call you, they are going to ask you whether your relationship with Neveah became sexual. I am going to fight like hell to keep that line of questioning out. But there's a chance I won't win that fight. Neveah has already told me that you and she, at one point, had an intimate relationship. You were sleeping with her."

His face soured. "That's an ugly way to put it. If you're even half good at your job, none of that should be a part of this trial."

"You're right," I said. "It shouldn't. But Simon Pettis wouldn't be the first defense lawyer in a rape trial who tried to slut shame the victim."

Web slammed his fist to the table. "I won't hear that. I can't even repeat that word."

"They're going to try to say that your relationship with Neveah was a business transaction. You understand that, right? Your characterization of the MOCA app is lovely, but that's not what most other people think of it."

"I don't care what people think of me or that app. Neveah and I had an emotional connection."

"She's thirty years younger than you," I said.

"She's an old soul. Neveah would be the first one to tell you that."

Oh brother. If Pettis put this guy on the stand, I would have my work cut out for me.

"The word he's going to use is sugar daddy. You know that, right?"

He waved me off.

"What do *you* know, Mrs. Brent? If you're so quick to judge Neveah's character, why are you prosecuting this case?"

"I'm not judging her character or yours. I'm of the firm belief that whatever two consenting adults do behind closed doors is no one's business but their own. Unfortunately, I'm about to go to trial on a rape case where the defense is going to claim Neveah Ward consented to have sex with the former and possibly future mayor of Waynetown. They're also going to use you to try to prove that's exactly what happened. So regardless of the ugly words I might use, I need to be very clear about what your relationship with Neveah was. And I need you to be prepared for what's about to happen to you."

"I beg your pardon?"

"You get that Pettis probably considers you his star witness. He paints a picture with you. Here's this poor, young girl who has a pattern of hooking up with older, rich men. They're going to try to make it look like Neveah was preying on Denny Sizemore, not the other way around. They'll use you to do it."

"I am not privy to the things Neveah does when I'm not with her."

I sat back. It was an odd thing for him to say. If he said it on the stand, Neveah's credibility was in trouble.

"You think she's lying about being raped by Sizemore?"

"They can't ask me that on the stand," he said.

"No. I'm asking you. Right now."

"I hope she's telling the truth," he said. "That would be a very vile thing to accuse a man of if it wasn't true. In this day and age ..."

"In any day or age," I said. "You saw Neveah though. After her attack. Didn't you? In fact, you picked her up at the hospital. You were the first person she called after talking to the police."

"She was very distraught."

"Distraught and injured," I said. "She had a fat lip. She was bruised."

Silence.

Web Margolis squirmed in his seat. He gestured to the server, asking for his check.

"Web," I said. I didn't want to ask the question. At the same time, I knew Pettis would ask it. I had to know his answer now.

"Web, did you at any time tell Simon Pettis or anyone else that Neveah likes it rough? Or did Simon Pettis tell you or imply that's what you should say if he puts you on the stand?"

"I think I've said all I wish to say to you," he said. He stopped, waiting for the check. Instead, Margolis placed a fifty-dollar bill on the table, threw his napkin onto his plate, and stormed out of the dining room.

He hadn't directly answered my question. But his demeanor told me all I needed to know. Neveah's case would implode if I couldn't keep Web Margolis off the stand.

7

I had a pre-trial ritual. I stood in the center of the conference room with photocopies of my evidence laid out. I stared at the board at the end of the room. Two pictures stared back at me. One, the accused. Two, the victim.

They could not be more different. Denny Sizemore's cap-toothed smile beamed in two dimensions. The American flag draped behind him, his red tie matching to perfection. A confident, handsome politician. Polished and propped up by his handlers.

Then there was Neveah Ward. The photograph I chose was taken in the emergency room the night she reported the rape. Her haunted gaze was slightly off center from the photographer. She looked to the left and downward. Her lower lip cracked and bled. Her left eye was nearly swollen shut. Her hair, which she normally wore so meticulously braided, stuck out in curled wisps. Still, she was beautiful. Broken, but strong.

A soft knock on the door drew my attention. Caro poked her head in.

"Hey, Mara, sorry to interrupt. Your, uh, date is here." She smiled.

I'd completely lost track of the time. I glanced at my smart watch. Six o'clock exactly. This would be one of the last days I'd stay at the office this late. The trial started Monday. Sunday night, Will and Kat were flying back from D.C.

I missed him terribly. Our nightly FaceTimes weren't the same. He'd seemed mostly upbeat, but I knew my son. He was worried about something. Jason promised he didn't discuss the custody hearing with him. But Will could always sense when something was wrong with us.

"My date," I said. "Right."

"He's cute, Mara," Caro said.

"Cute?" I laughed. As Maumee County's medical examiner, I wondered how many times David Pham had been called cute.

"And polite," she said. "He brought you flowers."

My face got hot. "You're kidding."

"Wild flowers," she said. "They're perfect. Not ostentatious or presumptuous, like roses. I'll get a vase. They'll brighten up your office."

I raised a brow. I knew Caro had an ulterior motive. It would give her an opportunity to pop her nose back into my office while I talked to David.

"You do that," I said. Rolling my eyes, I moved past her and out into the hall. My office door was open. I could see David's gleaming, polished leather shoe as he sat with one leg crossed over the other in a chair in front of my desk.

"Hi, David," I said. David leapt to his feet. Just as Caro said, he held a bouquet of blue and yellow wildflowers mixed with baby's breath and wrapped with the florist's green tissue paper. It crinkled when he handed them to me.

"They're lovely," I said. "Oh, they smell good."

Caro appeared, holding a glass vase. "Let me take care of those," she said. "What a gentleman you are, David. I can't remember the last time I got flowers."

"Well, I'll make sure to bring you some the next time I'm in the office," he said, smiling.

Her hand fluttered to the strand of pearls around her throat. She was blushing. So was David. She was right. He was cute. Adorable, actually. And suddenly, all my nerves dissipated. David Pham was a truly nice guy. It had been a while since I'd gone out with one.

"You ready?" he asked. David grabbed my coat off the coat rack near the door and held it out for me. "How do you feel about Giorgio's?"

"Oooh, fancy," Caro said as she hovered in the hallway.

My stomach growled, answering for me. It occurred to me that I hadn't stopped for lunch today.

"That's how good." I laughed. It was obvious David had heard my gurgly tummy.

"Can I help you?" Caro said. Something had drawn her attention out in the lobby. It gave David and I some privacy finally.

"Thank you for saying yes to this," David said. "I gotta admit. I've been working up the courage to ask you out for quite a while."

"I'm flattered," I said. Sam's words rose up in my consciousness. He said I wasn't ready. I pushed those thoughts away.

David helped me put on my coat. I grabbed my briefcase, then thought better of it. There'd be no work for me tonight. This could wait until tomorrow morning. I set it down beside my desk, grabbing only my purse instead.

"Should I follow you?" I asked. Though we hadn't preplanned it, taking two cars would give me peace of mind. We could eliminate any awkward after-dinner drives up my secluded section of Waynetown. Whatever happened, we would end the evening out in the open. Casual. Light. Sam was right about one thing I wasn't yet ready for.

"I'm parked right out front," he said. "I can drive you back to your car after dinner. It'll be on the way."

"Okay," I said. Perfect. Casual. Light.

We headed toward the lobby. Caro stood there with her hands on her hips. Her mouth turned downward in disapproval at whoever had just come in after hours.

"Ms. Brent is gone for the day," Caro said, before she realized I was standing right behind her. The woman in front of her was Bree Wharton. For the last year, she'd been dating Jason's sister, Kat. Her expression sent ice through my bloodstream.

Something was wrong.

"It's okay. Bree, is everything okay?" Her puffy eyes told me she'd been crying. Bree was still wearing purple scrubs and her ID badge. She was a cardiac nurse at University of Michigan Hospital.

"I'm so sorry to barge in on you like this," she said. "I didn't know what else to do. Kat's going out of her mind."

"What's wrong?" I said, though my mouth felt as though it had filled with hot ash. Kat. Kat was supposed to be in D.C. with Will. She was flying back with him and staying at my place next week while I was in trial.

"Will's okay!" Bree quickly said. "Oh my God. I'm sorry. You must have thought ... no. He's okay. It's not that. But is there somewhere we can talk for a few minutes?"

"I can wait, Mara," David said. "Let me walk Caro to her car. Then I'll come back for you."

"Thank you," I said. Caro gave me a pained expression. She wanted to hover. But she took David's offered arm and left Bree and me alone.

"What's going on?" I asked.

"Mara," she said. "Jason canceled Will and Kat's airline tickets. He has no plans to put Will on a plane back home."

It was as if a trap door opened beneath my feet. I grabbed the nearest desk for support. No. No. No.

"What are you talking about?" I said. But I knew. I'd feared it. Every time I put my son on a plane since the divorce, I worried about this very day.

"I just got off the phone with Kat," she said. "She's a mess. She and Jason got into a huge fight. You have to know she does not support this. She wants what's best for Will. But she's afraid to go against her brother. She's afraid to leave Will's side."

"Start from the beginning," I said.

"Kat's been very upset about what's going on between you and Jason. She's worried about Will."

"So am I," I said, my anger rising.

"Things came to a head last night," she said.

"I talked to Will last night," I said. "He seemed fine. Kat seemed fine. She was there. I saw her on FaceTime."

"This happened after Will went to bed. Jason told Kat he wasn't comfortable sending Will back here to Waynetown. You're going to be in trial in a few days so he decided it would be better to just keep Will with him."

"He never said anything about that," I said. "That's not our agreement."

"I know," she said. "And Kat knows. She told him that. But Jason has made up his mind. He asked Will if he'd like to stay until after your trial. He promised to take him to an air show he's been wanting to go to. The Blue Angels."

"He bribed him," I said. "Let me guess. Will said yes. He doesn't want to disappoint his father. He manipulated him."

Bree didn't answer. "Well, whatever you want to call it, Jason went ahead and canceled Will's flight. Kat found out and went ballistic. Jason told her she was welcome to come back to Waynetown on her own. He won't stop her. But he knows she's not going to leave Will. It's too much. She loves you both. She loves Will like he was her own. I know you know that."

I couldn't breathe. Couldn't think. "When was Jason going to tell me?"

"I don't know," Bree said.

"Does Kat know you're here?"

"No," Bree said. "She was beside herself when she called me. She doesn't know what to do. Jason's her brother. She loves him too. The two of them, they're all each other had growing up. He got her out of foster care when he was old enough to take care of her."

"I know their history," I snapped. Though Bree wasn't the one I wanted to attack.

I fumbled in my purse for my phone. Jason's number went to voicemail the first try. I called two more times. On the third attempt, he finally picked up.

"Hi, Mara," he said. "It's a bad time. I'm in a meeting. I'll call you back."

"Cancel your meeting," I said. "Is it true you're planning on kidnapping my son?"

Bree withered in front of me.

Jason's haughty laugh on the other end of the phone incensed me. "Don't be dramatic, Mara. We have joint custody."

"We most certainly do not," I said. "We have joint legal custody. That means we consult each other on decisions. But Will lives here, with me. And he better be on a plane Sunday morning. Is there any reason to think he won't be?"

"Mara, I was going to call you. At this point, I think it's better if we communicate through our lawyers. You're clearly not capable of a rational conversation."

I wanted to murder him. I wanted to reach through the phone and strangle him. I took a breath.

"So you canceled his flight," I said. "Is that true?"

"We have some things to work out," he said. "It'll be good for you to keep your focus on your trial ..."

"You don't get to decide that," I said. "We have a routine in place. You know how detrimental it is for Will when that gets disrupted. You send him home, Jason. I don't want to hear ..."

"I know what's best for my son," Jason said. "I'm going to end this conversation now as I don't feel it's productive. You're getting hysterical."

My cheeks were on fire. I wanted to call him every filthy name I could think of.

"Will belongs at home," I said. "We have an agreement that you send him home on Sunday. I expect you to honor it. I'll be calling Will later tonight as usual."

"My lawyer will be in touch, Mara," Jason said. Then he hung up on me.

This couldn't be happening. He couldn't actually be trying to keep Will away from me.

"Mara?" Bree said.

"Thank you," I said. "For coming to me. I get how hard this is on you and Kat. I never intended for either of you to get caught in the middle."

"I love that kid too," Bree said. "I'm breaking Kat's confidence by coming here. I just know she's beside herself. She's feeling pulled in three directions. So please work this out with Jason. Don't make Kat have to choose between the two of you."

I remembered Jeanie's words. Kat was Jason's sister. When push came to shove ... When. Jason was shoving now. Hard.

The door opened. David walked back in. I covered my face with my hands.

"Oh," David said. "Mara, if this is a bad time ..."

I looked at him. "I'm so sorry, David. It is. It's a disastrous time. I have to go home. I have to call my lawyer. I have to ..."

"It's okay," he said. "I understand. We can do this some other time."

I felt like an ass. I felt sick. David offered to walk Bree back to her car on his way out. A true gentleman. A good guy. I said my reluctant goodbye and went back to my office.

I dialed Jeanie's cell phone. She answered on the first ring.

"Hey, kiddo," she said. "I was just going to call. Your lout of an ex just filed an emergency motion for temporary physical custody starting now. We're in for a fight, I'm afraid."

I crashed my head to the desk. My nightmare had come true.

8

The true seriousness of Jason's actions became clear when Jeanie Mills decided it was worth a house call.

She sat at my kitchen island thumbing through my divorce judgment. She'd seen it before, of course, but today she wanted a visual aid.

"What hurts you is this," she said, folding back a page and sliding it across from me.

I knew the passage she referred to. I kept my gaze locked with hers.

"You don't have specific schedule language."

"We agreed we could work things out between us," I said. "Up until now, we have."

"Up until now," she said. "But without specific language in a court order mandating Jason return Will to Waynetown by a certain date and time, you don't have a case for parental kidnapping. The D.C. police aren't going to go out there and get him for you."

"I don't want that. My God. That would scare Will to death."

"And Jason knows it," she said, her tone becoming more harsh. "He's banking on the fact that you're not going to do anything that will upset that kid."

I buried my face in my hands. "This whole thing has to be upsetting to him. Will thrives on routine. He marked it in his calendar that he's coming back on Sunday morning. He's got school the next day. Jeanie, we were just finally settling into a routine where he felt safe and comfortable again. This thing has the potential of setting him back."

"And that's what we'll argue to the court," she said. "I'm waiting on those reports from Will's therapist and the school counselor. The sooner they can get those to me, the better. I've got seven days to respond to Jason's emergency motion. Your hearing is in two weeks."

"Two weeks," I said, my voice shaking. "Two weeks before I can get my kid back?"

"If we prevail, yes," she said. "Sorry. When we prevail. We will, Mara. This whole thing is bullshit and Jason knows it. The second the press gets a hold of ..."

"No," I said. "That's the one thing I don't want. No media. That's not good for any of us."

"Not good for Jason, you mean? He's up for re-election. Mara, you don't have to protect Jason's career."

"I'm not trying to," I said. "I'm trying to protect my son. Jason's still his dad. He loves him. He idolizes him. Dragging Jason in the news isn't going to serve my son."

My smartwatch vibrated with the alarm I'd set.

"Jeanie, I have to FaceTime Will. I can't miss this."

"I don't want you to," she said. "In fact, I wouldn't mind listening in, if you don't mind. He doesn't have to know."

"I do mind," I said. "Because I'll know. It's a violation of Will's privacy. I won't do that. You can wait here though. I'll make the call in my office upstairs."

"That's up to you," she said. "But don't think for a second Jason isn't listening in. Keep that in mind."

It turned my stomach to think Jason might cross that line. But he'd crossed far worse than that. I tried like hell not to hate him for it.

I failed.

Jeanie agreed to wait. My heart racing, I headed upstairs and fired up my laptop. Before I made the call, I put a smile on my face. I couldn't let my son see how upset I was. He was too good at reading me. It's why the last year and a half married to Jason had been so excruciating.

I adjusted my screen. My bookshelf was behind me. The door was closed on the off chance Jeanie made any noise downstairs. Will would be shrewd enough to ask about it.

His face popped on screen and my heart soared. He'd gotten a fresh haircut. At eleven, the bones of his face were changing. The first hints of the handsome man he would become someday were beginning to show. A strong angular jaw. Bright-blue eyes with lashes thick enough to make any makeup artist jealous.

He looked just like Jason.

"Hi, guy!" I said, waving. "I like your haircut."

"Dad took me to his barber on Capitol Hill. His name is Jonas. I got a shoe shine on my dress shoes, too. The man showed me how to do it. Quick, slow. Quick, slow. Like this."

Will held up his black leather slip-on dress shoes. I'd bought them for him when he had to wear a suit to serve as a junior groomsman at a family friend's wedding last year.

"Those look beautiful," I said. "How are you?" I wanted to blurt out my most pressing questions.

Did Dad tell you you're not coming home? How do you feel about it? Jeanie's words stayed at the forefront of my mind. I had to assume Jason was listening in.

"We're going to the Air and Space Museum on Monday," Will said. "There's a new exhibit on the Mars missions. Dad's getting me VIP access. There's a lady from NASA who's going to go with us."

Monday, I thought. The day Will was supposed to be home and back in school.

"Wow," I said. "How do you feel about that?"

Will's gaze shifted to the right. He squirmed a bit in his seat.

"We have so much we can learn from the Mars missions," he said. "They're hoping to be able to make fuel once we have a reliable source of water up there. Someday that's how the astronauts will be able to get home."

"That's amazing," I said. "I miss you, buddy."

"I miss you too," he said, finally making eye contact. There were no tears. He wasn't fidgeting with his sleeve or chewing the inside of his cheek, his go-to stims when he was under duress.

"Your trial starts in two days," he said. "Do you think you'll win?"

"I hope so," I said.

"I think you will," he said. "You do eighty-two percent of the time."

I smiled. Will kept track of my win-loss averages more than I did.

"I'll keep that in mind," I said. "I really, really miss you, buddy. I can't wait for you to come home."

Will nodded. "I want to get a fish tank, I think."

"We can do that," I said. "Mr. Anderson has that pet store on High Street. We won't go to one of those chain pet stores you don't like."

Will nodded but didn't say any more about it. That was extremely odd for him. I expected him to give me a rundown of every type of tropical fish he wanted and why they'd make for a harmonious ecosystem with each other.

"I love you, Mom," he said.

"I love you too," I said. I put my hand up, wishing for all I was worth I could hug him.

"Tomorrow at 6:00 p.m.," he said.

"Yes!" I said. I could feel the tears coming. "I wouldn't miss it for anything."

"See ya," he said. Then the screen went black.

I took a breath. I shut my laptop and headed downstairs where Jeanie waited.

"He's been planning this for weeks," I said. "Maybe since before I sent Will out there for his visitation."

"How do you know?" Jeanie asked.

"Because he's scheduled things with Will," I said, my anger rising. "Things you couldn't do on the spur of the moment. He's been prepping him, Jeanie. So Will wouldn't get upset by a change. To Will this isn't a change. Which means he's also somehow gotten my son to lie to me."

"That rotten bastard," Jeanie said. "Write it all down for me. Will his therapist back you up?"

"I think so," I said.

"Good." Jeanie rose and gathered her paperwork. She stuffed it into her briefcase. "Mara, Jason's not afraid to play dirty. You know that, right?"

I gripped the edge of the granite island. "I get that."

"Which means you have to. This is going to get way uglier than you hoped. I'll need you to let me do my thing. If you don't, you won't get your kid back. Do you understand?"

"I understand," I said. My voice sounded so flat to my ears.

"Okay then," she said. "Then I know what to do. As much as you can, just focus on what you have to do. I've been watching the news. You pour yourself into fighting for that Neveah Ward. I'll pour myself into ripping your ex a new rear end. Deal?"

I met her eyes. "Deal."

9

On the eve of her trial against Denny Sizemore, I met Neveah Ward in the place she now felt most comfortable. She sat in the center of a group of three-year-olds, reading them the story of *Stone Soup*. She was animated, making broad gestures as she drew each of the kids into her tale. They squealed with delight as one by one they added imaginary ingredients to the pot of soup Neveah described.

"She's great with them," I said. I leaned against the wall beside Neveah's boss and mentor, Louella Holmes. She ran Maumee Valley Montessori on the north side of town.

"She has the gift," Louella said. Louella would know. At seventy-seven, she'd run this school for over forty years. She had a two-year waiting list. Parents had been known to call her the second they found out they were expecting a child.

"I've never seen her like this," I said. "In her element, I mean."

Every time I'd spoken to Neveah before, she'd been nervous and intimidated by me or the process. I couldn't blame her at all.

"They love her," Louella said. "I just wish she'd hurry up and figure out this is her true calling. She's been so set on pursuing a career in politics. What happened to her is so horrible. The only silver lining is it's disillusioned her from that career path. She's happy here though."

"I'm glad she found you," I said.

"A happy accident," Louella said. "I'm so glad I plucked her application out of the pile."

Another of Louella's aides came over to us, pushing a cart in front of her filled with wrapped snacks and juice boxes. "Getting ready to sugar 'em up before we send 'em home," she said.

"Just scoot those off to the side, Aimee," Louella whispered. "Neveah's just finishing up."

Aimee gave me a smile and did as her boss asked. I turned my attention back to Neveah.

"Neveah told me she's going back to take classes this fall," I said.

Louella smiled. "She told me that, too. I expect great things from her. Just look at her!"

Neveah got to the end of her story. The group of children sat in wonder. One of them climbed into Neveah's lap and gently touched her face. Neveah hugged her. She waited patiently for the little girl to climb down. Louella took her cue and called the kids over to the snack table, giving Neveah an out.

She came over to me, dusting off her jeans. "Thanks for meeting me here," she said.

"No," I said. "I'm glad you had the idea. You're great with them."

Neveah waved to Louella, who nodded in response. Then Neveah led me to a small office off the classroom where we could speak more privately.

"Most of those kids' parents work weekend second shifts at the hospital," she said. "Nurses and maintenance crew. That's why we run the daycare here on Sunday nights."

"I assumed as much," I said.

"I like it," she said. "I thought I'd want more of a nine-to-five gig, but this suits me. What their parents do? It really matters. And I get to help them do it. I always thought working in the government was where I could make a difference."

"Me too," I smiled.

"But this ... it's just so much more important. If I'd have figured that out sooner, maybe ... things ... would have turned out differently."

"Have you told Louella that? Because she thinks you belong here. She might be right."

Neveah crossed her arms. "I found out fewer of my classes are going to transfer than I hoped. I have to start over."

"Louella doesn't have an early childhood development degree, Neveah," I said. "Have you talked to her about your future here? If it's something you think you might want?"

Neveah got a far-off look in her eye.

"It won't make you rich," I said. "But Louella takes care of her people. She considers you one of them."

"Things have been so up in the air with me. I figure when this trial is over. When I can put it behind me. My therapist said I shouldn't make any major life decisions for a little while."

"That's good advice too," I said. "And I'm glad to hear you're seeing someone. Is it helping?"

She nodded. "Yeah. Turns out I was pretty messed up even before the rape."

"Your therapist said that?"

Neveah laughed. "No. I was just trying to make a dumb joke. But ... I've spent too much time worrying what other people think of me. And trusting the wrong people."

I nodded. "I met with Web Margolis."

"Yeah. I'd say Web would be next on the list of the people I shouldn't have trusted. Right under Denny Sizemore."

"If the defense calls him, we're going to have to assume Web will do what he needs to protect himself, not you."

"I get that," she said. "Web has stopped returning my calls and texts."

"You think someone got to him?"

"I think it's like you said. Web is looking to cover his own backside, not mine. Despite all the promises he made to me. But yeah. Maybe someone got to him. I'm not naïve, Mara. Not anymore. I know that when we walk into that courtroom, nobody is going to fight for me but you."

I took her hand. "I will fight for you. And I wouldn't be so sure about other people. I'd say Louella is a damn fine ally to have. Don't forget that."

Neveah wiped a tear. "Even my own father wants to call me a slut to anyone who will listen."

I wanted to tell her it would all be okay. Even if we won, it might not be. At that moment, I knew the best thing I could do was be there for her.

"It doesn't matter," she said. "That's what I've been working on in therapy."

"What doesn't matter?"

"If we win or lose. Well, I mean winning or losing has to be defined by something other than a guilty verdict. That's what my shrink says. She says winning is me getting up there and telling my story. No matter if the jury believes it."

"I suppose that's a good way to look at it," I said. "But I think they'll believe you."

She smiled.

"Miz Ward!!!!"

A small voice drew our attention. A little boy with wild blond hair stood outside the office window into the playroom. He held up a crude drawing he'd made of Neveah holding a big black cauldron. *Stone Soup*.

"That's Monty." Neveah smiled. "His mom's an EMT. She works until four in the morning tomorrow. When he first started coming here, he never talked. He used to wrap himself around his mom's leg when she tried to leave."

"Then you better get back to him." I laughed. Young Monty was jumping up and down, waving his artwork, proud of what he'd done.

Neveah left the office and scooped Monty into her arms. He hugged her tight. When she put him down, he raced off to join the rest of his friends.

I came out of the office. "Neveah," I said. "Your therapist is right. Winning means more than just a guilty verdict. But I plan on getting that for you, too. Are you ready?"

She took a breath. When she let it out, she was smiling. "Yes. I am."

"Good," I said, squeezing her shoulder. "Then let's go get that bastard once and for all."

10

Denny Sizemore was on from the moment he walked into the courtroom. He wore the same crisp, black suit and red tie he'd worn in every campaign poster and billboard seen plastered around town. His thick, salt-and-pepper gray combed and shellacked into place. I half expected Simon Pettis to stick the American flag behind him for the jury pool's further benefit.

"He doesn't look nervous," Neveah said to me. She sat behind me as I looked through my notes. "Why doesn't he look nervous? I'm terrified and I'm not the one facing prison."

"I'm sure he is," I whispered. "He's just gotten good at hiding it."

"It's how he is," she said. "You think he's one thing. But he's something else. I hope they can see through it. I wish I had."

"I know," I said. "You okay? Do you want me to go over what's going to happen again?"

She shook her head. "I'm clear on everything."

"You can sit in the courtroom through opening statements but then you'll have to leave. Judge Saul won't allow you to be in the courtroom until after you testify. Pettis will object to you listening to the other witnesses who testify before you."

"I'll take care of her," Louella said. She had promised to sit beside Neveah today. Neveah tried to talk her out of it. Louella rarely took days off from the school. I was glad for her support. Neveah needed her. She had no family support.

"If you need anything," I said, "those women back there in the red shirts are here for you."

Three members of the victim's advocacy group, the Silver Angels, had shown up today. I trusted them to answer any questions Neveah had while I couldn't.

Denny Sizemore had his own supporters. His wife, mother, members of his extended family, plus a dozen more paid staff and political operatives. They filled up the gallery benches behind him, leaving barely any room for casual spectators.

"All rise!"

Sizemore shot to his feet, a half-smile fixed in place. Simon Pettis towered over him. Up close, his formidable size drew attention. His hands looked like they could serve as dinner plates. He had a thick, barrel chest. The back of his neck reddened and I didn't think it was from nerves. The man might be one cheeseburger away from a heart attack.

Judge Saul took the bench. I was glad we drew her. Pettis's reputation wouldn't impress her. She suffered no fools and wouldn't stand for courtroom theatrics if Pettis tried to pull any. She wouldn't stand for any from me either.

"Counsel, are we ready to go?" she asked.

"Yes, Your Honor," Pettis and I said in unison. He had a deep baritone that reverberated off the marble floors.

"Let's get the jury seated," she said.

We'd spent the better part of the morning in voir dire. The selected twelve members and two alternates filed in. It was a good mix. Seven women. Five men. My favorite was a retired female postal worker who stared down her glasses at Denny Sizemore. Pettis tried to challenge her for cause as her son was a deputy sheriff. Saul didn't buy it. So juror number four stayed on the panel.

Once the jurors took their seats, Judge Saul looked at me.

"You may proceed if you're ready, Ms. Brent," she said.

"Thank you, Your Honor," I said. I straightened my jacket and stepped up to the lectern. Behind me, I knew what they saw. Neveah dressed smartly in a blue suit with a pink scarf tied around her neck. She sat poised with her hands folded in her lap. Many of the jurors knew Louella. They had children or grandchildren who'd gone to Maumee Valley Montessori. Louella's presence beside Neveah wouldn't go unnoticed. She might be one of my best weapons and she wouldn't even take the stand.

"Members of the jury," I said. "Thank you for being here. Thank you for your time and attention. I've gotten the chance to get to know a little about all of you this morning. You've all told the court you know of the defendant, Mr. Sizemore. Many of you have seen his picture on television, on billboards and flyers around town. He served as your mayor four years ago. Some of you have even voted for him.

"He's a leader in this community. Well known. Liked and revered by many. Enough to get him elected. You've heard him speak. He's charismatic. Likable. Authoritative. He had all the characteristics and drive to get him elected mayor. A hometown hero, even.

"But Dennis Sizemore is wearing a mask."

I gestured toward him. Every member of the jury had their eyes on Sizemore. He kept his half-smile in place. I had counted on it.

"He wants you to think you know him. To like him. To trust him. To vote for him. But I put it to you today. Denny Sizemore is hiding his true nature.

"Eleven months ago, Denny Sizemore used that same charm and authority to become Neveah Ward's nightmare. She trusted him. Believed him. Was charmed by him into thinking he was interested in helping her.

"On that night, Denny Sizemore gave a lecture in one of Neveah Ward's college classes. He talked about civic duty, the nobility of working in local government to try to make a positive change at the grassroots level. Neveah was captivated. She was a twenty-year-old student who had dreams of working in politics to make the kind of positive impact Denny Sizemore talked about.

"When the class ended, they talked some more. The evidence will show that Denny Sizemore dangled a lucrative internship in front of her. He wanted to talk more about it with her. He talked so long it became dark outside.

"Neveah lived just a few blocks from campus. She was accustomed to walking home. In what she thought was an act of chivalry, Denny Sizemore offered to drive her because he'd kept her for so long. She said yes. And that was the only time she used that word with Denny Sizemore.

"The evidence is incontrovertible. The data from both Neveah and Denny Sizemore's cell phones will track exactly where Sizemore took Neveah that night. He didn't take her home as she asked. Instead, he took her to a dark corner in the parking lot of McCauley. He parked his car in the only spot in that lot where the street lamp didn't shine. Where the security camera couldn't reach. He knew it. He planned it.

"When Neveah demanded he take her home as he promised, Denny Sizemore's mask finally slipped. The evidence will show he attacked her. Struck her in the face. Pinned her down. Bruised her. Scratched her. Bit her. Ripped her clothing. And then ... Denny Sizemore brutally raped Neveah Ward.

"You'll see and hear the medical evidence. Neveah was raped. There is no doubt. There is no other individual involved. There is only Denny Sizemore and what he did to this woman sitting before you.

"I'm confident that when you see the physical evidence, the medical evidence, the cell phone and security camera evidence, there is only one conclusion you can draw. You'll see beyond a reasonable doubt that Denny Sizemore assaulted and raped Neveah Ward. And you'll return the only verdict appropriate in this case. You will find Dennis Sizemore guilty."

I walked back to my seat. Neveah's face had also become a mask. She stared straight ahead, gripping Louella's hand so tightly her knuckles went white. Louella took it. She squeezed back. Then Simon Pettis made his way to the lectern.

He leaned on it with one elbow, parking himself there. Some attorneys liked to move around, use the space in front of the jury. Making them follow, holding their attention that way. I was a mover when questioning witnesses. Pettis wasn't. He preferred to draw the jury's gaze right to him, positioning Sizemore over his right shoulder for them. He never even gestured with his hands.

"Ladies and gentlemen," he said. "Ms. Brent is good at her job. She's one of the top prosecutors in the state. She wins more than she loses. There's a reason for that. Well, there are a lot of reasons for that. But one of them is that she doesn't bring cases to trial unless she thinks she can secure a conviction.

"That's smart. On this one, she's promised you a parade of physical evidence. She might even be able to deliver it. The only problem is, she has to make you believe her story of what that evidence means.

"That's the thing. A good prosecutor is also a good storyteller. She just told you a great one. I was riveted too. But just because she says her evidence means something, doesn't mean it does. You have to buy what she's selling. You have to take her version of the story the evidence tells.

"Well, I've got a different one to tell you. The truth. In order to buy what Mara Brent is selling, you have to believe Neveah Ward. You have to believe that Denny Sizemore would be willing to risk his career, his marriage, his reputation, his freedom for one dalliance with Neveah Ward.

"Most of you have lived in this town for years. Your whole lives even. You know McCauley Park. Maybe your kids play there. Maybe you played there when you were a kid.

"There's nothing secluded about it. Think about that. Think about the kind of risk someone like Denny Sizemore ... or anyone ... would have to take in order to do the things Mara Brent is going to try to make you believe. That Neveah Ward wants you to believe.

"Remember that. Dennis Sizemore isn't a perfect man. He's a sinner like we all are. He makes mistakes like we all do. He has moral failings, like we all do. But he is no rapist. He is no monster. He's just a man. An imperfect man trying to do the best he can in the world. He fails sometimes. He fails a lot. But he's no rapist.

"Mara Brent is a storyteller. A good one. But ladies and gentlemen, remember this when she weaves her tale over the next couple of days. There's far more to the story than what she'll try to present. There is doubt. And where there is doubt, there is only one verdict you can reach. Denny Sizemore is no rapist.

"When you hear his story, and trust me, you will. Then you'll understand. I know you'll reach the right verdict."

I held my breath. Pettis had just promised the jury that Sizemore would take the stand in his own defense. I would get the opportunity to cross-examine the bastard. I tried to keep my face neutral.

With that, Simon Pettis rapped his knuckles on the lectern. I would soon learn he concluded every cross-examination the same way. A signal to the jury. An exclamation point.

"Is the state ready to proceed?" Judge Saul asked.

"We are," I said. "Your Honor, the state calls Detective Gus Ritter to the stand."

11

Gus Ritter and I had danced this particular waltz together hundreds of times. He knew the foundational questions I would ask. I knew the answers he would give. The cadence to his speech. He was the oldest and longest-serving member of the Maumee County Sheriff's Detective Bureau. He had just two more years in DROP, the Deferred Retirement Option Plan, and the county cops had a running bet whether he'd actually leave when that day came. The truth was, if someone you loved got killed in Maumee County, Gus was the one you'd want catching the case.

"Detective," I said. "How did you come to be involved in Neveah Ward's case?"

"I got a call from the hospital," he said. "Her treating physician at the hospital had a legal obligation to report evidence of sexual assault. It was my understanding that the victim, Ms. Ward, was also willing to file a formal report. I caught the case. I went to the hospital to talk to her. I arrived at seven twenty-eight on the morning of April 12th."

"What happened next?" I asked.

"Ms. Ward was still in an examination room. When I found her, she was in pretty rough shape. She was still bleeding from a cut on her lip. There were fresh scratches and bruises on her arms. The nurses were getting ready to administer a rape kit. That usually takes a couple of hours so I requested I be able to speak to Ms. Ward before that happened."

"Did you?"

"Yes," he said. "She was still pretty shaken up. But she was cooperative. She asked if one of the nurses could remain in the room. Her name is Kelly Smith."

"Nurse Smith was there the whole time when you spoke to Ms. Ward?"

"She was."

"All right. Then what happened?"

"I asked Ms. Ward to tell me in her own words what happened. She did."

"You didn't ask her if she'd been raped?"

"Not at that time. No. I deliberately asked her an open-ended question. In your words, tell me what happened. Then, I listened to her story."

"What did you do then?" I asked. Soon enough, Neveah would take the stand and explain to the jury exactly what happened to her.

"Ms. Ward identified her attacker as Dennis Sizemore, the defendant."

"She knew his name?"

"She did. She had her phone with her. She pulled up a picture of former Mayor Sizemore. She showed it to me and told me that was the man who raped her."

"Then what did you do?" I asked.

"At that point, I was concerned with Ms. Ward's well-being. And the nurses, as I said, were getting ready to administer the rape kit. Again, that can take hours. I called my lieutenant, Sam Cruz, and explained the situation. He agreed that I should go and talk to Sizemore as soon as possible. He sent a female officer to the hospital to stay with Neveah Ward. I waited long enough to speak to the doctor who had initially examined her."

"The one who had called your office to report a sexual assault?"

"That's right. Doctor Chloe Hernandez. I interviewed her next to her office in the hospital as soon as Officer Patel arrived. She stayed with Neveah. I went and talked to Hernandez."

"What was the outcome of that conversation with Dr. Hernandez?"

"Dr. Hernandez told me Ms. Ward had injuries consistent with a brutal sexual assault. There was significant tearing of her genital region."

"Objection," Pettis said. "The detective isn't a doctor. He's not here to make a diagnosis."

"He's here to explain the investigative steps he took," I said. "What he was told by Dr. Hernandez forms the basis of that."

"Sustained in part," Judge Saul said. "Detective Ritter, please confine your answers to what you did based on information you received rather than getting into the realm of diagnosis."

"Sure," he said. "Based on the information Dr. Hernandez gave me after examining Ms. Ward, and based on getting my own look at her. She was bleeding. Her lip was swollen. She was covered in scratches. She had bruises around her neck. Bruising on her arm. One of the bruises on her arm was consistent with her having been grabbed forcibly."

I moved to enter the series of photographs Ritter took of Neveah as she lay in her hospital bed. None of these showed anything below the waist. What they did show was horrific enough. On her left breast, she had a very clear bite mark that broke the skin.

"Detective," I said. "What did you do next?"

"Well, with Neveah in good hands and with Officer Patel and Nurse Smith by her side ... the two of them developed a good rapport right off the bat. Kelly's top notch as far as that goes. I gave both Neveah and Dr. Hernandez my cell phone number. I wanted to know the minute they had anything. As in, if there was DNA they could test the presence of semen, anything we could use to make a positive physical identification. Then I went to Denny Sizemore's house to talk to him."

"Was Mr. Sizemore at home?"

"He was."

"You spoke to him?"

"We had a conversation. I arrived on his doorstep at ten fifteen a.m. I asked him where he'd been the night before."

"What was his demeanor?"

"He was calm, holding a cup of coffee. He was fully dressed, wearing a dress shirt and tie. His wife, Claire Sizemore, kind of hovered in the living room behind him. I asked him if he'd rather step outside to talk to me."

"What did he tell you?"

"Not much. I asked him where he'd been between the hours of six p.m. and ten thirty the previous evening. He told me he'd given a guest lecture at the community college. He'd gone for a drive after that and then came home a little before midnight. I asked him if he knew Neveah Ward. He said he'd just met her the night before. She was a student with the class he taught and he admitted to giving her a ride home."

"He admitted that?"

"He did. He didn't at all seem surprised that I was asking. If anything, I believe he knew I was coming."

"Objection, calls for speculation," Pettis said.

"Your Honor, the detective's powers of observation are one of his investigative tools. Again, they form the basis for the actions he took in this case."

"Overruled," Saul said. "But I'd remind the witness his job is to answer the questions asked."

"Sure thing, Judge," Ritter said. The two of them had their own sort of waltz.

"Detective, what did you do then?"

"I asked Sizemore if he'd be willing to come down to the station for a formal interview. I told him he wasn't under arrest at that time and was free to decline, but that I had more questions about his involvement with Neveah Ward."

"What did he say?"

"That's when he started getting angry. He asked, 'What the hell has she been saying?' I told him I was more interested in his version of what happened. I asked him again to follow me down to the station."

"Did he come?"

"He refused. Said he was done speaking with me without his lawyer present. He told me he didn't care for the tone I was using or the look in my eye. That's what he said. Then he slammed the door in my face."

"Then what happened?"

"Then I went back to the hospital. Neveah was finished with her examination. The doctor was ready to release her. They had a positive rape kit. Semen and hair samples were sent off to the lab. I got a warrant for Sizemore's DNA."

"Then what happened?"

"I went to the Parks Department. That's who owns and operates McCauley Park. I got a warrant for the footage from the security camera on Crawford Street. That's the one that points at the parking lot. I reviewed the footage."

At that point, I entered the security footage into evidence. Denny Sizemore's black Mercedes could be seen driving to the darkest corner of the lot at nine forty-one. It sat there for forty minutes. The footage was grainy. The car had tinted windows. You couldn't make out faces or figures. Once or twice, you could see what looked like an arm in the window, but nothing else. Then, at ten eighteen, the car pulled out and headed north on Crawford and out of view. The only thing clear about it was the license plate. Ritter testified about how he ran the plate. It was registered to Dennis Sizemore.

"Then what happened, Detective?"

"In the meantime, Sizemore showed up with Mr. Pettis and submitted to a cheek swab. That was compared with the DNA collected from Neveah Ward's rape kit. Two weeks later, we got the results from the lab. It was a positive match. At that point, I felt I had probable cause to arrest Dennis Sizemore for sexual assault against Neveah Ward."

"Thank you, Detective," I said. "I have nothing further."

Simon Pettis practically mowed me down while making his way to the lectern. He gripped the sides of the thing, threatening to rip it off the floor.

"My client told you the truth about his whereabouts on the night of April 11th, didn't he?"

"He told me he taught a class at the community college."

"But more than that, he told you the truth. He'd just met Neveah Ward. He admitted he drove her home."

"He said he drove her home, yes," Ritter answered. "Nice of him, considering everything else he did."

"Your Honor, will you please admonish the witness not to editorialize?"

"Ask your questions, Mr. Pettis. Make your objections. If there's admonishment to be done, I'll do it as I see fit," Judge Saul said.

"You took Neveah Ward's word for what happened to her, didn't you?" Pettis said.

"I took her statement," Gus answered.

"But it was her word against Mr. Sizemore's, wasn't it? That's what this really boils down to."

"I took her statement. That was part of the basis for probable cause in this case. But the physical evidence was pretty clear, Pettis."

"The physical evidence. There was evidence of sexual intercourse. Is that what you're saying?"

"No," he said. "That's what you're saying. I'm saying there was evidence of sexual assault. That girl was beaten. Bruised. Battered. Held down against her will. Raped and sodomized. That's not sexual intercourse. That's a crime."

"If there's no consent it's a crime," Pettis said.

"What?"

"All of those acts you described. They're only a crime if there's a lack of consent. I mean, you can consent to any of them. Isn't that true?"

"That girl didn't consent," he said.

"Because that's what she told you, isn't that correct?" Pettis said.

"And what her brutal injuries were consistent with, yes."

"Detective, have you ever heard of a dating website called MOCA?"

"I have."

"Can you tell me what it is?"

"You just said what it is. It's a dating app."

"But it's not just a dating app, isn't that right? Isn't it also true that MOCA is one of the most commonly used apps to solicit prostitution?"

"Objection," I said. "This is irrelevant and highly prejudicial."

"Your Honor," Pettis said. "It's relevant to the issue of consent in this case."

"Is defense counsel planning to argue his client was soliciting prostitutes?"

Pettis fumed. I didn't care.

"Move off it, Mr. Pettis," Saul said. "Unless you can show a direct bearing on the case."

"I can, Your Honor," Pettis said.

"Short leash," Saul said. "Very short."

"Of course," Pettis said. "Detective, isn't it true that during your investigation, you became aware that Neveah Ward has an active profile on the dating app called MOCA?"

"She has a profile, yes. And also one with Tinder, Facebook, Match.com. Yes."

"But MOCA specifically, you're aware of its reputation?"

"Mr. Pettis," he said. "Your client didn't meet Ms. Ward through MOCA or any other dating app. He abused his position of authority and lured her into his car after a class where she was a student, then he brutally raped her and beat the crap out of her in McCauley Park."

Fire shot out of Pettis's eyes. For his part, Denny Sizemore kept his face neutral. Only a thin bead of sweat along his brow belied his distress.

"All right," Saul said. "That's enough out of both of you. Move on, Mr. Pettis."

"Gladly," Pettis said. "Detective, you don't like Denny Sizemore very much, do you?"

"I'm not a fan of criminals, no."

"But you hate him, don't you? You've hated him for a long time, haven't you?"

"I've never really had an opinion about the guy one way or another."

My heart dropped. It was my turn to keep my face as neutral as I could. I wished I could burn my thoughts into Gus Ritter's brain. This was a set-up. Whatever Pettis had, Gus was walking straight into it.

"Never had an opinion," Pettis said. "Well, then I guess that makes you a liar, Detective."

"Objection!" I shouted.

"Sustained!" Saul said, almost talking over me. "Mr. Pettis, you're going to get a handle on that temper of yours right quick. Are we clear?"

Pettis didn't respond. His nostrils flared as he stared Gus down. "Detective, isn't it true you've been out to get Dennis Sizemore for years?"

"What? It is most certainly not."

Pettis rifled through some papers on the lectern. "In fact, you sat in a corner booth at the Brass Monkey and made a promise to take care of Denny Sizemore, someday, somehow, sometime. Isn't that right?"

It was too specific. What the heck did Sizemore have?

"I don't recall that, no," Ritter said. He had his temper in check. That scared me even more.

"So if someone overheard you vowing to 'take care of that son of a bitch Sizemore someday' that person would be lying?"

"I said I don't recall that," Ritter repeated.

"You were at the Brass Monkey on December 14th, three years ago, for a retirement party, weren't you?"

"I've been to the Brass Monkey plenty," Gus said. "I've been to plenty of retirement parties. I can't give you dates and times."

"Did you or did you not say at the Brass Monkey on December 14th, three years ago, that you wanted to take Dennis Sizemore out. That you wanted to make sure he had what was coming to him?"

"I don't recall that!" Ritter said. I couldn't breathe. Could barely see straight. I knew Gus. He wasn't stupid. If he hadn't said what Pettis claimed, he would have denied it straight out.

Dammit. Pettis had something. A witness.

"I have nothing further," Pettis said, his tone smug. Gus sat rod straight, chin up. But if he had lasers for eyes, he would have incinerated Simon Pettis where he stood.

12

There was no time to deal with Gus. No time to figure out what the hell I could do about Simon Pettis's bombshell. I stood at the prosecution table and did the only thing I could.

I called my next witness.

"The state calls Dr. Chloe Hernandez," I said.

Hernandez hadn't been in the courtroom when Gus testified. She had no inkling of the turmoil going on inside me as I gathered my notes and got through her foundational testimony.

Board certified in emergency medicine for over a decade. She served on the Sexual Assault Response Team at Maumee County Hospital. At roughly my age, Hernandez looked a good ten years younger. She had a bright, cheery smile and soothing voice that I'm sure made her the perfect fit for her patients while in perhaps the worst crisis and trauma of their lives.

"Dr. Hernandez," I said. "Did you treat Neveah Ward on April 12th of last year?"

"I did," she said. "She was brought into the emergency room by a friend ... a Jennifer Hobbs. Ms. Hobbs stayed with her through most of the examination."

"What were Ms. Ward's injuries?" I asked.

"Well, from top down, she had a number of superficial wounds to her head and neck. The worst of those was a cut to her bottom lip. It required two stitches. She had bruising to her throat consistent with and reported by her to have been caused by being choked. There was also significant bruising to Ms. Ward's torso and a bite mark on her left breast just above the nipple. She had bruising on her arms. She had significant tearing of the labia and vaginal wall and rectum."

"Did Ms. Ward tell you what happened to her?" I asked.

"She did. She reported that she'd been raped and beaten a few hours prior to coming to the emergency room. At that point, I contacted the authorities and we ordered the administration of a sexual assault medical forensic exam. What's commonly referred to as a rape kit."

At that point, Dr. Hernandez cataloged all the evidence collected from the kit which had previously been entered into evidence. She had collected blood, semen, and hair samples as well as skin beneath Neveah's fingernails. My next witness, Dr. Felice Uhlman, would carefully present the DNA evidence. Every single sample was a positive match for only one person. Denny Sizemore.

"Dr. Hernandez, how bad were Ms. Ward's injuries?"

"Well," she said. "None of them were life threatening, if that's what you're asking. My biggest concern from a medical standpoint was making sure she wasn't suffering from a concussion. And there is, of course, always a concern about infection, particularly with the bite wound, and the transmission of sexually transmitted diseases. But she had no broken bones or major internal injuries. Having said all of that, Ms. Ward had just experienced significant physical and emotional trauma. I wanted to make sure she had a support system in place. I referred her to a counselor who works with victims of sexual assault."

"Did you admit Neveah Ward to the hospital?"

"She wasn't formally admitted, no. But she did spend most of the day with us. The rape kit unfortunately takes several hours to conduct. I was also keeping an eye on her for, as I said, any signs of a concussion. But she was alert and oriented for her entire stay."

"Dr. Hernandez, you said you contacted the authorities. Can you tell me again why you did that?"

"There was clear medical evidence that Ms. Ward was the victim of a violent sexual assault. She also confirmed that when I questioned her. I'm duty bound to contact the police in that situation."

"Did you tell Ms. Ward you were going to call the police?"

"I discussed it with her, yes."

"Was she agreeable to that?"

"She was," Dr. Hernandez said. "She was reluctant at first. Scared. But she agreed with me that it was the right thing to do."

"So she never tried to prevent you from reporting the rape?"

"She didn't, no."

"She never indicated her injuries were caused by anything other than a nonconsensual sexual encounter?"

"Oh no. No. And her friend, Ms. Hobbs, spoke to me first before I even went into Ms. Ward's room. She confirmed ..."

"Objection," Pettis said. "Whatever Ms. Hobbs did or didn't say to this witness, it's hearsay testimony."

"Sustained," Judge Saul said. "As it relates to this other witness, you may not testify about what she said to you. It's not the same thing if your patient is reporting things to you during the course of your treatment of her. Do you understand that, Doctor?"

"I do," she said.

I paused. Dr. Hernandez had been clear, concise, and consistent. If Pettis were smart, he wouldn't spend a lot of time going after her.

"I have no further questions, Your Honor," I said.

"Mr. Pettis?"

"I've just got a couple for you, Dr. Hernandez," he said, barely looking up from his notes.

"You indicated that you initiated the call to the police. Is that right?"

"I called them, yes," she said.

"It was your idea, isn't that right?"

"My idea? I don't know if that's how I'd describe it. I had a patient who presented with some very clear, physical signs of having been the victim of a sexual assault, so I ..."

"Physical symptoms," he said. "She didn't tell you she was raped, did she, Doctor?"

"What?"

"She didn't say those words. Nowhere in your clinical notes do you indicate that your patient said the words, 'I was raped.' Correct?"

"It's correct. It's not in my clinical notes," she said.

"And you don't remember her saying it either, do you?"

"I don't recall if Ms. Ward used those specific words, no," she said.

"And it's not in your clinical notes anywhere that this friend, Ms. Hobbs, said Neveah Ward was raped either, is it?"

"Objection," I said. "Counsel can't have it both ways. If Ms. Hobbs's statements were hearsay on direct, they're hearsay on cross."

"Mr. Pettis?"

He looked up for the first time. "I didn't ask the witness if Ms. Hobbs said it. I asked her if she wrote it in her clinical notes."

"All right," Judge Saul said. "The witness may answer with that narrow parameter."

"My notes speak for themselves, Mr. Pettis," Dr. Hernandez said.

"Right. If Ms. Hobbs or Ms. Ward had said those words specifically. I was raped. I was assaulted. This guy attacked me. Any of that, don't you think it would have been important for you, the clinician, to have written it down?"

"No," she said.

"You made an assumption as to what happened to Neveah Ward and you acted on it. You told Ms. Ward you believed she'd been assaulted and you told her you were going to call the cops, isn't that right?"

"I made a clinical diagnosis based on the symptoms my patient presented," she said.

"Right. Got it. Yeah, I don't think I have any more questions for this witness," Pettis said, leaving me stunned.

"Ms. Brent?" Saul also looked stunned.

"Nothing more from me, Your Honor," I said.

I finished the day with my DNA witness. She was brief. Her testimony was conclusive and damaging. There was no doubt that the hair, skin, and semen found in Neveah Ward's rape kit belonged to Dennis Sizemore.

Pettis did the thing every criminal defense lawyer did in that situation. He got the scientist to admit she couldn't speak to consent with any of those pieces of evidence. As we wrapped up for the day, I went straight to the Sheriff's Department. Gus and Sam Cruz were waiting for me in Sam's office.

"Who does he have?" I said. My throat felt ragged.

"Mara ..." Gus started.

"Don't," I said. "Pettis has a witness. Someone who heard you at the Brass Monkey threatening to do something to Denny Sizemore."

"I never threatened to do anything to him," Gus said. "I told the truth on the stand. I don't recall saying that at the Brass Monkey."

I sank into an empty chair in front of Sam's desk.

"But you recall saying something like it," I said. "Christ, Gus. That was dangerous. You were under oath."

"And I didn't lie!" Gus shouted. "Yeah. I've said crap like that about Sizemore. Hell, half the guys in this department have. More."

"That's not helpful, Gus," I said.

"Mara, calm down," Sam said. "Gus has a point."

"Which point?" I asked. "That he technically didn't just commit perjury. Or that your department has been looking for an opportunity to stick it to Denny Sizemore all along."

"He raped that girl!" Gus said. "You saw what he did to her. She's telling the truth. He's not being framed. I didn't make this up."

"That's a great little story," I said. "Only Pettis is going to tell a different one. You didn't deny saying that stuff about Sizemore because you couldn't. Thanks a lot for that. It *might* let me block him from calling anyone to corroborate a lie. Might. But he scored some direct hits, Gus. My lead detective is pretty much on record with a personal beef against the accused."

"It's bullshit," he muttered.

"It's reasonable doubt," I answered back.

"That creep has been beating his wife for years. You think Neveah Ward is the first girl he's done that to?"

He got in my face. Gus leaned over my chair, forcing me to crane my neck to look at him. I wasn't having it. I got up and pushed him back.

"You don't have proof of any of it. God, I wish you did."

"He's protected," Sam said. "That's the beef, Mara. He uses the Chatham Township boys as his clean-up crew. There has always been friction between our departments."

"Departments," Gus said. "They're not a department. They're glorified rent-a-cops out there. They can't even handle so much as a fender bender without calling for back-up. Back in the day when I was still in field ops, we used to get calls from their command officers asking us to roll their garbage out to the curb when they were on vacation. Can you believe that? Oh, I took care of their garbage. Threw it all over their chief's lawn."

"Brilliant," I said. "Stories like that don't help me, Gus."

"I'd do it again!" he said. "They have been protecting Sizemore and worse for years. Open your eyes, Mara. That's why Chatham Township voted to contract out for police and fire in the first place. So they could take care of their own and get away with worse crap than what happens to Sizemore's wife and Neveah Ward. He was just stupid enough to hurt that girl in my backyard instead of his own."

I shook my head. "You still don't get it. What you said at the Brass Monkey, what you're saying now. It looks bad, Gus. It makes you sound like the very thing Simon Pettis is going to paint you as in his closing argument."

"I don't care what Simon Pettis says," he said, waving a dismissive hand.

"Gus," Sam said. "Think. Who was there with you at the Brass Monkey at that retirement party? Mara's right, that Pettis is no dummy. He's not going to go on a fishing expedition without live bait."

"Hell if I know," Gus said. "Nine out of ten people who retire outta this department have their parties at the Brass Monkey. End of the year, we go to 'em every week. How many specific shindigs do *you* remember over there, Sam?"

Sam conceded the point with a nod. "Yeah. I don't know."

"But it's primarily cops who go?" I asked.

"Yeah," Gus said.

"Gus," I said. "I get it, okay? My office has its own issues with Chatham Township. But I also know you. You would never have said something like that unless you were around people you trusted."

Gus dropped his head. "Yeah." he said. "Son of a bitch. Yeah."

I looked at Sam. "Which means someone around you is selling secrets to Simon Pettis or Denny Sizemore."

Sam was generally even-tempered. But when he lost it, it was legendary. Today, only a small tremor in his jaw belied what he was thinking. That was two seconds before he picked up the mug on his desk and threw it against the wall, shattering it into pieces.

13

"I'm sorry," Neveah said. "But I don't understand."

We had a few moments before we needed to head back into the courtroom to start the second day of trial. I'd secured space in the empty jury room across from Judge Saul's courtroom. Though Neveah hadn't heard yesterday's testimony firsthand, her advocate with the Silver Angels had filled her in on the highlights.

"What difference does it make if that detective hates Denny Sizemore or not?" she asked. "He still raped me. He wasn't even there or involved at all until after I went to the hospital and Dr. Hernandez started to examine me."

"Which is exactly what I'll argue in closing," I said. "And you'll have the chance to tell your story."

"When?" she asked. "Why can't I just go up there now and get it over with?"

"I haven't decided when to call you yet," I said. "Getting the physical evidence and Detective Ritter's testimony in first gives the jury all the things that aren't in dispute. It's powerful. No matter what Sizemore says when he gets up there, there's no denying what that rape kit showed."

She sat slouched in one of the hard wooden chairs, her hands resting on her knees. "His lawyer. Pettis. He's going to try saying Detective Ritter planted the evidence against me or that Dr. Hernandez talked me into calling it rape."

"He'll try, yes. That was certainly the way his cross-examination was headed."

"They can't believe that. It's insane! He thinks they'll believe I asked for it? That I wanted to get strangled and beaten and ... and all the other things he did to me? This can't be how this is going to end. They cannot believe that about me. They just can't! How could anyone?"

"Neveah," I said. "You have to stay calm. That's the best way you can fight right now. Let me do what I do. I'm putting Jennifer Hobbs on next. Do you have someone who can wait with you today? There's a good chance I won't get to your testimony today, either. I'm going to see how it goes."

"You'll put me on last?" she asked.

"Maybe. I know the uncertainty is tough. That's why I don't want you waiting around here alone."

"I'll be fine," she said. "Those ladies from the Silver Angels will be here. They're nice. I just hate how they seem so sad when they look at me. I'm tired of everyone thinking of me as just a victim."

"They don't just think that of you," I said.

"Everyone else does, though," she said. "No matter what happens with the jury, that's what everyone is going to think of first when they think of me at all. He made me what he did to me."

"No," I said. "That's the one thing he can never do, Neveah. I know it feels like that right now because of the focus on the trial. But this is just one part of your life. It will get better. There are people you can talk to. The Silver Angels ..."

"I know," she said. "They've given me all the numbers and the names and resources."

A soft knock on the door from the bailiff, and I was out of time with Neveah.

"You can hang out here for as long as you want," I said. "Just keep your cell phone with you. I'll text you when I can talk to you again."

She nodded. "Thanks, Mara. And I'm sorry to unload on you. My mental health isn't your job."

I put a hand on her shoulder. The urge to say trite things like 'hang in there' bubbled up. But I kept my mouth shut. It was enough Neveah knew I was fighting for her. I hoped. When I walked into the courtroom, Sizemore and Pettis were already at the defense table. Denny was laughing about something Simon had just whispered in his ear.

Behind them, Claire Sizemore sat with her hands folded and her legs crossed at the ankles. She was in full, professionally applied makeup but it couldn't hide her hollow cheeks and puffiness under her eyes.

I stood as Judge Saul took the bench. Sizemore and Pettis were still speaking in hushed whispers, oblivious to her presence. It didn't go unnoticed.

It wasn't until the jury filed in that Pettis straightened up. The wry smile at the corners of his mouth faded as he went all business. Sizemore, too, had new fear in his eyes. They both knew Neveah might take the stand as early as this afternoon. Keeping them guessing about that was part of my strategy.

"Ms. Brent," Judge Saul said. "Are you ready to proceed?"

"I am, Your Honor," I said. "The state calls Jennifer Hobbs to the stand."

A sheriff's deputy ushered twenty-two-year-old Jennifer to the stand. She had a slight, willowy build and long brown hair she wore parted in the middle. She dressed sensibly in a pink cardigan over a white blouse and navy-blue pencil skirt. Her hand shook as she raised it to swear her oath.

"Ms. Hobbs," I said after a few preliminary introductory questions. "How are you acquainted with the victim in this case, Neveah Ward?"

"She was my neighbor last year," she said. "She used to live in the apartment across the hall from me. We got to be friends. We also had a couple of classes together."

"Would you consider her to be a good friend?"

"More a casual acquaintance," she said. "We never really hung out socially. We studied together before Neveah dropped out of school. We would talk and text. Mostly about classes. I don't see her very much anymore since she moved out of the apartment a few months ago."

"I see," I said. "Jennifer, I want to direct your attention to the evening of April 11th last year. Did you see or speak to Neveah that night?"

"Yeah," she said. "Neveah had class from six to nine. It was a Thursday. I saw her as she was about to leave. Neveah usually walked to class because the apartment building was only a few blocks. She had a car, but it wasn't very reliable. Anyway, I was out picking up my mail and I saw her as she was leaving."

"You spoke?"

"Briefly."

"Then, as far as you knew, she went to her class?"

"Yes."

"When did you next see her?"

"It was maybe eleven, eleven thirty. I heard keys outside Neveah's door. Our units were right next to each other. Then I heard Neveah outside her door, trying to get in. I don't know what made me go out there. I heard something. She was breathing weird. So I went out on the porch and I could see her fumbling with her keys. She didn't look right."

"In what way?"

"Well," Jennifer said. "Neveah is very neat with her appearance. She's got these beautiful braids and there's never a hair out of place. She always dresses up for class. Like in business suits and stuff. I teased her about it. Not meanly. I used to call her Madam President. Anyway, she was a mess that night."

"What do you mean?" I asked.

"Her hair was messed up. With flyaways sticking out. And her blouse was torn. I went out there to see if she was okay. I could see she clearly wasn't."

"How so?"

"She had a fat lip and she was bleeding. Shaking like crazy. She could barely get her key in the door."

"What did you do then?"

"I asked her what happened, of course. She just kept shaking her head. Wouldn't talk."

"What did you do next?" I asked.

"I took Neveah's keys and opened her door for her. Then I walked her inside and made her sit down on the couch in her living room. I got her a glass of water and a wash cloth. She was hurt. Shaking. Bleeding."

"Then what happened?"

"I sat across from her and kept asking her if she was okay. Asking her what happened."

"Did she tell you?" I asked.

"No," Jennifer said. "Not then. She was kind of in shock. But it was obvious what happened."

"What do you mean?"

"With her clothes like that? The fat lip? And there was blood running down her leg. Like from the inside of her thigh."

"What did you think happened?"

"Objection," Pettis said. "Calls for speculation."

"Sustained," Judge Saul said. "You can speak to what you observed, not what you guessed."

"Fair enough." I smiled at Jennifer. "What did you do then?"

"I told Neveah we needed to call the police. But she wouldn't. Or she just kept shaking her head."

"Did you call the police?"

"No. Not then. I was starting to get really worried about Neveah. So I finally decided I wasn't going to take no for an answer. I told her to sit tight. I ran back to my apartment and got my car keys. We don't have parking on-site. There's a lot across the street with a carport. So it took me maybe five or ten minutes before I pulled back up into the driveway."

"Where was Neveah during all of this?" I asked.

"She was just sitting on the couch where I left her."

"Then what did you do?" I asked.

"I put her in my car. Like I physically stuck my hands under her arms and got her to stand up. She was like a zombie. She didn't fight me or say anything. She just went along. She let me put her in the passenger seat, buckle her in, and off we went to the E.R. I took her to the hospital."

"I see," I said. "What happened next?"

"I got her out of the car and we walked into the emergency room. We waited maybe ten minutes. Luckily, there was a nurse there who spotted us right away. Neveah was in terrible shape. I think she saw what I saw pretty quick. They got her into an exam room and things started moving pretty fast after that."

"How so?"

"They got a doctor in there, Dr. Hernandez. And there were all these other nurses flocking around Neveah. They had me wait in a chair in the hallway. That's when Neveah started to come around. She started crying. Like, hysterical crying."

"What did you do?"

"I waited. After a while, Dr. Hernandez came out and asked me pretty much the same questions you just did. And I gave her the same answers. They asked me to wait with Neveah. So I did."

"How long did you wait?" I asked.

"Oh, it was hours. The police came. I was interviewed by Detective Ritter. I told him the same things I told you and Dr. Hernandez. About how Neveah got home. How she looked. How she was acting."

"Did you see Neveah again that night?" I asked.

"Sure," she said. "She asked for me. While they were examining her, I stood beside her bed and held her hand. It was awful. Just ... awful. She barely got through it."

Jennifer broke down in tears.

"Did Neveah ever tell you what happened?" I asked.

"Objection," Pettis said. "To the extent this witness is about to testify about what Neveah Ward said to her, it's hearsay."

"Once again," Judge Saul said. "You'll need to stick to what you observed."

"Got it," Jennifer said.

"Your Honor," I said. "I have no more questions for this witness."

Pettis stood behind me like a ghoul as I gathered my notes. I stepped aside and took my seat at the table.

"Ms. Hobbs," Pettis started. "You indicated that Ms. Ward usually walked home from class, but that's not true, is it?"

"What? Yes it is," she said.

"But you've seen Neveah come home in cars with other men plenty of times, haven't you?"

"What? I don't ..."

"In fact, you've routinely seen Neveah Ward getting dropped off by other men."

"I wouldn't say routinely. But she's gotten dropped off, yes."

"Did you notice what kinds of cars they were then?"

Jennifer looked confused. "I mean ... I guess. Sometimes."

"Have you ever seen her dropped off by a man driving a blue BMW?"

"Uh ... sure. Yes."

"When was this?"

"I don't know the dates. A few times. Yes."

"Enough so that you commented on it to other friends, isn't that right?"

"I might have, yes," Jennifer said.

"And you've seen Neveah being dropped off by a man driving a silver Mercedes, haven't you?"

"Yes."

"These were dates she was going on, isn't that right?"

"Objection," I said. "This is highly irrelevant."

"Sustained, Mr. Pettis," Judge Saul said. "Move on."

"Ms. Hobbs, are you familiar with a dating app called MOCA?"

"What? I mean, sure."

"In fact, you maintain a profile on MOCA, don't you?"

"Objection," I said. "Irrelevant."

"Mr. Pettis?" Judge Saul said.

"If you'll grant me some leeway," he said.

"No," Judge Saul said. "Counsel, please approach."

We met her at a sidebar. Saul leaned over, covering her microphone.

"Knock it off, Mr. Pettis," Judge Saul said. "The dating life of this witness isn't relevant by any means."

"Well, the dating life of the victim sure is," Pettis said. "This witness and Neveah Ward indulged in certain proclivities.

Those proclivities absolutely relate to the claims Ms. Ward has made."

"You gotta be kidding me," I said. "You cannot seriously be going there."

"The girl has a MOCA profile," Pettis said. "She's a prostitute."

"You're unbelievable," I said. "There's no evidence of that. Or are you actually planning to argue that your client was her john?"

"Enough," Judge Saul said. "We aren't going to settle this in a sidebar. We're going to need a full evidentiary hearing. Though I'm warning you, Mr. Pettis, if your plan is to just try throwing out unwarranted accusations, I'll smack you down hard."

"All I'm asking for is the right to argue my point."

I was livid. It wasn't that we hadn't seen this coming. But now that Pettis was actually saying the words, it was hard to believe. He was going for the 'she asked for it' defense.

"In the meantime," Saul said. "You're done asking this particular witness about her dating life or whether she subscribes to MOCA or any other app of the kind. So you can resume your cross with that caveat. Then we're in recess until after lunch. At which time I'll hear oral argument on the evidentiary question of whether Ms. Ward's dating profile should come in if she takes the stand. But only when she takes the stand. Got it? You don't get to back door this through anyone else."

"Got it," Pettis said.

We broke. I tried to keep my temper out of my expression as I went back to the table. As Pettis took the lectern, he had a beaming smile for Jennifer Hobbs.

"Ms. Hobbs," he said. "Thank you. I have no further questions."

With that, we were in recess. I had just enough time to get word to Neveah that she wouldn't take the stand until tomorrow. Then I raced back to my office to prepare for Simon Pettis's next salvo.

14

I came in hot. Blazing. It took everything I had not to launch myself across the courtroom as Simon Pettis stood there and argued to the judge.

"Your Honor," he said. "The prosecution has attempted to paint a false picture of Neveah Ward's lifestyle. Her story, to the police, is that she merely expected a ride home from the defendant. We have the right to explore the veracity of that claim."

"Ms. Brent?" Judge Saul said. I stood gripping a pen so hard I could have turned it to powder.

"Her lifestyle? Your Honor, if that isn't a signal for slut shaming, then I don't know what is. Ms. Ward's lifestyle, as Mr. Pettis seems to imagine it, isn't relevant. This is the twenty-first century. The introduction of a rape victim's prior sex life is inadmissible."

"Mr. Pettis," Judge Saul said. "I'm on Ms. Brent's side here. What exactly are you trying to accomplish with this?"

"Your Honor," Simon said. He was sweating. "It's not Ms. Ward's sex life that's relevant. We're not talking about who she's dating. We're talking about her proclivity to engage in sexual activities that are ... well ... borderline violent. The defense will be able to show that Ms. Ward routinely solicits men for sex. And that when she does, she indulges in rather violent sex play. The issue of consent is really the only relevant question of fact for this jury. Look, this is distasteful to me, too. I'm not out here trying to ruin the girl. But my client is on trial for his freedom. For his reputation. It's within his right to challenge Ms. Ward's assertion that whatever happened between them wasn't consensual."

"Your Honor," I said. "With all due respect to Mr. Pettis, this is a complete load of bull he's peddling. He's twice now tried to introduce evidence of Ms. Ward's online dating profiles. There is absolutely no evidence that any of that had anything to do with how Denny Sizemore got her into his car that night. They didn't meet online. They met because he was teaching her class. Quite frankly, the fact that he's even been allowed to mention the MOCA app is extremely prejudicial and has zero probative value to the issues in this case. I'd also like to move that the jury be instructed to disregard any testimony regarding it."

Judge Saul let out a great sigh. She pinched the bridge of her nose. After a moment, she focused a laser-like stare on Simon Pettis.

"Mr. Pettis, I agree with Ms. Brent regarding this dating website. At least as the evidence has been presented so far, I see no relevance to it. So to that extent, I won't allow any more references to it or questions regarding it. Now, on the issue of consent, you're right. Of course, it's relevant in this case.

However, it's only relevant as it relates to the interaction between the defendant and the victim. You don't have carte blanche to question witnesses about other sexual encounters Ms. Ward may or may not have had."

"Your Honor," Pettis interrupted. "You cannot cut off my ability to explore the existence of a pattern of behavior."

"Mr. Pettis, you're on dangerously thin ice with me. If Neveah Ward takes the stand, you're welcome to explore the issue of consent. If you have any other witnesses who have firsthand knowledge of what happened between these two people, you're welcome to call them in your case in chief. Firsthand knowledge. Not innuendo. Not rumors, gossip, or anything else. That's my ruling. Are we clear?"

Pettis opened his mouth as if he were about to unleash another tirade. Something made him think the better of it. He closed his mouth.

"We're clear, Your Honor," he said.

"That is all," she said. "It's three o'clock already. I'm inclined to let the jury go home for the day. Ms. Brent, how many more witnesses do you have left?"

The true answer was one. But if I said it, it would signal to Pettis that Neveah was up next. "Potentially four," I said.

"All right," she said. "I've got my schedule cleared for four more days of trial. Can you be done in a day and a half of that?"

"I would think so," I answered.

"Deputy Comstock? Would you be so kind as to go back there and tell the jury they're free to go home with our standard admonishment regarding discussion of this case?"

"Yes, ma'am," her bailiff said.

"Then we're back here at nine a.m.," Judge Saul said, briefly banging her gavel.

Pettis and Sizemore were already in a huddle. I packed up my things and headed out of the courtroom. I didn't want to make contact with either one of them. They made me sick.

I slid open my phone and sent a text to Neveah. I'd sent her home for lunch with instructions to stay close in case there was time to put her on the stand today.

"You can stand down," I texted. "We're back in court at nine and you'll take the stand first thing. We can meet again this evening to go over whatever you need."

I waited a moment as three dots blinked.

"Okay on tomorrow," she texted back. "I'd rather meet in the morning and just try to unwind tonight. Is that okay?"

"Sounds good," I answered. "I can pick you up at seven. We'll head over to my office before going to court. Wear the blue suit we bought."

She texted back, "Okay. I'll be ready by seven. I just want this over."

"I know," I said. "We're almost there."

15

I got home just in time for my six o'clock FaceTime call with Will. I waited as the staccato bleeps rang out and adjusted my iPad to fix the lighting. The hanging copper pots gleamed behind my left shoulder. I used to let Will bang on them with a wooden spoon when he was little.

The screen lit up. I smiled at my son. Only it wasn't his face on screen. It was Kat's and she was frowning.

"Hey, Kat," I said. "Where's my little man?"

"He's with Jason," she said, plastering on a smile. "He got called back for a floor vote and thought Will might like to tag along."

It was a lie. What's worse? Kat knew I knew it. Will looked forward to our nightly calls. They were part of his routine. My son wouldn't have just blown one off to do something spontaneous like that. It wasn't how he was wired.

"Kat," I said. "Don't. You better tell me what's really going on."

Kat blinked rapidly. She was fighting back tears. "I'm sorry," she said. "Jason was supposed to get a hold of you. I told him to. I don't want to be in the middle of this."

"But you are," I said. "And I'm not the one who's trying to change everything. Will is supposed to be here right now. With me. Back in school. I didn't cause this disruption."

Kat looked tortured. I loved her as if she were my own sister. She *was* my own sister. But at the moment, I didn't care. I was too angry and I wanted my son home.

"I'm looking out for him," she said. "I always will. But you and Jason need to work your stuff out."

"You know Bree came to see me," I said. "She's upset too, Kat. She's worried you're going to move to D.C. permanently if ..."

I couldn't even say it. I would not entertain the possibility that I'd lose custody of my son. At the same time, I was doing what Jeanie Mills made me swear I wouldn't. I was not about to discuss the case with Kat or anyone else besides Jeanie.

"He's going to have Will call you tomorrow," Kat said.

"Did he tell you to tell me that?" I asked. "Is he making you be the messenger now?"

There was movement behind her. It was just a flash, but I saw someone quickly walk through the living room.

Callista. She was Jason's latest girlfriend. What on earth was she doing in Jason's townhouse if he wasn't there?

"Is that Callista? I can see her, Kat. What's going on?"

Except I knew. There was only one reason Callista would be there without Jason. She was staying there. She was living there. With. My. Son.

"Callista!" I yelled. "I can see you."

Kat covered her eyes with her hand. Her jaw quivered. I supposed it should have made me feel better that she was in distress. It didn't. I loved her. She loved Will. And I hated Jason.

"Hey, Mara," Callista said, waving from behind Kat's shoulder. "I just stopped by to grab some things."

She was lying. It's why Kat was in the state she was.

"Hey," Callista went on. "Will's doing great. He's really happy. You don't have anything to worry about."

"Go away, Callista," I said. "I don't have anything to say to you."

Callista went white and straightened. She was every nightmare in a tight tank top and workout pants. Her smile soured and she disappeared off screen.

"Kat," I said. "Is she living there?"

"Mara, you need to talk to Jason. I can't be your intermediary. I'm trying to be there for Will."

"It's not fair of Jason to ask you to be. Your life is here. Bree is here. Will is my son, not yours."

"Do you want me to leave? Now?" She almost shrieked it. "Will can't handle that. This has been really hard on him."

"Then that's what you need to tell the mediators, Kat. The truth. That's all I ask. That's all Jason should be asking."

"I need to go," she said. "I just wanted to make sure you knew Will was okay."

"Is he?" I asked. "Is he really? He has to have questions. He has to be regressing. I know him. This is killing me, Kat."

"I know." Her tone went soft. "I know. I love you too, Mara. But I also love my brother. I'm ... I'm trying."

"I know," I said. I couldn't bear it.

"Will will call you tomorrow. Six o'clock. I'll make sure of it."

"Jason should be making sure of it," I said. "I hate what this is doing."

"Good luck," she said. "I know you're in trial. Focus on that for now. I'll make sure Will's taken care of. I promise."

"Thank you," I said. God, I missed Kat. And I hated everything about this. We clicked off and I shot off a text to Jeanie.

"Jason made Will miss his FaceTime call with me tonight. Looks like the girlfriend is also living with him. That's also a violation of our custody order."

A moment later, Jeanie texted back. "Bastard. I'll file an emergency ex parte motion to move up your hearing. Keep documenting everything. And good luck in court tomorrow. I expect you to rip Simon Pettis a new one. We're all rooting for you down here in Delphi."

"THX," I texted back. Then I went for a bottle of wine.

I couldn't sleep that night. I went over the questions I needed to ask Neveah a thousand times. I knew her direct examination by heart. She'd been rock solid during all of our prep sessions. We were both ready. And I was grateful for the distraction from my personal life.

I finally got out of bed at five a.m., showered, and put on my best black suit. By six thirty, I was ready to go. I grabbed my phone.

I had three unread texts. One from Kenya wishing me good luck. One from Jeanie telling me she'd file my ex parte motion this morning and pop into the courtroom if I didn't mind. I texted her quickly back telling her that sounded fine. The third text was from David Pham.

"Thinking about you today," he said. "Knock 'em dead or break a leg or whatever you're supposed to say in this situation."

I smiled. I owed him a rain check for dinner. I wondered if my life would ever stop being complicated enough to honor it.

"Thanks," I texted back. "That means a lot."

I slipped my phone in my briefcase and headed across town to pick up Neveah.

I pulled into the driveway and headed up her walk. The lights were on and I could hear music playing. Rhianna. It made me smile. It was Neveah's hype up music.

I knocked on the door, but the music was too loud for her to hear me. Cautiously, I pushed on the door. It wasn't locked.

"Neveah?" I called out. I took a step inside. Just one step into her living room. I gripped the door handle, afraid to let go. Afraid to breathe.

"No," I said, my voice sounding far away and foreign to my ears. "God. No."

Then my heart dropped straight to my knees.

16

I'd been here before. Watched this scene play out. The shocked witness sitting in the back of a patrol car. Someone hands her a cup of coffee or a water. There are lights flashing. There is the heavy, thrumming diesel engine of the ambulance as it idles nearby. A soothing voice asking questions no one ever wants to answer. In a space no one ever wants to be in. Their tone is gentle at first. Always. But at a certain point, the witness must focus. Must be pulled out of whatever protective daydream they've retreated to. Anything to shield them from the trauma their body knows they are experiencing. Their brain just hasn't caught up yet.

Yes. I've seen it happen hundreds of times. Watched as the witness slowly slides back into the present and focuses on the person asking the questions.

Only this time, the witness was me.

"Mara," Sam said. He squatted down in front of me, holding coffee in an insulated cup. He handed it to me. Gus Ritter stood beside him, his expression grim.

"I'm sorry," I said. "What did you ask me?"

Gus held his notepad. His gun and badge were clipped to his belt. I don't know what made me focus on that. He kept a black pen slid inside the holster, tucked along the barrel of his weapon.

"When did you last speak to Neveah?" he asked.

I took the offered coffee from Sam. "Um ... it was last night. We texted. My phone. I can pull it up."

"Your purse is here," Sam said. It was lying on the floor of the car beside me.

"God, what is wrong with me?" I said. "I had a man blow his head off right in front of me. And worse ... I ..."

"She was your friend," Sam said. Was. I squeezed my eyes shut. She was there. Neveah. That beautiful, vibrant, tragic girl. She was slumped sideways on her living room couch, lips blue, lifeless eyes bulging, with a needle sticking out of her arm.

"What can I do?" I asked. "What do you need?"

I fumbled for my phone and pulled up my text exchange with Neveah. I handed it to Gus. He took it. Wrote it all down in his old-school notepad.

"The last time you spoke to her in person?" Gus asked.

"Yesterday. In court. We had the evidentiary hearing. Judge Saul isn't going to allow Pettis to delve into Neveah's sexual history. It took the better part of the afternoon and I told Neveah to go home. She was ... yesterday. She seemed fine. Normal. Ready to testify. She's ... she's my last witness."

Gus and Sam exchanged a look.

"She knew that?" Sam asked. "She knew you were putting her on first thing this morning?"

I rose and stepped out of the car. "I need to get to court. I need to let them know what's happened. We'll need a continuance."

"I've already done that," Sam said.

"Mara," Gus said. "Did you know she was using?"

"What? No. Wait. What? No!"

"Mara," Gus said.

"No," I said. "She wasn't using. She was fine. She was ready to take the stand. She was solid. Rock solid. Gus, this doesn't make sense. She never once hesitated or wavered. She was nervous, yes, but ... God."

"We found paraphernalia," Gus said. "In a cigar box near her bed."

"No," I said. "She was clean. I'm sure of it. I never saw any track marks on her. Ever. I know what to look for. She was clean."

"Do you know who her next of kin was?" Gus asked. "They need to be notified."

"No," I said. "I mean, her father's still around. He lives over on Gantry Street. Gary Mosely. But Neveah didn't want anything to do with him. He tried to sell her out to the press when this whole thing started. She never came out and told me directly, but I got the impression there was some physical abuse there growing up."

"Who were her close friends?" Gus asked. "I've got a crew heading out to Jennifer Hobbs's place."

"I don't even think they were communicating very much since the trial started," I said. "If she's close to anyone, it's Louella Holmes. Louella's been a rock for her. A mother figure. Lord. This is going to crush her. Louella loves Neveah. Those kids at the Montessori. They love her too."

"We'll get a hold of her," Sam said.

"Mara," Gus said. "Do you think she did this on purpose?"

"Killed herself?" I said. "I don't know what to think. I know that's not very helpful. But no, there's nothing she's said or done as far as I know. That would have given me a clue she was thinking of taking her own life."

"Well," Gus said. "She's got a dealer. We'll start there. Lab guys will run her cell phone. That usually tells us what we need to know."

"I just don't buy it, Gus," I said. "She shows up dead a few hours before she's supposed to testify? Promise me you'll look hard at this one."

"I look hard at all of them, Mara," he said. "If there's something to find, we'll find it."

"I know," I said. "I'm sorry. I didn't mean ..."

"It's okay," Gus said. "This one's gonna leave a mark on me, too. That kid's been through enough."

The M.E.'s van pulled up. It felt like another blow straight to the stomach. I knew she was dead. Of course I did. But the thought of them rolling Neveah Ward out in a body bag just opened up another black hole of despair.

I saw it written on Gus's face.

"I thought she had a shot," Gus said. "I really did."

"Me too," I said. Instinct took over and I went to him. Gus wasn't a hugger, but he opened his arms and grabbed me.

"I'm sorry," he said.

"I should have sat with her," I said. "I should have had her come over to my place and spend the night. If she was upset. If she was ..."

"You can't take this on," Gus said, letting me go. "Neither of us can."

"Just take care of her," I said.

"Yeah. I'm gonna head in there with the M.E.'s people. Make sure everything's secure."

"I want to ride with her," I said.

"You don't have to do that," Sam said.

David Pham stepped into view. He walked over to the three of us.

"You okay?" David asked me. "I heard them call it in. You're the one who found her?"

"Yes," I said. "Sitting on the couch in the living room. She was already dead. Looked like she had been for a while."

"Can you bump her to the head of the line?" Gus asked.

"You think this is foul play?" David asked.

"I don't know what to think yet," Gus said. "I just want to make sure this kid gets taken care of."

David nodded. "Of course."

"You'll do the post mortem yourself?" I said to David. "Can you promise me that?"

"Of course," he said again. "I'll take care of her. Do you have any info on her next of kin?"

"We're trying to get that settled," Gus said.

"Got it," David said. "Well, let me get in there. I'll let you know what I can do when I can. It'll be later this afternoon or early tomorrow morning."

"Take whatever time you need," Gus said. "I'll head in there with you."

Gus squeezed my hand. David watched him. He pursed his lips and gave me a soulful nod, leaving me there with Sam.

"Come on," he said. "Why don't you let me drive you home?"

"I've got my car," I said. "And I need to get to the office. I need to figure out where we go from here. How long do you think I have before the media gets a hold of this?"

"I think you're gonna need to assume they already have it. She's got neighbors on all sides. Everybody knows she's the one accusing Sizemore of rape and they know the trial's going on."

"Right," I said. "Which means I should expect a call from Pettis any second."

"What are you going to tell him?"

"I need to talk to Kenya," I said.

"You sure you're okay?" Sam asked. He stopped me, put a hand on my arm.

"No," I said. "I'm not okay. I'm angry."

As I said it, I felt my temper rising. I wanted to break something. To punch someone. To scream.

"Pettis is going to be out in front of the cameras any minute," Sam said. "I think you can pretty much guarantee that."

"She didn't get to tell her story," I said. "Which means Sizemore is going to try to control the narrative from here on out."

"The evidence is still the evidence, Mara," Sam said. "No matter what he says, Sizemore can't change that."

I nodded, though I didn't feel hopeful. I felt lost. We stood frozen together, Sam and me, as David's team passed us with the stretcher and the empty body bag that would soon hold Neveah Ward.

17

Louella Holmes took two halting steps toward me, then fell to her knees in the hospital corridor. She knew. She'd been my first call as soon as I had a moment to make one. But now that she was here, as she saw me standing under a sign that pointed to the morgue, it hit home for her as it did me in the back of that police cruiser.

I went to her. She clung to me as I helped her to her feet and into a chair.

"What happened?"

"We're not sure," I said. "I don't have any good answers for you. When was the last time you spoke with her?"

Louella sniffed. "Two days ago."

"How did she sound to you, then?" I asked.

"Nervous," Louella said. "But determined. You know how Neveah gets. She was anxious to get it over with, you know? She sounded like ... Neveah. Oh God. I don't know how I'm going to tell those kids. They love her."

Louella doubled over, burying her face in her hands. There was nothing I could do for her except be there.

"That baby," she whispered. "That poor baby. What happens now? Are they going to take care of her?"

"Dr. Pham is a friend of mine," I said. "The medical examiner. Yes. He'll take good care of her."

"She wrote me down as her emergency contact," Louella said. "Does that mean I have to make arrangements for her?"

"Usually that's done by her next of kin," I said. "Obviously, you know more about Neveah's family situation than I do. I'm sure her father's already been notified. He'll have to … um … claim the body."

"Oh no. Oh no, no, no. She wouldn't want that. That won't do at all. Neveah wanted nothing to do with that man. He can't have her back. Not now. What can we do?"

"Let's just wait and see," I said.

"I need to see her," she said. "That's why I came. Do you think they'll let me see her for myself? Since I'm her emergency contact?"

"I'm not sure that's a good idea," I said. In Louella's emotional state, there was no way she could handle seeing Neveah like this. I barely could. Her blown pupils. The bluish cast to her skin. It wasn't Neveah in there on that slab. Not the girl Louella loved.

The elevator doors opened down the hall and Gus came toward us. His already dour expression darkened further when he saw Louella with me.

I patted Louella on the back, gestured to Gus, then met him close to the elevators and away from Louella's earshot.

"What's she doing here?" he asked.

"She keeps saying she was Neveah's emergency contact. Also ... I think she just felt like Neveah should have someone here who loved her."

Gus nodded. "Yeah. I get that. That kid didn't have too many friends in the world. Louella's a good one to have."

He walked over to her. "Hey, Louella, I'm so sorry for your loss. You holding up okay?"

Her whole face fell like melted candle wax when she looked up at him.

"I know this is a terrible time," he said. "But do you mind if I ask you a few questions?"

"Anything I can do to help," she said.

Gus asked her the same things I had. When was the last time she saw Neveah? How did she seem? Louella gave the same answers.

"Was she seeing anybody?" Gus asked. "A new boyfriend? An old boyfriend?"

Louella shook her head. "I never saw her with anybody. She just came to work and did her job."

"Louella, I know this is tough. But was there anything, anything at all about her behavior or how she looked in the last few weeks that would have led you to believe she might be using drugs?"

Louella's eyes widened. "No. Oh, no. There was nothing. Neveah wasn't into anything like that, as far as I know. She never even drank alcohol, I don't think."

"Do you drug test your employees?" he asked.

"Yes," Louella said, her face brightening. "It's a condition of employment."

"When was the last one Neveah had?"

"Right after I hired her," she said. "Six months? I can check my file. She passed though."

"Of course," Gus said. "You're sure though? No new boyfriends or other people in her life that you hadn't met?"

"I didn't see her outside of work. Not until the trial," Louella said. "But no. Nobody ever dropped her off. She drove herself. She never even really socialized with the other teachers or aides. Neveah kept to herself. It was me she was closest with."

"What about this man?" Gus asked. He pulled up a picture of Web Margolis on his phone. It was the exact question I wanted to ask Louella. "Have you ever seen Neveah with him recently?"

Louella looked at Margolis's picture. She rapidly shook her head. "No. I don't know him. Never seen him before in my life. Was he a friend of Neveah's? Do you think he knows what happened?"

"I'm just trying to gather facts at this point," Gus said. "What about him?"

He pulled up another photo of Gary Mosely, Neveah's father. Louella shook her head no again. "I don't know that man either."

Louella started to sob. She wasn't able to give verbal responses to the next few questions Gus asked. He finally gave up and patted her on the shoulder. "You should head on home, Louella," he said. "There's nothing you can do here."

"I'll stay," she said. "Someone should stay."

Gus caught my eye and gestured over his shoulder for me to follow him. We walked out of Louella's earshot around the corner.

"Have you been able to find anything else out?" I asked.

Gus looked uncomfortable at the question. "I just came from her old man's place. Father of the Year, that one."

"How did he take it?" I asked.

"I could barely get him to open the door," Gus said. "He was drunk off his ass. Hazy-eyed. When I came to the door he just asked me what's Neveah done now? When I told him she passed, he kind of shrugged it off. Shut the door in my face."

"Lovely," I said. "Louella's worried about what happens to Neveah next. She knows Neveah didn't want anything to do with her dad."

"I hate this for her," Gus said. "Louella's not in the best of health herself. She's had two heart attacks in the last five years. There's nothing she can really do here right now. I'm going to give her son a call and see if he'll come get her. Sit with her."

"That's a good idea," I said. "What other leads are you following?"

"I should have her phone forensics back in a few hours," he said. "Hopefully, I'll be able to track down her dealer that way."

"I just can't believe it, Gus. I told you before, I would have sworn it up and down that Neveah wasn't using."

"Yeah. I know. Let's just see what Pham has to say."

As if on cue, David emerged from the windowless steel doors at the other end of the hall. He wore scrubs and a surgical hat still. He took one look at Louella and went to her. She cried against his shoulder as he embraced her.

We couldn't hear what they were saying, but whatever David told her, it calmed Louella. She smiled through her tears and nodded as he rose and walked back toward Gus and me. Louella sank to a chair in the hallway, staring straight ahead.

"We can talk in here," David said. He led Gus and me to a small office down the hall.

The two men waited while I took a seat at a round metal table. Gus sat on my right. David stayed standing, leaning against the wall.

"What do you have for me?" Gus asked.

"Nothing you'll like," he said. "She was about as healthy as they come. No malformations to the heart or brain. Her lungs were clear. No signs of a stroke, heart attack."

"Any evidence of trauma?" Gus asked.

"Some bruising around the injection site in her left forearm," David answered. "She had a superficial cut behind her right ankle. There was a Band-Aid over it. She probably gouged herself shaving. But no, nothing. No obvious signs of trauma. No bruising, no scrapes, no broken bones."

"You're sure?" I asked.

"Of course," David said.

"What about her stomach contents?" Gus asked.

"Almost empty. Some partially digested lettuce. She probably had a salad for dinner. Based on her body temperature and a few other factors, she hadn't been dead very long. You said it was just after seven when you found her, Mara?"

"Yeah," I said.

"She likely died within an hour of when you found her. Two, tops."

"She was dressed in the blue suit I told her to wear," I said. "She was waiting for me to pick her up. If I'd just gotten there sooner."

Gus and David stayed silent for a moment, letting me process it. After a few minutes, David continued.

"And you found drug paraphernalia in the home?" Pham asked Gus.

"In her bedside table, yes," he answered.

"It's gonna take a few weeks for toxicology to come back, but that will probably be conclusive. There's no evidence of the cause of death from her physical exam. This was a drug overdose. I'll be able to confirm that when I get those labs."

"Yeah," Gus said. "Dammit. I've seen this thousands of times. These kids are playing Russian roulette any time they shoot up."

"Absolutely," David agreed. "I know what the labs are going to say. There will be a high concentration of fentanyl. I'm sorry, Mara."

I pressed my thumbs to the corners of my eyes. My head began to throb.

"Neveah is a lot of things. Was. But she's never been stupid," I said.

"I'll find who supplied her," Gus said.

"Has anyone talked to Web Margolis?" I asked him.

"Was she still seeing him?" Gus asked.

"I honestly don't know. But Neveah didn't have a lot of extra money. Certainly not enough to support a drug habit."

"You think Margolis might have been supplying her?" he asked.

"I think he's worth a conversation."

Gus nodded. "He'll be my next stop. Though I can't imagine he's going to admit to anything. I'll find out when he last spoke to her. Neveah's phone will be helpful. The forensics team will have that back to me by morning. We'll go from there. I'll be in touch."

"Thanks, Gus," I said. "You're going above and beyond on this one. Don't think I'm not aware."

He pursed his lips. Our eyes met. I knew Neveah's death was hitting him hard. He softly knocked his fist against the table. Then he got up and left David and me to talk alone.

"You okay?" David asked as soon as the door shut behind Gus.

"No," I said. "Actually, no. I feel like everything's just falling apart right now. I don't know how I missed it. I should have seen something was wrong. I should have made sure someone stayed with Neveah."

"You can't blame yourself for this one," he said. "You've been her champion. You know a lot of other prosecutors wouldn't have even taken her case. Denny Sizemore is a weasel, but he's a powerful weasel."

"I made some headway," I said. "But it was going to be her word against his. Now? I just don't even know. I can't even think about it."

David took the seat Gus had vacated. He reached across the table and gathered my hands in his.

"I'm sorry for your loss," he said. "I really am."

"Thanks," I said. "You're a good friend, David. A better one than I am. I'm sorry. You just caught me when everything in my life has just been ... messy."

David smiled. "I don't mind," he said. "And I'm not in any hurry. I think you might be worth waiting for."

I didn't know what to say. Then I realized there was nothing to say. I just sat and received David's sentiment. I leaned across the table and kissed him on the cheek. He blushed.

We sat for a moment. Then David became all business again. "What about Neveah?" he said.

"That's the million-dollar question. Her father is her next of kin but they were estranged. I don't know if he's even going to bother coming down to claim the body. That's kind of why Louella is here. She was worried Neveah didn't have any loved ones that would honor her wishes."

"Does she know what those were?" David asked. "Did she leave a will or any other instructions?"

"I have no idea," I said. "She was twenty-one years old. I doubt it. Gary Mosely, her dad, probably doesn't even have two nickels to rub together, much less anything to pay for a funeral or a proper burial."

"Well, she's safe here for the time being," he said. "I don't have to release her right away. I'll talk to Louella. See what arrangements can be made."

"That's very sweet of you," I said. "It'll ease Louella's mind."

"I'm glad to help in any way I can," he said. "That goes for you, too. Is there somewhere you have to be? It's getting late. I have a few things I have to finish up paperwork-wise, but then would you like to grab a bite?"

"How late is it?" I asked. For the first time all day, I looked at my phone. It had been on silent since after I found Neveah. I had over a dozen missed calls. Three were from Will. Two were from Jason.

"Oh no," I said. The day had gotten completely away from me. It was after six. I'd missed my evening FaceTime with Will.

"Everything okay?" David asked.

I shook my head. "It never is lately," I answered. "I'm so sorry to do this to you yet again. But I have to get home and put out a different kind of fire."

David's affable smile put me at ease. The man was the most even-keel human I'd ever met.

"Then I'll talk to you maybe tomorrow," he said.

I touched his cheek. Did he never get angry? Or have an ego?

"I'd like that," I said. "Oh, but Louella ..."

"I'll talk to her," he said. "We're old friends. She goes to my church."

"You're something, David Pham," I said. As I turned to leave, my phone rang yet again with Jason's ringtone.

18

Six days later, Jeanie delivered on her promise. My emergency hearing fell on the same day as Neveah Ward's funeral. I raced down the hallway of the Maumee County Domestic Relations Court searching for meeting room 14. I was four minutes late.

Four minutes that Jason would soon use as a weapon against me.

Jeanie sat alone on one side of the table. Jason sat opposite her, flanked by not one, but two lawyers and a paralegal. At the end of the table, the judicial attorney for Judge Brandon Small lobbed a deathly glare at me as I entered the room, breathless.

"Good of you to join us, Mrs. Brent," the judicial attorney remarked. Her name was Catherine Kent and everyone called her a cold fish. Until this moment, I'd always hated that misogynistic description. Now, it seemed apt.

"I apologize," I said. "There was a matter across town that I ..."

"See?" Jason barked before I could finish. "This is exactly what I'm talking about. Your absence was work-related, wasn't it?"

I expected at least one of his lawyers to tell Jason to zip it. They could have been twins. Both wore jet-black suits and had wavy brown hair, tanned skin, and shiny Rolexes. His lead attorney, Doyle Stratton, was about as expensive as they came.

"Actually, my absence was human-being-related," I said casually as I took a seat beside Jeanie. She shot me a withering stare. If Jason's lawyers weren't going to keep a lid on him, Jeanie's look told me she aimed to handle me differently.

"I've reviewed the pleadings," Catherine said. "I just have a couple of questions on behalf of Judge Small. Mr. Brent. You were going to provide a supplemental report from Dr. Marjorie Hammond?"

The lawyer on Jason's left, Stratton, had pulled a stack of papers out of a file folder. He slid a copy down to Catherine and another to Jeanie. I read over her shoulder.

"As you'll see," Stratton said. "Dr. Hammond specializes in treating children on the spectrum like Will. She's nationally renowned. It was a bit of a coup getting her to clear her schedule to see Will."

"What is this?" I asked, my heart racing. Jeanie put a hand on my arm.

"We didn't approve this," she said. "As it stands, Mr. Brent and Mrs. Brent have 50/50 legal custody. Mr. Brent isn't even asking for a change in that in his current petition. Treatment decisions regarding Will have to be agreed on by both parents."

"Actually," Lawyer Number Two said, "we're filing to amend the petition to change that portion of custody as well. Mr. Brent feels Will's best interests will be served by his securing full physical and legal custody."

"On what basis?" Jeanie asked.

"On the basis that I'm able to provide a more consistent, stable home life for my son," Jason said.

"You never have before," I said. "And you've violated every part of our existing custody agreement."

"The judge will take all of this under advisement," Catherine said. "I think I have what I need. Is there anything you'd like to add?"

"We have one more affidavit," Lawyer Number One, Stratton said. "On the issue of nightly video calls with the respondent. My client would like to limit those to three times a week."

"That is most definitely not in Will's best interests," Jeanie snapped. "Catherine, Judge Small needs to be aware that the petitioner's conduct was borderline kidnapping. It is well established that Will Brent benefits from consistency in his routine. There's no argument between the parties on that. It's Mr. Brent who has been making drastic, life-altering changes in Will's routine. He's pulled him from school. He has invited a live-in girlfriend into the home. Mr. and Mrs. Brent agreed that they wouldn't even bring dates home yet. Everything this man has done has been aimed at eroding Will Brent's relationship with his mother. She has been his primary caregiver since the day he was born. What he's shown is an inability to follow the orders of this court at a minimum. But ultimately, he's shown he's not capable of acting in the boy's best interests."

"We, of course, vehemently deny those allegations," Lawyer Number Two said. I gripped the edge of the table, wanting to launch myself across it and scratch Jason's eyes out. He stared at me. His expression dripped with hatred. Something I'd never seen from him toward me.

"Even today," Lawyer Number Two went on. "Mrs. Brent couldn't be bothered to get to this meeting on time. She's the one who requested it. My client flew out here from D.C., had to rearrange important government business, but he still managed to make it early because he has shown he prioritizes his son's well-being."

"Mr. Brent's actions are the entire reason why we're even in this situation," Jeanie shot back. She grabbed my hand beneath the table and held it in a death grip.

"All right, all right," Catherine said. "Judge Small will take all of this under advisement. I think we can safely say the parties are too far apart for further mediation to have any real benefit. You've both conducted ample discovery. Seeing as the minor child is eleven, Judge Small will want to hear from him. We can schedule it in camera with a social worker present."

"You can't," I blurted. "You cannot make my son come here and choose between his parents. Jason. Stop this. We can't allow that to happen. We can't put him through that. What are you doing?"

He didn't answer. His jaw twitched and it was the only outward indication he gave that Catherine's words distressed him as much as they did me.

This would kill Will. He would shut down.

"I need to stress that Will Brent is a neurodiverse eleven-year-old," Jeanie said. "The stress of having to come in and talk to the judge, forcing him to pit his parents against each other. Judge Small cannot think that's in this boy's best interests."

"I'll talk to the judge," Catherine said. "But he's going to want to hear from Will one way or the other. In person is best. If he's willing to write a letter, perhaps ..."

I couldn't hear this. I couldn't believe it.

"We're adjourned for now then," Catherine said. "I'll get Judge Small's decision on Will's testimony as soon as possible. We can get you on the schedule for a two-day custody trial by the middle of next month."

"In the meantime?" Jeanie said. "My client hasn't seen her son in six weeks. I need to renew my motion that Will be restored to his mother's care pending the outcome of the custody trial."

Catherine nodded. "The judge will get a decision to you on that within three days. That's a promise."

Then it was over. I wanted to vomit.

"I need a minute," I said. "Jason?"

"Mrs. Brent," Stratton said as Jason and his entire team rose. "I'm going to request that all your communications regarding Will go through my office from your attorney."

"It's okay, Doyle," Jason said.

"It's not okay with me," Jeanie said. I put a hand on her.

"Five minutes," I said. "Just give us the room."

"Mara ..."

I looked at her. She mouthed 'bad idea' to me. But Jeanie knew me well enough not to argue anymore. Jason's team knew him, too. He waved them off. My heart thundered in my chest as all our lawyers filed out.

"What is this?" I asked. "What is this really? You want to punish me for something? Fine. I went off script. I couldn't be the dutiful wife you needed. I couldn't stand there next to you, beaming up at you behind podiums while you campaigned. So now you're in a real re-election fight and that's coming back to haunt you. So you think you're going to use Will to save you?"

"This isn't about you or even us, Mara," he said. "It's about what I think is right for Will."

"That's crap," I shot back. "We had an agreement. Will was doing fine. More than fine. He was thriving. We moved to Waynetown for you and for him. You want to punish me, you've done it."

He shook his head and smiled. "When are you going to climb down off your cross, Mara? You want me to shoulder all the blame for what happened with us? For a while, I took it. I had an affair. I admit it. But I'm done taking it. My affair was the symptom. We were the illness. You and me. And I'm done letting you make all the decisions about Will. He's my son. And he's happier with me than he is with you. He has more opportunities with me. He has a support system. He has Kat."

"You'll sacrifice her too? She wants to come home. She has a life here. You've manipulated her. Chained her to your life instead of letting her build her own. You've made her think she can't survive without you. Maybe that was true when you were kids. She's not a kid anymore and what you're doing is cruel."

"Have you asked Kat what she wants?" Jason said. "Don't be so sure you know everything, Mara."

"You're going to let them drag Will in here. You're going to stand by while they make him choose between us. You know what that'll do to him."

Jason's plastic expression, the one I'd seen on billboards and campaign literature, came over his face like a mask. For an instant, it reminded me exactly of what I'd seen on Denny Sizemore's face as he sat in the courtroom. It chilled me.

"Don't be so sure you know what Will really wants, either. I'm not afraid to ask him. Think long and hard about why you are."

I was shaking. I curled my fists so hard my nails cut into the well of my palms.

Jason smiled. "Yeah. That's what I thought. See you in front of the judge, Mara. Will's not coming back here without a court order."

I was still shaking as Jeanie came back in and Jason left.

19

"We have no other choice, Mara," Kenya said. I sat in the chair in front of her desk. This was a formal meeting. One I'd dreaded for seven days, two hours and nineteen minutes. Every second that had passed since I found Neveah Ward's body.

I should have told her I understood. I should have told her I knew what had to be done. Instead, I sat there, hands folded, trying hard not to explode.

"Without Neveah's testimony, all we have is evidence that Denny Sizemore had sex with her."

I looked up. "Sex? It's not just sex, Kenya. We have a catalog of injuries. We have Sizemore's skin under her nails. We have Dr. Hernandez's testimony that those injuries were consistent with a violent sexual assault."

"But only Neveah could identify Sizemore as the one who perpetrated it. And that she didn't consent. Not to mention Pettis will come forward with a pretty credible constitutional rights violation if we don't dismiss. He has the right to confront his accuser in court. Pettis can't cross-examine a dead witness."

"I'm not afraid of Pettis," I said.

"You're not thinking straight," she said. "Neveah was more than just a witness to you. She became a friend. She's a hundred girls we couldn't bring a case for. And now we can't do it for her either. I'm so sorry. But you know there's only one way this can go. I've already communicated with Pettis. We have no choice but to dismiss the charges against Dennis Sizemore."

I squeezed my eyes shut, hating every second of this but knowing there was something worse yet to come. Within the hour, I'd have to stand in court and say the same thing.

"I'm more than happy to handle the hearing on our office's behalf," Kenya said.

"No," I said. "I have to do it. It's my job."

"For what it's worth, I hate this as much as you do. He did this. Denny Sizemore is a rapist. And he's going to get away with it this time. If it's any consolation, maybe at least now he knows he's on our radar."

I met her eyes. "No. This isn't going to clip his wings. It's only going to embolden him. He's always believed he was untouchable. This just proves it. There will be another girl. He'll just be a little smarter, maybe about making sure he can't get caught."

"I hope you're wrong," she said. "What about Neveah's death? Where does the investigation stand?"

"I don't know," I said. "Gus is trying to track down Neveah's dealer. He's hit a brick wall. We're still waiting for final toxicology. Her phone forensics didn't help. There were no calls coming or going that raised any red flags. As it stands right now, there's no viable path to hold anyone accountable for what happened to that girl. Not while she was alive, and not for how she died. "

Kenya winced. "Well, keep riding Gus on it. Whatever he needs. I'll run interference with the mayor and city council."

I barked out a laugh. "They all just want everyone to forget that Neveah Ward ever existed. Even though Sizemore's gunning to take back Mayor Loomis's seat, it's still a good old boy network. If we can come after the last guy, we can come after the next one. They'll want to sweep all of this under the rug."

"Well I don't," she said.

"You should be careful," I said. "You're up for re-election soon yourself."

"I don't care," she said, her voice flat and cold. "If I did, I never would have signed off on the charges against Sizemore in the first place. In for a penny, in for a pound. Let the good old boy network do its worst."

Her face fell at the same time mine did. In life, and now in death, it was Neveah Ward who had paid the price of that network's worst.

"I better get to court," I said. "This lousy week is about to get even lousier."

Kenya rose with me. "I'll meet you over there. There'll be press to deal with."

Kenya grabbed her suit jacket off a hook behind her. She got waylaid by Caro before she could follow me. I went ahead without her, eager to get this thing over with.

Judge Saul's courtroom was packed. Denny Sizemore's family and friends took up every gallery bench. On Neveah's side, there was only me and three members of the Silver Angels. I pressed a fist into my heart when I saw them. They were in tears, knowing full well what I would have to do here today.

"Ms. Brent," Judge Saul said, her expression somber. "Are you ready to proceed?"

"Your Honor, in light of the untimely death of the victim in this case and thus her inability to give testimony against the accused, the state has no choice but to dismiss the charges against the defendant. So we'd like to formally move to dismiss the case against Dennis Sizemore without prejudice."

"Your Honor," Pettis boomed. "This case should be dismissed with prejudice. There is absolutely no evidence that he committed the crime he was charged with. There is no basis in the law for a dismissal without prejudice under the circumstances. Double jeopardy applies in this case. As tragic as Ms. Ward's ending was, and I can promise you, we are praying for that poor girl's soul, the circumstances as they are warrant a dismissal with prejudice."

"Ms. Brent," Judge Saul said. "I'm sure you and the state are aware that double jeopardy attaches once the jury is sworn in or the first witness testifies. In this case, we got through both. I find the defendant's point is well taken. Double jeopardy does indeed apply and the state is therefore precluded from bringing new charges stemming from the same facts. As such, the law requires me to dismiss this matter with prejudice. So ordered. Bailiff, can you please inform the jury that they are free to go with my thanks for their service? Mr. Sizemore, you are also free to go. Dismissed."

With that, Judge Saul brought her gavel down on Neveah Ward's fate. I felt numb. I don't even remember gathering my things and walking out of the courtroom. I just remember the rush of people moving toward a jubilant Dennis Sizemore. He was in full campaign mode yet again. Smiling. Glad-handing. The press would wait for him on the courthouse steps. He and Pettis would claim victory. He would begin the process of reclaiming his own narrative. The hero. The wrongly accused.

I felt sick. Kenya was waiting for me somewhere. As much as it sickened her, she would have to hold a press conference. I should be there beside her.

I needed air. I snuck out a side door and found a quiet space in the alley between the courthouse and the Sheriff's Department. Around the corner, I could hear the crowd starting to gather. That's where Pettis and Sizemore would stake their claim. He'd have the perfect backdrop for his photo op with the courthouse behind him and the American flag flapping over his shoulder.

I wished I smoked. I wished I drank heavily. There was only one place I really wanted to go. Someone should be with Neveah today. The earth was still soft and turned over her grave. I would plant some flowers.

I don't know how long I stood there. Long enough that I finally heard the crowd disperse. My phone buzzed with a series of missed calls and texts. Kenya was looking for me. There was a message from Jeanie Mills.

"Sorry about this one, kid," she texted. "But karma is a bitch and Denny Sizemore has his coming."

I slipped my phone into my pocket and started to make my way to the parking lot. I needed a drive before I could face the press myself.

As I rounded the corner, I walked smack into the two people I never wanted to see again.

Sizemore and Pettis.

"Denny," Simon said, trying to pull his client away.

"Mrs. Brent," Denny said. "Rough day for you. I'm sorry for your loss. Truly."

"Which loss?" I said. "Do you mean Neveah?"

He gritted his teeth. "I know you don't believe me, but she was a tragic girl ... she ..."

"Denny," Pettis cut him off. "We need to go. There's nothing left to say here."

Anger bubbled up inside of me. For Neveah. For every other woman Denny Sizemore had victimized, but that I couldn't prove. Including his wife.

"Nothing left to say?" I said. "How about this? We both know what happened in that car. You're a predator, Denny. You think you've gotten away with something. Maybe this time you have. But let me be perfectly clear. We're watching you. All of us. You do so much as jaywalk ..."

"I'd advise you not to threaten my client, Ms. Brent," Pettis said. He pulled at Denny's sleeve. But something shifted behind Denny Sizemore's eyes. I swear for that split second, I saw into his soul. He wasn't used to women standing up to him. His contempt for me dripped off of him. This wasn't just about the case or my job. This was something much more evil and primal within him.

"I'd like to see you try something," he said. "You're nothing. Less than nothing. Just like ..."

"Denny!" Simon shouted. "That's enough."

"You son of a ..." I snapped. My anger turned to white-hot rage. I saw Sizemore as he must have looked to Neveah. He'd treated her like a piece of garbage. She was powerless. I wasn't.

Before I knew what was happening, I was in his face, jabbing my finger into his chest.

"I see who you are," I said. "Know that. I see you."

I felt heat flood my face. Sweat poured down my back. I lost control.

I never touched him but for that quick jab to his chest. I never said anything more than those words. But it didn't matter.

Simon Pettis put his sizable form between me and Denny and pushed him back toward his waiting car. Behind him, at least six people stood there with their cell phones up, snapping and recording the entire exchange.

20

"We have a long road ahead. A lot of work to do. I'm just grateful that justice has prevailed. But none of that is the truly important part. Neveah Ward was a tragic, troubled girl and I regret any part I played in what happened to her. I know you are eager to hear my story. Just as I'm eager to tell you. But for now. For today, I'd like to lead a moment of silence in prayer for the soul of Neveah Ward."

"He did not just ..." Caro stood beside me as we stared at the playback from Denny Sizemore's press conference on her computer screen.

"He did," I said. "The bastard just led a prayer on the courthouse steps."

"There was no justice," Hojo said. He stood on the other side of the room. "He wasn't found not guilty."

"He's going to spin it that way anyway," I said, the words leaving a bitter aftertaste in my mouth.

"I can't listen to any more of this," Caro said. She reached over and closed her laptop.

"He's going to win," Hojo said. "Denny Sizemore is like a cockroach. He's going to figure out a way to make himself the victim and he's going to be mayor again."

"I have to go," I said. "I'll be across the street at the Sheriff's Department. I want to see where we are on Neveah's death investigation."

"You're clear for the rest of the day," Caro said. "You were supposed to be in trial all this week. Take all the time you need. We'll hold down the fort here."

"Thanks," I said, grabbing my briefcase. I made the short, one-block walk into the police station and up to the detective bureau. Gus wasn't at his desk but Sam saw me and motioned for me to come into his office.

"Close the door and have a seat, Mara," he said.

"What do you have for me, Sam?" I asked. "Please let it be good news."

He gave me a sad smile. "I don't know what constitutes good anymore. Do you?"

I paused. "Yeah. I guess not."

"Gus is downstairs re-interviewing Web Margolis."

"I want to be there for that," I said, rising. Sam motioned for me to sit back down.

"He's got it under control. You can head down there in a few minutes. I'll go with you. In the meantime, we got the full forensic report back on Neveah's phone and laptop. I wish I had something interesting to tell you. But Gus isn't seeing anything out of the ordinary. No surprises."

"So you're nowhere," I said. "Those drugs came from somewhere. They didn't just drop from the sky."

"We're working on it," Sam said. "But you have to be prepared for the fact we're about to run out of investigative road. David says he'll get the final toxicology back in a few days."

"You're going to close the case, aren't you?" I said. "That's what this grim face of yours is all about."

"I didn't say that," he said. "I said you need to prepare yourself for what might be coming."

"She didn't kill herself," I said. "Neveah was making plans. She was building a future for herself for after this trial was over."

"She was about to take the stand against Sizemore," he said. "She was nervous. Scared. She might have just been looking for some courage."

I shook my head. "She wasn't a junkie."

"Mara," he said. "You don't know what she was. You saw a piece of her. This girl led a complicated, sometimes dangerous life."

He picked up a stapled set of papers off his desk and slid it across to me. "I said we didn't find anything out of the ordinary on her phone or laptop. But we did find something. Neveah was active on her MOCA account as recently as last week."

"What?" I said. I took the sheets of paper from him. It was a log-in sheet from the MOCA app.

"I don't understand," I said. "You said you didn't find anything out of the ordinary on her phone or laptop."

"She didn't log in to the app or the site from either of those," he said. "She was using public Wi-Fi. A couple of different places. The library four blocks from her house. The coffee shop over on Melbourne. The student union on campus."

"Did she meet with anyone she met off of MOCA?" I asked.

"That's where we are with this. Gus is trying to track that down. That's one of the things he's trying to get out of Web Margolis."

"But she wouldn't have communicated with Web through the app anymore. She had his private number."

"And it doesn't look like she called him on it in months. That part of this tracks with what Margolis already told Gus."

"Do you think someone she met on MOCA gave her the drugs that killed her?"

"It's a possibility."

"She swore to me she was done with all of that. Sam, I went over this with her in detail. We knew Pettis was going to try to use it against her on cross. You're telling me that Neveah was hooking up with men on MOCA as recently as a week before she was going to take the stand? It makes no sense. She wasn't stupid. Have you considered the possibility someone logged in to Neveah's MOCA account without her knowledge? To smear her?"

"Everything's on the table at this point," he said. "Like I said. That's one of the things Gus is trying to get from Margolis."

"I need to go down there. I need to hear it for myself. I've talked to this guy too. I know how he operates."

"All right," Sam said. "But you need to trust Gus to do his job."

"I do trust him," I said. "I trust you, too. I just want ..."

"I know," Sam said as he held the door to the stairwell open for me. "We all do."

Sam and I walked the two floors down to the interview rooms. Before I could ask which one Gus was in, a door opened up and Web Margolis walked through wearing the same Gucci suit he'd worn the last time I saw him. He turned and extended a hand to shake Gus's. Gus kept his hands to his side.

"Exit's that way," Gus said. Web saw Sam and me. The man at least had the decency to look uncomfortable. Sam put a hand on my shoulder as if he were ready to hold me back. As if I'd break into a run and try to tackle the guy. The thought did cross my mind.

"Mr. Margolis?" I said.

"Ms. Brent," he responded. "It's good to see you. I wish it were under more pleasant circumstances. I'm so sorry for what happened to Neveah. I wish there was something I could have done. As I was telling Detective Ritter here, I hadn't spoken to Neveah in quite some time. I knew she was anxious about testifying. I just had no idea she'd go to such lengths to self-medicate. Believe me, had I known, I would have ..."

"You would have what?" I asked.

He threw up his hands. "Right. Well, I suppose ultimately we can't save people from themselves no matter how much we try."

"We're done for now, Margolis," Gus said. "Answer your phone if I call."

"Of course," Margolis said, visibly relieved at the reprieve. He disappeared down the hall.

"Gus ..." I started.

"He's clean," Gus said. "Of this anyway. He just got back from Dubai the day before yesterday. He showed me his passport. I confirmed it with the airlines. He was out of the country for a week before that. There's no record of Neveah contacting him in her phone dump. He's agreed to provide me with copies of his own cell phone records."

"He was under a subpoena," Sam said. "He skipped the country until the trial was conveniently over?"

"It wasn't my subpoena," I said. "It was Pettis's. I was never going to call him during my case in chief. But you're sure. I trust your read on people, Gus."

Gus let out a hard breath. "As much as I can't stand the guy, I think he's telling the truth. He hadn't seen or talked to Neveah. I don't think he's directly involved in what happened to her. Smarmy as he is, he cooperated today. He seemed surprised Neveah was active on MOCA again. If anything, he was wounded by that."

"We're not going to find anything, are we?" I said, my voice going robotic. "There's nothing but dead ends."

Gus and Sam looked at each other. Sam's phone buzzed with a text. He didn't look at it right away.

My own phone started to blow up. I looked at it. I had incoming texts from both Kenya and Jeanie Mills. I tapped Jeanie's first.

"Have you been online? Call me. We need to figure out a game plan."

"Mara," Sam said.

I opened my text from Kenya. "Get back to the office as soon as you can. Don't panic."

"Mara," Sam said again.

"Something's going on," I said. "Jeanie said ..."

Sam turned his phone toward me. He had it open to a local news site. There was a headline in red font and all caps. "Top Prosecutor Becomes Unglued."

There was a picture of me, my face contorted in rage, looking almost grotesque. I was pointing a finger in the air. It happened outside the courthouse when Sizemore and Pettis confronted me. The next photo showed me jabbing my finger into Sizemore's chest.

"What?" I started to sweat. I pulled up the news app on my own phone. There were more local headlines, but all with the same flavor.

"Was It a Witch Hunt All Along?" The picture of me below had been distorted even further, elongating my nose to look witchy. It got worse from there.

"Unhinged Prosecutor Assaults Former Mayor After Losing Case."

"You gotta be kidding me," Gus said as he read the headlines.

"This is Sizemore," Sam said. "These stories have to be planted."

"No," I whispered. "This isn't Sizemore. At least not by himself. Dammit, Sam. This is Jason. I don't know how. But this is about way more than the Sizemore case."

I left Gus and Sam staring after me as I ran toward the exit and punched in Jeanie's number.

21

By day three, the video of me had gone viral. By day four, I was a meme. Waynetown's local version of that unhinged Desperate Housewife of Wherever stabbing a finger into the air.

Jeanie warned me not to respond to it. My calls to Jason went unanswered anyway.

"He's going to use it to argue to the judge I'm unstable, isn't he? Or that my job is affecting my mental health."

Jeanie laughed on the other end of the phone. "Everyone's job affects their mental health. He's just trying to take the shine off you from the circumstance of your divorce. It doesn't matter, Mara. The only thing that matters is how you parent. He's trying to bait you. Promise me you won't take it. I'm glad Jason wouldn't take your calls. Don't make any more. We have our trial next month."

"So what happens if I just fly out there?" I said. "If I show up on his doorstep and just take my kid. If it wasn't kidnapping where he was concerned, it can't be for me either."

"Mara," Jeanie said. "You've been a lawyer your whole adult life. You know exactly what happens if you do that. The court hasn't made a ruling. Four weeks. You have to wait it out."

She was right. I didn't want to hear it.

"Take some time for a little self-care," Jeanie said. "Not because I think any of that crap they're posting online about you is true. But because you actually deserve it. Go get a massage. Have a spa day. Or even just hide out in that big house of yours in the woods with a glass of wine and a bubble bath."

"It's too quiet in that big house in the woods, Jeanie," I said, trying to keep my voice from breaking.

"Yeah. I know. I'm sorry. I'm going to fix this though. It's just going to take time."

I assured her I wouldn't do anything crazy. I would play by the rules even if Jason wasn't. And I would hate every second of it.

As soon as we ended the call, Caro stepped into my office.

"Hey, Mara," she said. "I got a call I don't know what to do with. It was Neveah Ward's landlord. She says nobody's come to claim her personal belongings. It's been over two weeks and she's eager to get it cleaned and get a new tenant in there. She says the police have cleared the premises."

"What does she want from me?" I asked. "I'm not an eviction lawyer. Have her call the local bar association."

"Yeah," Caro said. "I don't think the eviction process is her issue. She doesn't know what to do with Neveah's things. She said she doesn't feel right about just renting a dumpster like she would have if a tenant skipped out without paying the rent. And Neveah was paid up through the rest of the month. I'm sorry. I can just call her back and tell her we can't be involved. It's just ... I thought maybe you wouldn't want her things thrown in a dumpster either."

"No," I said. "You're right, Caro. You always are. Is the landlord over there now?"

"Until four o'clock," Caro said. "Her name is Diane Merrick. She's a sweet lady. She goes to my church, actually."

"Okay," I said. "I'll head over there. And thanks, Caro. You're a good egg, you know that?"

I grabbed my purse off the hook near the door. I got to Neveah Ward's rental house by two thirty. Just as Caro said, Diane Merrick met me in the driveway. She was a tiny, old woman with cotton-candy, white hair. She wore a fuzzy pink cardigan and a rhinestone, daisy-shaped brooch.

"Hi, Mrs. Merrick," I said.

"Oh, I'm so glad you came," she said. "It seemed like someone who cared about the girl should go through her things. She had nice ones. I've made arrangements for a truck from St. Vincent de Paul to come pick up most of it. But I thought maybe you'd know if there was anything of sentimental value her friends or somebody might want."

"I appreciate that," I said as Diane Merrick unlocked Neveah's front door. I took a steady breath as she opened it. The last time I'd walked over this threshold, I found Neveah dead.

The house had been cleaned. The living room couch where Neveah had lain was gone.

"I got rid of a few things already," Diane explained. "That couch needed to be replaced even before ... well ... you know. Habitat for Humanity already came by and took most of the big things."

"It looks nice in here," I said. In fact, it already looked fairly well-staged for when Mrs. Merrick was ready to show it to prospective tenants.

"She was a good tenant," she said. "One of the best I ever had. Clean. Orderly. She treated this house as if she owned it. I don't mean that in a bad way."

"I know how you meant it," I said as we walked toward the kitchen. Neveah had rented the entire first floor of the house. Mrs. Merrick had a different tenant on the second floor with access from a set of stairs in the back. Neveah once told me she never saw the other tenant or even knew her name.

"Mrs. Merrick," I said. "When was the last time you talked to Neveah?" I trailed my hand along the tile countertops. There was scarcely a crumb in the grout.

"I live in the house in the corner down there. Me and my Larry. That's my husband. He's a handyman of sorts, though his back and knees are shot. I'd see Neveah when we'd come out to get the mail. Larry used to like checking on the girls once a week. You know, to make sure they didn't have any leaky faucets or some such. We bought this place when Larry retired. Seemed like a perfect project to keep him busy and out of my hair. We've always rented to college students. I got a waiting list two years out."

"It's a great location," I said.

"Larry redid all the wood floors," she said. "Aren't they something? There was purple shag carpet in here when we bought the place six years ago. Can you imagine? Why do people do stuff like that?"

I turned to her. She hadn't really answered my question. "Did you see Neveah the day before she died? Did you talk to her?"

I moved through the kitchen and down the hall to the back bedrooms. Neveah had slept in one and used the other for storage. She didn't have much. She had a few labeled boxes against the wall of the spare room. Winter clothes. Textbooks. But nothing else.

"I didn't see her the day before, no," Mrs. Merrick answered. We walked into Neveah's bedroom. The bed was made. She had two nightstands. I opened one. Neveah's hand lotion and melatonin were tucked neatly in a drawer divider. The other nightstand was pulled away from the wall. Gus had found drug paraphernalia on the floor behind it. I moved the nightstand back into place.

"Such a tragedy," Mrs. Merrick said. I wondered how much she knew about the items removed from the house. "Stay right there. There's a box of things you might want."

She left me alone in Neveah's bedroom. I trailed my fingers over the bedspread. I wished I was clairvoyant. I wished I could see the last few hours of Neveah's life just by touching her things. If she could have only held on a little longer.

"Was someone watching you?" I whispered. "Were they here when you got home?"

I looked inside the lampshade on Neveah's nightstand. I checked the light fixtures on the wall. Had Gus thought to sweep the room for bugs?

"This has got some of her school stuff in it," Mrs. Merrick said. "Notebooks. A couple of textbooks. I know they buy those back."

I looked in the box. It was as Diane Merrick described. I flipped through the pages. There was nothing there of interest. Just a conscientious student taking notes.

"You should just donate these too," I said. "Textbooks are so expensive these days. Maybe another student can use them."

"That's a good idea," she said.

"Did you have occasion to observe Neveah's comings and goings?" I asked. "Did you see her with anyone you didn't recognize? Anyone new in her life lately?"

"You know," she said. "That detective asked me the same thing. I couldn't tell him much more than I can tell you. I know she dated. Not a lot recently though. Not for months. She'd get picked up by an older man in a silver Mercedes quite a bit last year. Not so much recently. I figured they had fallen out."

I knew she meant Web Margolis in the Mercedes.

"I wish she'd have dated boys closer to her own age. I told her that once. I was worried she was going to get taken advantage of again. Seems like that's maybe exactly what happened. I never liked Denny Sizemore. Never liked any politician. I know that poor girl was probably telling the truth about what he did to her. I think she was just afraid nobody would believe her in the end."

"Did she seem down or depressed or even scared the last time you talked to her?" I asked.

Mrs. Merrick shrugged. "I never asked her about her personal business. She had enough of it splashed all over the news and the internet."

"Did your husband Larry come into the house once a week? When he checked on the tenants, I mean."

"Sometimes," she said. "You know. That's the thing. Larry was always looking for signs of misbehaving."

"What do you mean?"

"Well, see, Larry was a home inspector before he retired. He was used to going into all kinds of homes. Did some work for H.U.D. and a bunch of different government agencies. He knew what he was looking at, you know?"

"No," I said. "I'm not sure I do."

"Drugs," she whispered. I wasn't sure who she thought might overhear us. "He said he could always tell when he was in the house of a junkie. Sure, there are obvious things. But there was subtle stuff. Stuff in the garbage. Pens taken apart. Lots of plastic spoons. Balloons. Anyway, Larry was always right. His sixth sense on these things when it came to our tenants was spot on. He blames himself a lot. He wants to sell this place. He's so upset. But we never would have guessed that girl was doing drugs. I told the cops the same thing."

"What would you have done if you suspected though?" I said, trying to make her feel better.

"I don't know," Mrs. Merrick said. "But that girl just didn't have too many people looking out for her. I like to think Larry and me were."

She started to cry. I went to her. I put an arm around her waist and she sank to the bed, sitting on the edge.

"You sure you don't want any of her things?" she asked me.

"No," I whispered. I don't know what I thought I would find here. Now that we sat in Neveah's room, it just made her feel more gone than before. Maybe that's the best I could have hoped for.

"She liked you," Mrs. Merrick said. "I can tell you that much. I asked her about you. Asked her if she thought you were the one to handle this case against that Sizemore. She told me you were the best."

"Thanks for that." I smiled. "She was lucky to have you in her life too, Mrs. Merrick."

"We're just a parade of well-meaning people who couldn't do anything for that girl in the end."

"That we are," I said.

"Well, you go on home," she said. "I don't believe anything they've been saying about you on the internet. Just so you know."

I smiled. She meant well. But if that video of me had made it in front of the likes of Diane Merrick, it truly was everywhere.

"Am I doing the right thing?" she asked. "With St. Vincent de Paul?"

"Yes," I said. "I think Neveah would approve."

Except it was a lie. I felt like I knew less about her than I did before. It was what Diane Merrick needed to hear though and that was at least something.

She seemed more at ease as I left and drove back home. I couldn't face the office again. I knew by tomorrow or the day after, Gus would call to tell me he had no choice but to close Neveah's case for good.

I was thinking about it as I pulled into the driveway. The bubble bath Jeanie suggested didn't sound half bad. I walked into my too quiet house and only made it as far as the kitchen.

Something was off. The chairs were pulled away from the table and placed at odd angles. I heard movement off the kitchen.

Heart racing, I crawled my fingers across the countertop and reached for a knife.

"Mom!"

My heart stuck in my throat. Will came flying around the kitchen island. His hair was too long. His pants were too short. He barreled into me with an embrace that nearly knocked me flat.

"What? Well, hi! My God." I held my son tight. It felt like a dream.

It was then Kat came around the corner, a sad smile on her face.

"How?" I mouthed to her.

"Will asked me to bring him home," she said, tears filling her eyes. "I couldn't say no."

"Jason?" I mouthed to her over Will's head. He hadn't hugged me this long since he was a toddler.

Kat shook her head no. Oh dear. Her meaning was clear. My sister-in-law had just kidnapped my son to bring him to me.

Thank God.

22

Those words. "I missed you, Mom." They were the last ones Will spoke that night and into the next day. He retreated to his Lego room upstairs and continued working on a model of the ship the S.S. *California*. The one rumored to have ignored the *Titanic*'s distress calls on the fateful night it sank.

He let me sit at the table beside him and watch. His brow knit in concentration as he saw the model ship in his mind, then found the pieces to bring his vision into three dimensions.

"I missed you so much, buddy," I said. "I'm glad you're home."

He didn't answer. If anything, he worked even more furiously. He'd started this particular project last summer. Had he been home, he would have finished it by now and moved on to the next thing.

I wanted to tell him it wasn't my fault that he hadn't come home. I wanted to tell him how hard I'd been fighting to bring him here. I said none of it. Even now, I would not bash his father in front of him. I wondered whether Jason had been capable of showing me the same courtesy.

Well, whatever he'd told him. Will was here. Now. He'd told Kat he wanted to come home.

Kat was downstairs. I could hear her puttering in the kitchen, agitated.

"I'll be downstairs, okay?" I said. "I need to talk to Aunt Kat. After that, I want to make an appointment for you with Dr. Vera. So you can see her in person, not just on Zoom. Is that okay with you?"

He nodded, but didn't look up from the Legos.

"I'll be back," I said. "Start thinking about what you want for dinner. We can go out. We can stay here and make one of your favorites. Whatever you want."

Again, just a nod. No words. I brushed a hand over his hair. He stiffened, but let me.

Kat waited for me at the kitchen island. She'd poured herself an iced tea and offered me one. I waved it off.

"He won't talk," I said. "How long has that been going on?"

"He's been quieter lately," she said. "Not like this. He just needs some time."

"Where is Jason?" I asked.

"He's in California for a couple of days. Some kind of congressional summit."

"He doesn't know you left with Will, does he?"

"I just thought it was silly for Will to be in Jason's townhouse while he was gone. He can pick him up on his way back," she said.

I resisted the urge to tell her that it would be over my dead body. I would not put Will on a plane again. No chance.

"You didn't answer my question," I said. "Jason has no idea you brought Will home, does he? If he did, my phone would be blowing up."

"I'm trying to do what's best for Will," she said. "I hate this. You know I love you. I love my brother. But I'd like to knock both of your heads together. You have to figure this out. Jason said you're making Will talk to the judge and choose between you. Is that true?"

My vision went white. "He said I'm making him do that? I am most certainly not. I've begged your brother to honor the agreement we had in place. It was working fine."

"No, it wasn't," Kat said. "That's the thing, Mara. It wasn't. Will isn't doing well with the back and forth. I told you that. I've been telling you that. Both of you. I don't know what the answer is. If he should live here. If he should live in D.C. with Jason. I don't know. I just know that Will can't be the one to decide. It'll break him."

"I don't want that," I said. "I have avoided saying anything negative about Jason in front of you. I'm not even going to ask you if he's done the same for me. You know why we aren't married anymore. I've always left it at that."

"I respect that," she said.

"But you should know," I said. "If you or Jason try to put that boy on a plane again ... well ... I won't let it happen."

Kat's face went pale. She knew I was serious. Just then, a new text came through. It was from Dr. Vera, Will's therapist's office. She had an opening first thing in the morning to see Will. I texted them back to confirm it, then laid my phone back down.

"Thank you," I said. "I owe you. I love you too. But I will fight for my kid. No matter what. No matter who I have to fight against."

"Are you sure about that?" she said. "Because my brother says the same thing. Mara, he always wins. Always."

There were tears in her eyes. It was one more thing I could lie at Jason Brent's feet. He would drive a wedge between Kat and me if it meant he could get what he wanted.

"I love you, Kat," I said. "But you should go home now. I'm sure Bree's anxious to see you. This has been really hard on her, too."

"Bree," she said through a bitter laugh. "Let's just say she hasn't been very supportive of my life choices lately."

"She loves you," I said. "She wants you to make your own life choices, not the one your brother maps out for you."

She looked at me. "I thought that's what I just did."

"Go talk to her," I said. "Tell her you love her."

There was nothing left to say. I slid off the stool and hugged Kat. God, I'd missed her too.

23

Will was in good spirits as we pulled into Dr. Rita Vera's office. Before he left for D.C., he met with her once a week right after school. Every Thursday. He looked forward to it. They were supposed to keep the same appointment time via Zoom while he was with Jason. But Jason had stopped it and said he was looking for a new therapist closer to him. It was one of a thousand points of contention.

I waited outside Dr. Vera's office. She had soft, New Age music playing. Just loud enough so that none of the waiting parents could overhear their child's therapy sessions. A saltwater aquarium with colorful fish filled one corner. Another had a water fountain that I guess was supposed to foster tranquility. Usually, it just made me want to pee.

Fifty minutes to the second, Dr. Vera emerged with Will. He seemed relaxed and easy, but wouldn't say anything.

"Will?" Dr. Vera said. "Are you okay with hanging out in the touch room while I talk to your mom for a few minutes?"

The touch room was a sort of playroom down the hall where Dr. Vera kept toys and manipulatives. Will always liked sitting on the swivel seat and playing with colorful plastic beads she had hanging from the ceiling.

Will shrugged and headed off down the hall. My heart sank. I knew what Rita Vera would have to say. Smiling, she ushered me into her office.

"I'll be honest," she said, direct and to the point as she closed the door and showed me to the chair in the corner. She took the couch opposite me. "I'm worried."

"Me too," I said. "Did he say anything?"

I hated to ask. It was a breach of trust between Will and me. As his parent, with him being a minor, Dr. Vera could tell me anything they discussed. But I'd made a promise to him that I'd never ask unless absolutely necessary. That day was today.

"No," she said. "I got a couple of yeses and one no, but no conversation. He was happy enough to sit in here with me. He wanted to be here. But he's not talking, Mara."

"It's new," I said. I'd already explained the circumstances of how Will got back to Waynetown. "His aunt says he was talking somewhat normally before they got on the plane. He's been communicative when we had our nightly FaceTime calls. But since he got home, it's been the silent treatment. He's regressing, Dr. Vera."

"He's under stress," she said. "Will's smart. He knows what's going on between you and Jason even if nobody has explained it to him fully."

"Should I?" I asked. "I'm trying to figure out what the right thing is. I'm so angry with his father. But I've been careful never to say that around him. I've tried to just be excited for whatever new adventures he and his dad had. Whether it was a trip to a museum or the Capitol."

"That's good," she said. "But Will will be better served by a solid routine. Do you have any indication when the court will make a final ruling on the custody order?"

"Within the next few weeks," I said. "But Will may have to testify."

Dr. Vera took a breath.

"That's going to be difficult for him," she said. "If he's giving me the silent treatment, I don't know what the judge thinks he's going to get out of him. In the meantime, just try to foster the routine he's familiar with."

"So you think I should send him back to school?"

"That's one thing we talked about," she said. "I asked Will if he wants to go back to class. That's one of the yeses I got. That's a good sign. He's asserting himself. The more control he has over his environment the better. Do you want me to reach out to his teacher? I don't know how far behind he's gotten."

"She's been sending assignments while he was with Jason," I said. "He should be close to being caught up. Kat told me she's made sure he does his homework."

"Good," Dr. Vera said. "So take him to school Monday morning the way you always have. We'll take this one step at a time. I'll plan on meeting with him there Thursday afternoon. Back to our old schedule."

"Thank you," I said. "I'm worried about this refusal to talk. But the sooner I can get him back in a groove, I'm hoping that will get better."

"Me too. I'm optimistic. He's a strong kid. Stubborn though."

"Yeah," I said, starting to rise.

"How are you doing though?" she asked. "Are you seeing someone? It might benefit you to have someone to talk to. I can recommend a few people."

"Thanks," I said. "When I have time again, maybe I'll take you up on that."

She rose with me. "I was so sorry to hear about what happened to Neveah Ward. Such a tough case."

"It is," I said. "Thank you."

"She was really thriving, I thought."

I stopped short. "You knew her?"

Dr. Vera nodded. "Sure. I work with a few kids at M.V.M. Like I do with Will at Grantham, I meet with them at school. I've seen Neveah in action. She was wonderful with those kids. A lot of them come from troubled homes. Louella's scholarship program has been a godsend. Those kids' parents would never have been able to afford to send their children to her otherwise."

"How well did you know Neveah?" I asked.

"Not well at all," Dr. Vera said. "I teach as an adjunct at Maumee College. I pick up a couple of early childhood development courses. Neveah met with me for some advice about their program."

"I didn't know that," I said. "She never mentioned it."

"I was rooting for her," Dr. Vera said.

"Me too. Do you mind if I ask you? Did you ever see anything with Neveah that would have made you worry she was using?"

Dr. Vera shook her head. "I can't say that I did. But I wouldn't describe us as close. Like I said. I mostly just saw her at M.V.M. She'd enrolled in one of my classes, but never got to take it. She was serious. Conscientious. And she was great with those kids. Some of them are having a tough time with her loss. She's missed."

I nodded. "That's nice to hear. I'm glad she had people like you and Louella looking out for her in the end."

"I just wish it had been enough," Dr. Vera said as we walked out into the hall together. "I just wish I knew more about what she was going through. I don't know that I could have helped. But ... maybe."

Maybe and what ifs. There were far too many of those when it came to Neveah Ward. I wished I'd known her better. With each passing day, I realized how much about Neveah I never knew at all.

24

Within four days, Jeanie had earned every cent I'd borrowed from my mother to pay her retainer.

"We won the battle," she said over the phone. "Judge isn't going to order you to put Will back on a plane. He can stay where he is pending the final hearing later this month."

The closest thing I could grab on to so I didn't fall to my knees was a parking meter. I stood outside the Sheriff's Department readying myself for another patch of bad news I knew I had in front of me.

"Thank God," she said. "No. Thank you. Jeanie, I ..."

"Yeah, yeah, yeah," she said. I could hear the smile in her voice. "Just love on your boy. Plus, I said the judge is keeping the new status quo. I didn't say he was thrilled. As long as your sister-in-law truly acted alone, I don't think you'll take any shrapnel from Will's abrupt arrival in Waynetown."

"I didn't ask her to do that, I swear," I said.

"Good. So that all's just going to have to stay between Kat Brent and her brother. If she needs her own lawyer, let me know. I have a few names down there she can call."

"I'll keep that in mind," I said. "And Kat's still a wild card in terms of what she'll say in court. Jason has her believing it was my idea to put Will in front of the judge."

"Have you told him about that yet?" she asked.

"No," I said. "His therapist agrees it's a terrible idea. I'm working on getting an affidavit from her to that effect. I'll forward it as soon as I have it."

"Please do," she said. "No promises, but it'll help. But Mara, are you sure Will wouldn't tell the judge he'd rather stay with you? Especially now. We know he asked his aunt to bring him back."

I paused, letting my heart finish twisting in my chest.

"Jeanie," I said. "Even if I knew for sure Will would choose me, I just can't put him through that. We need to fight it for him. Do you understand?"

"I do," she said. "You're a good mom, Mara. Just keep doing your job and I'll do mine. We'll talk soon."

"Thanks, Jeanie," I said, then clicked off the call. I slid my phone in my briefcase and steeled myself for the next hard conversation I'd have to have.

Gus and Sam met me in Gus's office. Sam closed the door. They waited for me to settle in a chair. Sam sat behind his desk. Gus leaned against the radiator by the wall. "I know this isn't what you want to hear," Sam said. "But we're closing the investigation into Neveah Ward's death. It's being ruled as an accidental overdose. There's no one to charge, Mara. We have no probable cause that a crime was committed."

I squeezed my eyes shut. "But you both know it's bull, don't you?"

"I've got no new leads," Gus said. "Her phone and laptop are clean. The last person she talked to the night before she died was you. No other texts incoming or outgoing. There's nothing. She didn't even log into the internet after that. She had paraphernalia on her nightstand. No one saw anyone coming or going. There's just nothing else to chase down."

"There's your gut," I said. "And mine."

"And you know we can't make a case on gut instinct," Sam said. "I hate this as much as you do. That girl got a raw deal. Sizemore chewed her up and spit her out and there's not a damn thing we can do about it. There's no solid proof of anything other than the girl was scared about testifying and shot up either for courage or to escape it. We can go round and round about why that doesn't track with your impressions of her. But it's not enough to make a case. I know you know that."

"They knew," I said. "Sam, they knew. Neveah and I didn't tell anyone when I was going to put her on the stand. That's a decision I made as the trial progressed. It was up to me to decide when she was ready."

"I know," Gus said. "It's your gut instinct that something else went on with that girl. I wanted that to be true, too. You think I don't know how Sizemore is spinning this? That crap Pettis pulled on cross got leaked. People are out there saying this whole thing was my vendetta against that bastard. That's the spin."

"I won't let that happen," I said. "We'll put out a statement today."

Gus waved a dismissive hand. "It won't help."

"I'm not going to let that man ruin anyone else's life," I said. "You're the best detective I know, Gus. I don't care what kind of shop talk you had in some bar God knows how long ago. Denny Sizemore raped that girl. Period. I will never let the people of this town forget that."

Gus stared glassy-eyed out the window.

"I'm sorry," he said. "That's all I can say. I wanted to win one for that girl."

"Me too," I said. The weight of it settled on my chest like an anvil. This was truly the end of the road for Neveah Ward.

"He won't try anything like this again," Sam said. "He knows we're watching."

"It won't matter," I said. "There will be another girl. We all know it."

Gus slammed his fist against the radiator. Then he got up without a word and went back into the bullpen. I got up to go after him.

"Don't," Sam said. "Let him be."

I stopped. "Yeah," I said. I picked up my briefcase.

"Why don't you let me buy you lunch?" he said.

I shook my head. "Rain check. There's something I have to do."

Sam gave me a quizzical look, but didn't ask me questions. Just like Gus, he knew this was a time to let me be.

25

Neveah Ward didn't have a headstone yet. Louella Holmes ordered one a week ago but it would be weeks before it could be placed. So I set a bouquet of red and yellow roses on the ground. There was a bench at least just a few yards from where Neveah lay.

"I'm sorry," I said. "I wish I had better news."

The wind picked up. It rustled my hair, whispering against my cheek. It would get cold again soon before spring finally gave way to summer.

Mine weren't the only flowers laying on the freshly turned earth. They'd laid a patch of sod over it, but the rectangular outline of Neveah's grave was still clear. Someone had left her daisies. They were starting to wilt.

A man walked toward me. He wore a battered black coat over a navy-blue Carhartt jumper. Steel-toed work boots and calloused hands. When he saw me sitting there, his step faltered.

"You here for her?" he asked, pointing to Neveah's grave. I folded my hands in my lap.

"I am."

"That's my girl," he said. "That's my Neveah. Heaven spelled backwards. That was her mama's choice. I always thought heaven spelled backwards meant hell. Guess I was right."

"Mr. Mosely?" I said. I'd never met the man before. I only knew what Neveah had told me, none of it favorable. Her mother finally kicked him out of their lives when she was seven or eight. She never came out and said there'd been physical abuse, but I knew Neveah was scared of him as a kid. She came to Waynetown to try and get answers after her mother died.

"You're that lawyer," he said. "The one who put ideas into that girl's head."

"What ideas would those be?" I asked, rising. There were other mourners about a hundred yards to the east, standing in front of another grave. A hundred yards to the west, three grounds crewmen were working on landscaping.

"She shouldn't have took that man to court. The minute she did that, I knew she'd get nothing. He would have paid up. Types like that always do."

"Neveah was interested in justice, Mr. Moseley, not blackmail."

His lips curled into a smile, revealing badly nicotine-stained teeth. He was missing both upper incisors. "Baby girl was always interested in dollar bills, lady."

I looked back at the ground. "Well," I said. "I just wanted to pay my respects. I'll leave you alone to pay yours."

"Damn fool," he said, approaching the edge of Neveah's grave. "I told her a thousand times she was gonna wind up like this. Thought she knew better. Thought she was smarter. Well, look where it got her."

"Mr. Moseley," I said. "When was the last time you spoke to your daughter?"

He snapped his head around. "I'd say that's none of your business. Neveah and me had our own thing. She'd get mad at me. Run off. But she'd always come back one way or the other. 'Cept this time."

"You gave an interview," I said. "You told a reporter you thought your daughter got what she deserved from Denny Sizemore. Mr. Moseley, did someone pay you to say that?"

"You ask a lot of dumb questions."

"It's my job," I said. "Neveah's gone now. You can tell me the truth. If someone put pressure on you to lie to the press, I'd like to know."

He shook his head. "She was fine when she listened to me. It's when she listened to you she got hurt."

"I never even met Neveah until after she reported her rape to the police, Mr. Mosely. She did the right thing."

He said nothing. I couldn't figure him out. Why come here at all? He pulled out a fresh bouquet of daisies from his deep pocket and laid them on the ground next to the old ones.

"Been coming here every week," he said, answering the question I hadn't yet asked. "Everybody wanted a piece of that girl. If she'd a just listened to me. Told her that her whole damn life. She never did. There are rules for a reason."

"What rules?" I asked.

He stared at me, his eyes narrowing in clear contempt.

"Not my Neveah, no. She thought she was special. Thought the rules don't apply to her." He turned back to the grave. "See what happens when you don't play by 'em. What it gets you?"

"Mr. Mosley," I said. "If you know something about what happened to Neveah, you need to speak up. I can protect you."

He laughed. "Like you protected her?"

"What do you know?"

He spit on the ground. The brutality of it shocked my heart.

"Don't know a damn thing," he said. "But at least I can admit it. Instead of walking around here like I'm above it all. Like she did. Like you do. Nah. I don't know nothing. But it's more than either of you."

He tossed the daisies to the ground and walked back up the hill.

I sank back onto the bench. The rules. New rage bubbled up inside me. I made a decision then and there. I was done playing by the rules where Neveah was concerned. And I no longer cared what it got me.

26

She was easy to find. High society in Maumee County, such as it was, hung out at the Poise Barre in Chatham Township. The Tuesday morning hot barre class was a particular draw.

Claire Sizemore walked out with a group of equally toned and tanned women carrying a neon green yoga mat slung across her shoulder. There were three of them. Laughing. They lined up together in front of the Poise Barre sign and one of the group took a selfie of the three of them that would no doubt make it into her Instagram story within the hour.

I parked behind Claire's blue Prius. She waved goodbye to her companions. She pulled her key fob out of her bag. Her step faltered as she noticed me sitting there finally. One final wave back at the others. She was making sure they were truly on their way and no longer paying attention to her.

I got out of my car.

Claire hurried her step. She'd parked at the end of the row right next to the alley separating the Poise Barre with a health food store.

"Mrs. Sizemore," I said. I dressed casually in my own pair of yoga pants and hoodie. Let anyone passing by think we were just two gym rats having a conversation.

"I don't have to talk to you," she said, whirling around to face me. Those were the words that came out of her mouth. But she moved into the alley so no one could easily see us.

"No," I said. "You don't. But you should talk to someone. This has to end."

"I'm sorry about what happened to your client," she said. "But it has nothing to do with me."

"Do you believe him?" I asked.

She blinked. Her mouth dropped open, staying frozen in an 'o'.

"I know you don't," I said. "I know you know he did exactly what Neveah Ward accused him of."

She clamped her mouth shut.

"If you don't want to talk to me, that's fine," I said. "But maybe you should listen. Guys like Denny, they don't get better. I've seen it before. Do you know how many assaults and murder cases I've prosecuted against spouses like him? He makes you promises, but he always breaks them."

"I can't do this," she said. "And you shouldn't be here. Go back to Waynetown."

"You aren't safe," I said. "He makes you think he's protecting you, but he's not. He's keeping you a prisoner. Someday he'll go too far with you like he did with Neveah. Probably sooner rather than later. Girls like her are what kept him from doing worse to you. He's got to be more careful now. But that urge he has. To dominate. To control. To hurt. It has to be fed. Pretty soon, you'll be the only prey left, Claire."

"Stop it," she cried out. The sun came out from behind the clouds. It lit her face and that's when I saw. She had fresh bruising beneath her right eye. It had been carefully covered with make-up, but her skin still glistened from her workout.

There was something else. Just below her hairline, I saw a healed scar. It was recent though and had been stitched.

"You've protected him," I said. "I know you're scared. You're strong, Claire. You've done what you had to do to survive. Only it's not enough anymore. The game has changed. He changed the rules when he went after Neveah Ward. There has to be a line you can't let him cross. It's not just you anymore."

"I'm not responsible for that girl," she said.

"Are you sure about that?" I asked. "You sat there in court. You saw the photographs cataloging her injuries. If she'd lived long enough to take the stand, you would have heard her tell the jury what he did to her. He choked her. Pinned her down. Clawed at her. She lost a lot of blood. She tore. They had to use fourteen stitches to sew her back up down there."

"Stop it," she said.

"He marked her," I said. "Branded her like cattle. Only he used his teeth. She would have those scars for the rest of her life. He knew that. He counted on it. He...he did it to you too, didn't he?"

It was a guess. But the flicker in Claire's eyes told me I'd hit my mark. Then she brought a hand to her chest, resting it right over her breast. I knew then she had scars too. Where Denny had bit her just like he'd done to Neveah.

"I'm not responsible for that girl," she said. "Denny told me what she was. I'm not judging her. But she made her choices too. It was her lifestyle."

"What, because your husband has you convinced she was a prostitute? As if that would have absolved him even if it were true? Did he make you think she deserved it?"

"Stop it," she said again.

I reached into my purse and pulled out the photographs I knew she hadn't yet seen. These weren't part of the trial. They were taken the day Neveah Ward died.

"Did she deserve this?" I asked. I shoved Neveah Ward's death photo in her face.

"Look very closely," I said. "This girl didn't just shoot up. Look at her. Look at what she's wearing. She got dressed up for court. She was ready."

"She was a junkie," Claire said. "It's awful and tragic. But it's predictable."

"She wasn't a junkie," I said.

"You don't know! You don't know anything."

"What else has to happen before you'll speak up?" I said. "Who else has to die? Because if you don't call this man out for what he is, you'll be another casualty."

Claire Sizemore's face contorted with rage. She curled her hands into claws and shoved me. Hard. She had me pinned against the brick alley wall. I didn't fight back. I let her rail against me. Maybe it would bring something out of her she needed to say.

"I'm not responsible for that girl," she repeated as she let me go. She wiped her nose on her sleeve. Claire Sizemore seemed more animal than human at that moment.

"Yes, you are," I said. "And so am I. She died because she was going to testify against your husband. I can't prove it. Not yet. But you have to know it's true. I think you already do."

She shook her head.

"Are you going to try to tell me Denny isn't capable of something like that? How many times has he threatened to do the very same thing to you if you told anyone what he does to you?"

She kept shaking her head.

"He's using her as an example to you, isn't he?" I asked. "Is that it? He told you to look at what happens to the women who tell."

Still nothing.

"I can help you if you'll let me," I said. "Denny isn't untouchable."

She met my eyes. "You don't know anything."

"This only ends one way if you keep doing what you're doing," I said. "Denny won't be able to hold back. One of these times, he'll kill you. Or he'll hurt you so badly, you'll wish you died."

"Are you going to tell me I can trust you?" She laughed. "That you'll protect me?"

I raised my chin. "No. I won't tell you that. I can't protect you. Only you can do that. And I want one thing. I want Denny Sizemore held accountable for what he's done. If you won't work with me and that ends up hurting you too, so be it."

"You're threatening me?"

"No. I'm giving you an opportunity. I'm giving you a heads-up. You can tell your husband, don't tell your husband. It's your call."

Her face broke into a slow smile. "You can't really be that naïve. You think my husband is the problem?"

"Tell me who is," I said.

"You're asking me that? I'm not afraid of Denny. I'm certainly not afraid of you. I thought you were smart. You think I'm turning a blind eye or protecting Denny?"

She readjusted the sling on her yoga mat and started to walk past me.

"Claire," I said.

She whipped around. "I don't need your protection. Save it for yourself. You're going to need it if you keep kicking this particular hornet's nest. So let that serve as your heads-up. I know what I need to do to survive. Do you?"

She was still holding on to the picture I'd given her of Neveah. "You may not believe this, but I really am sorry for what happened to her."

"She was murdered," I said.

"That's your story," Claire said.

"It's the truth. And it should bother you. It should scare you to death. It does me. It means there's no line Denny Sizemore won't cross."

She cocked her head, studying me. Then she let the picture fall to the ground.

"You're asking the wrong questions," she said. "You've always asked the wrong questions."

"So, what are the right ones?"

"You have a lot more to lose than I do," she said. "You think Denny's worst is the thing I should be afraid of?"

"What do you mean? Who's trying to hurt you?"

She shook her head and turned her back on me.

"Claire?"

She didn't answer. She just kept on walking until she got to her car. Her hands were trembling as she opened her door.

27

They had the same posture. I'd never noticed it before. But as my mother watched television with my son, they each sat with their right legs folded up against their bodies, their heads resting on their knees.

Natalie Montleroy wouldn't dare let anyone see her looking this way. Casual. No makeup except for the kohl black eyeliner she had tattooed on twenty years ago and didn't think I knew. She wore what passed for sweats in her world. An oversized cable-knit sweater over caramel-colored riding pants.

She was beautiful this way, my mother. Careful in the way she held herself next to my son. Knowing if she made any grand gestures of affection, he might fold back into himself. So she sat as close to him as he would allow. Breathing in his scent. Enjoying the wonder of Will's hyper-speed brain as he ticked off the inconsistencies of the evidence touted as gospel in the JFK assassination documentary he'd asked her to watch with him for about the twentieth time. It was his love language. My throat felt thick with emotion as I watched her hide her smile.

In some ways, theirs was the perfect relationship. My mother had never been one to show me affection, either. Her love language was control. Look the right way. Surround myself with the "right" people. Money. Status. Power. She would have made the perfect political wife if my late father had ever had that ambition. It was the great tragedy of her life that he hadn't. The great boon of her life that he'd left her an obscenely wealthy widow with political connections strong enough to catapult Jason's career when I refused to enter into the fray.

As the credits rolled on the documentary, Will got up to find a new DVD. He could have streamed anything he wanted but my son felt that gave the algorithms too much information about him. He was probably right.

My mother joined me in the kitchen where I poured her another glass of wine.

"He's doing great," she said. It felt more like an affirmation to herself than a real assessment of Will's state of mind. She needed to believe it. It was easier to let her for now. "When is that judge finally going to get off his rear end and put an end to all of this?"

"We've got another hearing tomorrow," I said. "The judge wants oral argument on whether Will should have to testify." The words burned in my throat.

"They're not seriously going to make him do that," she said, sipping her Merlot.

"Jeanie's fighting like hell against it," I said. "A lot of this is Jason trying to bury me in legal costs."

"For what I'm paying Ms. Mills, she damn well better win."

"If it were just about money, this would already be over," I said. "But thank you. I'll pay you back."

She set her wineglass down. "I don't expect that. What else am I going to do with it? You insist on staying in that menial job of yours in this godforsaken town. When this is all over, won't you please just come back home to New Hampshire with me? Go into private practice. You could make ten times what they're paying you now if you took the job with Chaney and Sanderson. Do you know how many insufferable bridge games I've played with Sylvia Chaney to get her to put a good word in with Beau for you? It has to be worth something, Mara."

"I didn't ask you to do that," I said. "And I can't keep having this same conversation with you. Waynetown is good for Will. It's home. He's had enough change and upheaval in his life."

"Do you want President Garfield or Lincoln next, Grandma?" Will asked. He had his index fingers through the center holes of two different DVDs.

"Um ... dealer's choice," she said. "I'm up for either. I'll be out there in five minutes. Let me pop some popcorn."

Will abruptly turned and headed back into the living room.

"It's good having you here," I said. "He's missed you."

"Jason's up in the polls," she said, changing the subject with whiplash-inducing speed as she was wont to do when she felt uncomfortable.

"Good for him," I said.

"I haven't contributed a dime this cycle," she said. "And won't. It's causing some friction within the party but I don't care. The rumor is this will be his last congressional race. Zeke Corbin's senate seat will be up for grabs in two years. Jason's positioning himself to run for it."

"I don't know how to feel about that," I said. "But it's always been the long game."

"I'm being pressured already," she said. "I've still got some influence with the leadership."

"With everything that's been going on," I said. "You're telling me these people still expect you to fall in line behind Jason?"

She poured herself a second glass of wine. "There's what's good for the family and what's good for the party. Some people don't see those as mutually exclusive."

"Do you?"

She paused for a moment, running a perfectly manicured finger along the rim of her glass. "I didn't used to. Now? Yes. Yes, I do. But there's a risk to me if I don't do what's expected. And by extension to you."

"To what?" I said. "To my political standing? I don't care about that. To your ability to get the best invites at Martha's Vineyard?"

"To my family's legacy," she said. "Which, by extension, means yours. They can't touch your father's money, thank God."

I bit my tongue from saying I didn't care about that either. There was only so much personal growth I could expect from this woman. I'd take what I could get.

"The things I do now will ensure that boy's future," she said. "Someone has to."

"That's what I'm doing too," I said.

"I know you want to live in a vacuum down here," she said. "It's a nice, peaceful, small-town dream. It's just not practical."

"It's us," I said. "And it's ..."

The world exploded in a rain of glass. Heat flashed across my face. I heard screeching tires, then the thunderous rumble of a motor revving.

"Mom!" Will shouted.

Cold air hit my back. My mother stood before me, her face a mask of shock. She was saying something, but no sound came out of her mouth.

"Get down!" I shouted to Will. He was a few feet away on the other side of the couch.

I came out from behind the kitchen island and grabbed my mother by the shoulders. I pulled her to the ground.

"Are you okay?" I yelled to Will.

"A brick," he said. "It landed right over there."

I tracked where Will pointed. Sure enough, a red brick lay just a few feet from where he sat. There was a piece of paper wrapped around it with a dirty rubber band.

"Don't touch it," I said.

"Mom, are you okay?" I asked her. My mother slumped against the wall, breathing heavy. She had shards of window glass embedded in her sweater, but she didn't seem to be bleeding.

"Mara," she said. "Your face."

"What?"

It was then I felt the heat again. I lifted a hand to my right cheek. When I pulled it away, my fingers were covered in blood.

"Mom!" Will said. He ran to me, barreling into my chest.

"It's okay," I said. "I'm okay."

"Are they gone?" my mother asked.

"I don't know. Everybody just stay down."

My phone was on its charger on the kitchen counter. I reached up and grabbed it.

"Why didn't your alarm go off?" my mother asked.

"It's not on until we go to bed," I said. "But I have cameras. Just hang tight and stay where you are."

I punched in Sam's cell phone number. He answered on the second ring.

"Hey, Mara," he said.

"Sam," I said. "I've got trouble at the house. Someone's thrown a brick through the window and I don't know if they're still out there or not."

His voice lowered an octave when he answered. "Don't hang up," he said.

He was still on duty. I heard some clicks and beeps as he got on the radio and called in a code.

"I've got help coming," he said to me. "Are you hurt?"

"No," I started to say. Then Will shouted toward the phone.

"There's glass everywhere! That was a big brick. It's right there! I won't let anyone touch it. Don't worry. But my mom. She's all cut up, Lieutenant Cruz. Send an ambulance Code 3."

"They'll be there in five minutes or less," Sam said to me. In the background, I could hear another motor rev. He was in his car and he'd just floored the gas. A second later, his voice was nearly drowned out by the sound of a siren. "Stay away from the windows. I'm on my way too."

I held the phone to my chest. I felt lightheaded as blood began to drip down my neck. I reached back up and pulled down the roll of paper towels I had sitting on the counter. I pressed one to my face.

Will sat beside me, his arms wrapped tightly around my waist. Then he reached up and took the towel from me. Our eyes locked as he gently held the towel to my cheek.

28

"You gonna tell me I should see the other guy?" Jeanie said. "Christ, Mara. What happened?"

I'd done my best to minimize the damage. I'd used a flat iron to straighten my hair over my right cheek. But five stitches below my eye, a shiner, and a giant bandage later, there really was no hiding it.

"It's a long story," I said. "And we're still trying to work out the details. But someone doesn't like the work I'm doing on the Neveah Ward case."

"There's a case there still?" she asked. We walked into the Common Pleas Court building. Jeanie would argue to Judge Small on our motion to block Will from having to testify. This was the last piece before a full custody trial if Jason wouldn't back down.

"Not according to the Maumee County Sheriffs," I said. "It just still doesn't sit right with me how she died."

"It's a hard one to let go of," Jeanie said. "We've all got 'em. She was just a kid, really. Such a shame. Well, I don't know what help I can be. But even if it's just another brain you want to pick ..."

"Thanks," I said. "And I might take you up on that."

"All right," she said. "I probably don't need to tell you. But I'm going to tell you anyway. You let me do the talking in there. Jason's best strategy is to rattle you. Not sure if Judge Small is planning on taking testimony from either of you but if he does, you gotta keep your cool. Everything you say has to be framed as what you believe is in Will's best interests. Resist the temptation to educate the judge on what an asshole your ex can be. It'll be strong."

"I got it," I said.

"Okay," she said. She reached up and brushed a piece of lint off my shoulder. She'd told me to dress like a mom today and not a prosecutor. I had no idea what that even meant. I went with a cream-colored suit instead of black.

Jeanie opened the door to courtroom number four. We were the respondents in this case even though this was my motion. So we sat at the table furthest from the empty jury box. A moment later, Jason came in with his team of lawyers. He'd added two more since the day of our status conference hearing. They surrounded him. Fawned over him. I'd been advised not to come in here as a prosecutor. Jason clearly came in as full-on Congressman Brent.

Thirty seconds after Jason's team settled, Judge Small took the bench. He got right to the point.

"Okay," he said. Judge Small was a bit of an outsider to Maumee County. He'd been appointed to his seat six years ago after only six months' residency at the very edge of town. He was one of the youngest members of the county bench at forty. Everyone assumed he planned to springboard himself to the appellate court at some point. His political aspirations worried me. Today could tell the tale whether he was in this to score political favor with Jason.

"I've read your pleadings, Ms. Mills. I understand the respondent's reticence to produce the minor child for testimony in this matter. I have some questions."

"Yes, Your Honor," Jeanie said.

"I've reviewed Will Brent's school file. He is under the care of Dr. Rita Vera for psychotherapy once a week."

"Yes, Your Honor," Jeanie said. "Dr. Vera has been working with Will since he was seven years old. That is one of the concerns we have in terms of the disruption the petitioner has introduced into Will's routine. I'm happy to report Will's back in school at Grantham and adjusting well. As you'll see in Dr. Vera's report, she does not feel it's in Will's best interests to provide testimony on the custody matter before the court. She's of the opinion it will do him more harm than good."

"She's met with him how many times since his return to his mother's residence?" the judge asked.

"Twice, Your Honor," Jeanie said.

"Your Honor, if I may." Jason's lead attorney stood. Doyle Stratton was a power player in Virginia. The lawyer beside him, Andrew Shay, was local. His one job was to sit by Stratton's side and vouch for him with the state bar so Stratton could appear in this court without being licensed here. Shay was star-struck. He stared up at Stratton, moony-eyed. Shay had political ambitions of his own.

"You may when I ask you to," Judge Small said. "Ms. Mills?"

"Your Honor," Jeanie said. "Will's emotional state is precarious at this point. Without going into the broader issues raised in the petitioner's custody motion, Will Brent has documented learning disorders and is on the autism spectrum. He thrives with routine and consistency in his daily life. More than thrives. He excels. This disruption in his life, by his father keeping him in Georgetown without agreement by the parties, did not serve Will at all. But he's home now. He's readjusting and getting back into his more successful routine. If I may speak frankly, putting this kid through the wringer of having to come to this environment, the courthouse, in front of you and the team of well-meaning, professional social workers, will be extremely disruptive and stressful for him. Will can't afford a setback like that. Will has strong bonds with both parents and my client has done everything in her power to foster that. He's eleven, yes. But his emotional maturity is much younger than that. We respectfully ask the court to take those factors into consideration and deny the petitioner's request to force Will Brent to testify in this matter."

"Mr. Stratton?" Judge Small said. "What's your response?"

"Your Honor, the respondent takes the position that this court would be asking Will to choose between his parents. That's not the case. We'd like to give Your Honor more credit than that. We agree. Will thrives on stability and routine. My client has shown he is better equipped to provide that. That's all we would ask the court to hear from Will about. How his life is going in Georgetown. Mrs. Brent wishes to paint a very false picture to this court. She orchestrated Will's removal from his father's care while he was away on a business trip. We're exploring whether a case can be brought for parental kidnapping. But that is even a separate issue. There has been a new development within the last twenty-four hours that we feel the court must consider. It's no longer just Will's best interests we are trying to protect. It's his physical safety."

"Excuse me?" Jeanie said.

I rose to my feet. Jason stared straight ahead at the judge.

"What's going on, Mr. Stratton?" the judge said.

"Your Honor," Stratton said. "We understand there was an assault at Mrs. Brent's home the night before last. Will was in the direct line of attack and witnessed what had happened. Mrs. Brent is being targeted by someone relating to her job as a prosecutor. She is unable to provide a safe environment for Will. She can't hide it, Your Honor. The result of this attack is quite literally written on her face."

I gripped the edge of the table.

"What happened, Mrs. Brent?" Judge Small asked.

"Your Honor," Jeanie interjected.

"No," Judge Small said. "I'd like to hear from your client."

"Mr. Stratton is grossly mis-characterizing what happened," I said. "There was a rock thrown through my window. Will was not in danger. I was not in danger."

"Your Honor," Stratton said. "This wasn't a random incident. Mrs. Brent lives at the end of a quarter-mile wooded drive. This was no drive-by. Someone with deliberation and purpose targeted Mrs. Brent's home while Will was present and in a position to be hurt. Badly. Whatever is going on, we don't care. We only care that Will Brent is not safe in his mother's home. And this is not the first time that Will's been involved in a volatile or violent incident directed at his mother. A few years ago, he was actually the target of a bullying incident that related to a case his mother was working on. He's not safe in Waynetown. Not emotionally, not physically. We respectfully ask the court to expedite its ruling on the custody issue. We need to get Will out of that home. Even if he needs to stay with a third party pending your decision."

"This is ridiculous," I said. I tried to remember what Jeanie told me. But there was no way I could keep my temper. "My son is safe."

"He watched you bleed on the kitchen floor, Mara," Jason said. "He's scared to death."

Jeanie put a hand on my arm. "Don't," she whispered.

"Your Honor, Mr. Brent is sensationalizing the incident. Time and again, he has tried to argue that Will's mother should be penalized for working. That her career somehow makes her unable to care for her son. It's revolting and sexist. If we're going to stand here and rehash ancient history, I would remind the court that it was Jason Brent's behavior that caused the breakdown of the marital home in the first place. From the very beginning, he has acted in his own best interests, not his son's. I didn't want to bring this up but he's left me no choice. Jason Brent filed his custody petition only after his campaign manager put a poll in the field that showed his favorability ratings went up when he was seen as a father. He's using this kid as a political prop. Don't let him fool you."

I felt sick. I'd long suspected it. But Jeanie pulled a file out and I knew without having to look at it what it was. She had the goods to back up the claim she'd just made.

Jason and Stratton began to shout over each other.

"Enough!" Judge Small banged his gavel. "I've heard enough for today. The issue before the court is whether Will Brent should be compelled to testify. So here's what I'm going to do. If I feel it is necessary to hear from Will, I will do so in chambers, not in open court. I'm appointing a guardian ad litem for Will today. You'll be contacted with the name by the end of business tomorrow. I want a social worker and Will's guardian ad litem to meet with him within forty-eight hours to advise the court on his capacity to meet with me. That is all."

Judge Small rose and disappeared into his chambers with a swirl of his robe.

I stood dumbstruck. Any love I had for Jason melted into hatred in that moment and I wasn't proud of myself for it.

"We're getting out of here," Jeanie said as she packed up her things. "Now. You need to resist the urge to say anything to him. Not one word, Mara. Let's go."

Quaking with rage, I followed her out of the courtroom. We got to the elevators and one mercifully opened. I felt swallowed by it as we stepped inside and waited for the doors to shut.

"This is far from over," she said. "But we need to prepare Will for what's coming."

"He won't understand," I said. "This G.A.L. and a court-appointed social worker ... the last thing he needs is more strangers coming at him. He knows it. Jason knows it. But he's doing this anyway."

"He doesn't care," she said. "I'm sorry I had to swing with that polling data. I should have warned you. I was hoping I wouldn't have to bring it up."

"It's okay," I said. "The court needs to know. God. I need to know."

"Are you okay though, Mara?" Jeanie said. "I mean, really?"

"Yes," I said. "It's just ..."

My heart turned to ice. Something had nagged at me as Doyle Stratton tore into me about the rock incident. Below the shock and rage, there was something ...

"Jeanie," I said, my throat feeling thick. "Will hasn't talked to Jason since before the incident at the house the other night. No calls. No texts. They aren't scheduled to talk until tonight. There hasn't been a police report filed yet. It hasn't been reported in the press. Kat doesn't know. No one knows outside of the people in my house, Sam Cruz, and the two sheriff's deputies that came to the scene with Sam. But Jason knew. He knew it was a rock thrown through my window. He knew Will was in the room and saw it."

Jeanie pressed the emergency button to stop the elevator.

"My God, Mara," she said. "Do you think he's behind it?"

Her words hit me like a blow to the chest. "I don't know. God. I don't know. He wouldn't. He couldn't ..."

One thing crystalized in my mind. Everything I thought I knew about Jason Brent before today had been blown to bits in the last twenty minutes.

29

"You don't have to do this," I said. I found Caro elbow-deep in files. She'd just finished boxing up the last of my trial materials on the Ward/Sizemore case.

"I was hoping to have it finished and out of here before you came back," she said. She held a packing tape wheel and ripped it across the top of the last open box.

"I didn't think you'd want to deal with it," she said.

"Ugh," I said. I leaned in the doorjamb. "It's all just so, I don't know ..."

"Meaningless?" she said. "Arbitrary. Three small boxes. That's all that's left. There's an evidence box at the Sheriff's Department, but that's it. That's all she gets."

I ran my hand across one of the boxes. Caro had digitized everything, but we still kept a physical file on a few important cases. Caro never even had to ask me whether this one would qualify. She knew.

"Are you getting much sleep?" she asked. God only knew what she thought as she looked at me. I wasn't even supposed to be here. I'd started a week's vacation. I was in capris-length spandex workout pants and a pink hoodie. I had every intention of going for a run to try to clear my head. But the office just drew me to it.

"I'm sleeping," I said. Caro gave me a sad smile but didn't press.

I felt a hand on my back. Hojo and Kenya came up behind me in the hallway.

"Well," I said. "As long as the band is back together, you might as well all come in."

"I'm on my way to Muni court," Hojo said. "Just wanted to say hi. You look ... well ... you know? I don't know if I've ever seen you when you weren't wearing a suit. Nice scrunchie."

I fake punched him. Hojo smiled and bounded off. Caro said a quick goodbye and hightailed it out of my office right behind him.

"Uh oh," I said, finally catching the sober look on Kenya's face. "They sure both scrammed in a hurry. You want to let me in on the doom?"

"Close the door," she said. "We need to talk."

Kenya motioned toward my desk. So this wasn't a casual conversation at all. I opted to sit in one of the client chairs rather than behind my desk. Kenya sat beside me and turned the other chair so we faced each other.

"What's going on?" I asked.

"First of all, how are you holding up? Word is your hearing yesterday was a little rough."

"If by rough you mean my ex has doubled down on trying to take my kid away from me for political capital? I would say yes. It was rough."

"What's your lawyer saying?" she asked.

"She's cautiously optimistic," I said. "Or she was, until Jason's lawyer tried to use this as a reason to grant Jason's petition." On the word this, I motioned to my still bandaged cheek.

"He argued that my home is an unsafe environment for Will."

Kenya sat back hard. "Of all the bottom-feeding tactics. Mara, I'm so sorry."

"Judge Small is going to issue a ruling on whether Will has to testify by the end of the week. If so, I have to produce him by next Monday afternoon."

"I'm so sorry. Dammit."

"Okay," I said. "So you didn't come in here just to ask about my custody mess. What's going on, Kenya?"

She heaved a great sigh. "I realize this is going to be the very last thing you need right now. First, I have to ask you. Did you have an altercation with Claire Sizemore?"

"I wouldn't call it an altercation," I said. "I spoke to her in the parking lot of her gym. It wasn't a particularly pleasant conversation, but it was just a conversation."

Kenya shook her head and rested her chin on her hand. "I really wish you hadn't done that. Was this before or after someone lobbed a rock through your window?"

"The morning before," I said.

"Does Sam think they're connected?" she asked.

"I don't know."

Kenya glared at me. "You don't know. Meaning you didn't tell him about you and Claire Sizemore?"

"I didn't see how it was relevant."

"Come on. That's crap. And you know I know that's crap. You didn't tell him because you knew he'd tell you the same thing I'm about to. Mara, you've got to let this one go."

"I'm not afraid of the Sizemores," I said.

"Sure. Great. Only that kind of heat is the last thing you need. You didn't ask me how I found out you went rogue at the Poise Barre. Care to be enlightened?"

I didn't say anything. I just blinked.

"Claire's lawyer called me. She filed a complaint with my office. He stopped just short of threatening to ask for a restraining order against you on her behalf. That might be next."

"That's ridiculous," I said. "I never threatened her."

"Well, she's sure ready to threaten you," Kenya said. "She's filing a formal complaint against you with the Office of Disciplinary Counsel."

"What?" I said. "I don't have an attorney-client relationship with her. She doesn't have a case."

"That's probably true," Kenya said. "But I don't know how far she's willing to take it. At the moment, it seems pretty clear that the Sizemores are going to try to paint a picture of you in the press. They're going to spin this whole thing with Neveah as the result of an overzealous prosecutor with a personal vendetta against them. I know you didn't have any sinister motives with Claire, but by contacting her at all, you've given them fuel for this thing."

"I said, I'm not afraid of them," I said.

"You should be," she said. "I told you, this is the very last thing you need. They want to portray you as unhinged. Can you think of anyone else who might get a side benefit from that?"

I felt sick. I hated the world. I hated that Kenya was right.

"Look," she said. "I've got your back. That's not even a question. But this thing has gotten too far under your skin."

"You know what happened to that girl," I said. "You know that Denny Sizemore raped and brutalized her. We were supposed to be her voice. I was supposed to protect her. I promised her that."

Kenya rubbed her brow. "Well, you shouldn't have. I'm sorry, but that wasn't your job. Your job was to put together the best case you could based on the evidence we had. You did that. But it ends when that gavel comes down, Mara. It has to."

"Does it end for you?" I asked. "You want to sit here and tell me you don't go home with these cases? My God, Kenya. If we didn't, we wouldn't be able to keep doing this job."

"This time you have to," she said. "This time, you have way too much to lose. There will be other Neveah Wards. I hate that it's true. But it is. If you give them the rope to hang you with, then you won't be able to fight for those other women. And they need you. I need you. Will needs you."

There was nothing more I could say. I knew Kenya was right. But so was I. A moment passed. Finally, I looked Kenya squarely in the eyes.

"He can't win, Kenya," I said. "No matter what else happens, Denny Sizemore can never hold another position of power in this town or anywhere else. He has to be exposed for who and what he is. If we don't stand up to him, who will?"

"I don't know. Today, at least, I don't know."

"What do you want me to do?" I asked. "You tell me."

She reached for me. "Go home. Spend time with Will. Prepare him for what's coming. Even if you win against Jason, it'll come at a cost to Will."

I fought back tears. When Kenya held her arms out, I let her hug me. I hugged her back. After a moment, we broke away.

"There's one more thing," she said. "I want you to talk to a malpractice lawyer."

"What?"

"Someone who can protect your interests if the Sizemores won't back off. I don't think you've done anything wrong. But you should have counsel of your own."

"I'll think about it," I said, rising.

Kenya looked up at me with worry-filled eyes. I left her there, sitting in front of my desk.

"You have a week off," she said. "Use it. I don't even want to see you anywhere downtown in the next seven days."

I straightened my shoulders and headed for the elevators.

30

There were still two more hours before Will would come home from school. After that, I planned to do exactly what Kenya said. It was good advice. None of the rest of this mattered as much as he did. Not even Neveah Ward.

Only I couldn't shake the feeling that she was watching me. Haunting me, even. When I closed my eyes, I could only see her amber ones staring back at me, filled with tears and pain.

She was alone. She trusted me. I should have been there that morning. I should have made her stay with me the night before her testimony. If only I had, she might still be alive.

I drove aimlessly, blaring music that suited my mood. Bikini Kill. Then Hole. I headed away from downtown Waynetown and took the scenic route along the river. These were the beautiful parts of Maumee County. Rolling hills and farmland. Evil things happened here too, just like anywhere. But these were good, hard-working people. People who counted on me to bring them justice when those evil things reared.

I don't know what made me do it. The clock, perhaps. It was twelve o'clock. Wednesday. I swear I hadn't consciously driven here. But I found myself heading up the winding hickory tree-lined drive of the Highland Hills Country Club.

They were protected here. The so-called county power players. I was supposed to be among them. The dutiful, political wife with the rich family who could catapult the likes of Jason Brent, their hometown boy, into the stratosphere.

Web Margolis's silver Mercedes was parked in its reserved spot at the base of the hill leading to the clubhouse. Noon. Wednesday. His standing lunch date. Margolis would be here.

Rage seized me. I had the urge to take a baseball bat to Margolis's taillights.

"Go home, Mara," I said out loud. I had the best of intentions when I left Kenya's counsel. I swear I did.

But Web was another one who would remain unscathed by the horror that befell Neveah Ward.

I paused, idling just behind Web's car. I could ram it. That was childish. It served nothing. Besides, there were, of course, security cameras all around. If I hadn't given Claire Sizemore fodder for her bogus grievances, that would sure do it.

Movement caught my eye. A couple were making their way down the steep sidewalk. I put my car in gear and backed up. No matter what else happened, I didn't need to risk anyone seeing me here.

I slammed back into drive, checked that my path was clear, then lost my breath.

It wasn't just any couple coming down the walk. It was Web himself. The woman beside him looked upset. She dabbed at her eyes and smiled up at him. Web put a comforting hand on the small of her back.

It was Claire Sizemore. She nodded quickly. Then she put her arms around him and kissed Web's cheek before breaking and pulling out her key fob. She walked to the opposite end of the parking lot. I ducked down behind my steering wheel so they wouldn't see me.

I waited a full minute before popping back up. Web's parking space was empty. I glimpsed the back of his car as he turned and made his way out of the club.

31

"I don't like the pretzel ones," Will said. He stared at the crust of the Pop-Tart he'd just devoured.

"Really?" I said, sitting across from him. He scowled at his plate, as if he blamed it for the offense of not being a "regular" brown-sugar-and-cinnamon Pop-Tart.

"I would have figured you'd be all over the pretzel-flavored ones," I said. "I mean, pretzel buns are the only kind you'll let me buy."

"Just because a flavor exists, does not mean they should make it into a Pop-Tart. Just sayin'," he said.

I smiled. Just sayin' was his new go-to phrase. Lately, he'd been adding it to the end of almost everything he said. But he was talking again. We could not afford anymore set backs. I tried to quiet the stirring rage inside my heart for what Jason wanted to do.

"You've got a point, my man. No more pretzel brown-sugar-and-cinnamon Pop-Tarts. You're a purist. I can respect that.

Now put your plate in the dishwasher and grab your backpack. Wheels up in ten minutes."

Will did as he was told, still grumbling about his toaster pastry. We'd been good this week. I loved our drives to school. He was the most talkative as he got on those trips. We avoided any discussion of his father or D.C. or the looming decision from the Domestic Relations Court judge. Jeanie expected a ruling on whether Will would have to testify by tomorrow morning. I had an appointment to produce him in the judge's chambers at four o'clock Monday if so. I'd have the weekend to prepare him. But how do you prepare a kid for something like that? Any kid? Let alone mine.

Will was in a good mood this morning. He rattled off statistics about the K-Pg during the Cretaceous Period, the mass extinction event that killed all the dinosaurs.

"There's a new traveling dinosaur exhibit that's coming to the Toledo Zoo in two months. Can we go?"

"We absolutely can," I said, trying not to think about what might be happening in Will's life in two months. I could not fathom that he might have to stay with Jason on a more permanent basis. The thought made me physically ill. I took a breath. One step at a time. It's what I told every crime victim as the trial process started.

I pulled into the drop-off line. Will leaned toward me, letting me put a kiss on his head. I was lucky. Most eleven-year-olds wouldn't want to risk being seen in such a moment. I knew my days were numbered on that score.

"Have a good day," I said. "I'll pick you up in the circle after school. Think about what you want for dinner. I can go to the grocery store."

"Okay," Will said. He adjusted his backpack and merged with the other groups of kids, heading in before the morning bell. I waited a moment, watching to see if he'd turn back and wave like he used to when he was little. He didn't. Another kid caught his attention and Will hustled to join him.

"Thank God," I whispered. But dread filled me again at the thought his own father wanted to yank him from Grantham Elementary.

The car behind me tapped on the horn. I had broken the rules. You don't stop and wait in the drop-off line. You keep on moving. I waved back and left the circle.

I had the entire day to myself. I couldn't recall the last time that happened. Maybe never. With a thousand other things I could have spent my time on, only one had my attention.

Sam answered right away as I hit his name on my dashboard contact list. "Are you in today?" I asked.

"Where else would I be?" he said, laughing.

"I just dropped Will off at school. Can we meet for coffee?"

A momentary pause. Then. "Um ... sure."

"I need to run something by you," I said. "I'd rather not do it on county property. I can be at DeLuca Coffee in about fifteen minutes."

"K," he said. "I'll be right behind you. Is everything okay?"

"See you there," I said, clicking off.

Kenya would kill me if she knew what I had cooking. She'd kill me if she knew where I'd been yesterday afternoon. For all

I knew, Sam might do the same. It was a chance I was willing to take for now.

Twenty minutes later, I sat in a back booth with a steaming vanilla latte in front of me. I waved off the offer of scones as Sam walked in and caught my eye.

"Just black coffee," he said to the waitress. "Oh, and one of those cronuts if they're fresh. You want anything else, Mara?"

"I'm good," I said. "Thanks for coming. I know you're busy."

"I've got a half hour unless Maumee County explodes in the next ten minutes. What's up?"

"Web Margolis," I said.

The server came with Sam's order. He smiled and waited until we were alone again.

"What about him?" he asked.

"I think he needs to be interviewed again," I said. "I don't think he's been completely forthright about his connections in Neveah's case. He's in a relationship with Claire Sizemore."

Sam looked around, making sure we were out of earshot of any other people.

"And you know this how?"

"I saw them together," I said, shaking a Splenda packet. "Yesterday afternoon. They were coming out of Highland Hills together and he had an arm around her. She was crying. He appeared to be consoling her."

"You think she's having an affair with him based on that? Everybody in Maumee County with a seven-figure income hangs out at the Highland. There are any number of reasons why the two of them would have been there at the same time. How were you in a position to see them?"

"I drove out there," I said. "It was sheer luck, Sam. I swear. I saw Web's Mercedes. It's hard to miss. Then, all of a sudden, the two of them were walking out together. I saw them. They didn't see me. I'm sure of it."

Sam's expression darkened. He took a sip of his coffee.

"I heard about your run-in with Claire Sizemore. Hell, it's all over town. She's saying you're unglued. Is it true she's filing a grievance against you?"

"She can do whatever she pleases," I said. "We had a conversation. That's all."

The furrow between his eyes deepened.

"Don't give me that look," I said. "I am not unglued. Gus may not feel he can go talk to her again but there was nothing stopping me from doing it. I wanted to see her face, hear her answer firsthand. She's covering for Denny. She knows what kind of man he is. I needed to see her eyes."

Sam put both palms flat on the table on either side of his coffee cup. "Well, you've kicked a hornet's nest, that's for sure."

"I don't know," I said. "I can't prove it. I couldn't hear what they were saying, but I think Claire went to Web Margolis yesterday because I rattled her. I think they were talking about Neveah's case and everything that's been going on. I think he was telling her he would handle it."

"Based on what?" Sam asked. "Intuition?"

"You've followed leads based on less," I said.

"Gus interrogated Margolis," Sam said. "Twice. He's clean. He has an alibi. There's absolutely no evidence that he had anything to do with Neveah's death."

"It doesn't bother you at all that Neveah Ward's ex-boyfriend seems to have at least an intimate friendship with the wife of the man who raped her?"

"Everybody knows Web Margolis," Sam said. "This is Waynetown. He's one of the richest business owners we have. Of course, people like the Sizemores know him. It doesn't have to mean anything."

"I want Gus to talk to him again," I said.

"Mara."

"Don't Mara me," I said. "If Web Margolis is bankrolling Claire Sizemore's attempt to cause me trouble, you don't think that's evidence of something?"

"I just want you to be careful," he said. "This might not end up leading where you think it will. Or where you want it to."

"Or where *you* want it to." I bit out my words. Sam wasn't the one I was angry with. Not really. But his seeming indifference surprised me.

"Mara, we have no probable cause to suspect Web Margolis of any crime. We don't just go around harassing people. And I can't believe I'm explaining this to you. I'm telling you. Lie low on this one. Get some perspective."

"Perspective," I said. "Sam. None of this passes the smell test. I've been doing a lot of thinking. I spent five minutes in a parking lot with Claire Sizemore. The next thing I know people are throwing bricks through my window. Then Doyle Stratton, Jason's lawyer, seems to know the intimate details of the incident and uses them against me at my custody hearing less than twenty-four hours later. I didn't tell anyone about that but you. There might be a leak in your office, Sam. Don't forget, somebody told Simon Pettis about Gus's beef with Sizemore. Someone repeated what they heard him say at the Brass Monkey. Sizemore tried to kill Gus with it on cross-examination."

His scowl was back. But at least he was listening.

"Nobody knew when I was going to call Nevaeh Ward to the stand. As far as Judge Saul or Simon Pettis knew, she was going to be my last witness. And yet, she just happens to die right before I pick her up to take her to court. Just before she's about to testify. She was ... the way I found her. Sam, it felt personal. Like it wasn't just about getting Neveah out of the way. It's like someone wanted me to find her the way I did. She was dressed in the suit I helped her pick out. She was waiting for me. Me specifically. I've been over this and over this."

Sam rubbed his brow. "Did you talk about the order of testimony with anyone in your office?" he asked.

"No," I said. "Nobody. I was completely solo on this case. And the rock. How would someone have gotten access to the police report within twelve hours of the event? Stratton knew how close Will was to it. That wasn't even in the report. You're the only person I called."

He sat back against the booth cushions. His face fell. My blood turned to lava and it got hard to breathe. I replayed the words I'd just uttered at the same time he did.

Sam had been the only one I called. I was the last person who called Neveah before she died.

"You talked to Neveah on your phone," he said just as it dawned on me.

"Yes," I said.

"You were the last contact Neveah had on her cell phone. We ran it. There was nobody else she called or texted."

"I called *you* first," I said. "The rock. Sam, I *only* called you."

My phone lay on the table between us, face down.

"Mara," Sam said, his voice flat, all business.

Without him asking, I slid my phone across the table to him. "Sam?"

"Yeah," he said, staring down at my phone. My heart thundered in my chest. I grabbed a napkin and wrote my phone's lock screen password on it. I slid that across the table to Sam.

"I'll take care of it," he said. "I'll have the forensics team run it this afternoon. It might take a day or two before I find anything out. If ... if there's something to find."

"Okay," I said.

"Is there anything on there you don't want me or them to see?"

I shook my head. "There's nothing. I have nothing to hide."

Sam nodded. He took my phone and slid it into his breast pocket.

"Okay," he said. "In the meantime, get yourself one of those prepaid burner phones from the supermarket. Text the number to me right away so we can stay in touch. And Mara, be careful. I'll arrange for an extra patrol around your house. They know to be discreet enough so Will won't catch on."

"Okay," I said. It seemed the only word I was still capable of uttering.

Sam reached across the table and covered my hand with his.

"I'll let you know," he said. "We'll figure this out."

I nodded. Sam rose and put a twenty on the table. "We'll figure this out," he said again. "I promise."

But as he left, I felt like the ground had opened up beneath me, threatening to suck me under.

32

I called Jeanie on my new burner phone. Friday morning and the news wasn't good.

"He wants to hear from Will," she said. "Judge denied your motion to block him from having to testify."

I sank into the kitchen chair. Two hours ago, I'd dropped Will off at school. I had five more before I had to pick him up and figure out what to say.

"Monday at four," Jeanie said. "I should be hearing from the court-appointed guardian ad litem within the hour. She'll want to meet with him before he goes in to talk to the judge. I can set something up for, say, two thirty Monday, right after he gets out of school."

"An hour before the meeting with the judge?" I asked. "How in the world can she properly assess Will's state of mind? They'll have no rapport. Will's going to freak out. That's three new people. Three new adults with authority between the judge, the G.A.L., and the social worker they're sending."

"I know," Jeanie said. "And I'm sorry. But we're up against it now."

"I have to talk to Jason," I said. "He needs to understand that this is not okay."

"There's more," she said. "Jason's side is also insisting you not be the one to bring him to court. Kat's agreed to do it. You should expect a call from her. Can I give her this number?"

"I'll call her myself," I said. "Kat won't be happy about this, either. Maybe she can talk some sense into Jason."

"I wouldn't count on that. Mara, has it occurred to you Jason's doing a King Solomon routine with this? He's banking on the fact you know this whole thing is bad enough for Will you'll capitulate and just give him what he wants."

"Give up my son? My God."

"I know," Jeanie said. "He's a rat bastard, Mara. I'm beside myself too. But this isn't the ballgame. As far as I'm concerned, every other factor weighs in your favor for a permanent custody arrangement. And Will might surprise you. Odds are he's going to tell Judge Small he's happier in Waynetown with you. Don't forget, Kat brought him home because he asked her to. Begged her to. That's going to come up."

"Is that supposed to make me feel better?" I said. "Will is always going to know he was forced to pick between his mom and dad. Always. And he'll know I wasn't able to protect him from it. What am I even supposed to say to him?"

"You need to be careful about that," she said. "The judge will for sure ask him that too. Any inkling that you tried to coach him on what to say will kill you."

"I wouldn't coach him."

"Judge Small has been at this for a very long time. I trust he can be sensitive to the situation. It might not be as bad as you think. In some cases, it actually gives kids a sense of empowerment and control. Talk to his therapist. She should be on board. See if she can clear some time to meet with him, maybe before and after his session with the judge."

"I will," I said, but I felt sick. This was the one thing Jason and I swore we would never let happen. And here we were.

"I'll get a hold of the G.A.L. I'll call you either later today or first thing in the morning. We've got three days to get him used to the idea. It's going to be okay."

"How?" I asked. But I didn't wait for Jeanie's answer. She didn't have one.

I called Kat next. She was in tears within the first ten seconds. It comforted me to know this whole thing upset her, too. A little anyway.

"I just want this to be over," she said. "You guys promised me I'd never get thrown into the middle of it."

"I'm sorry for that," I said. "I really am. But I wasn't the one who filed a custody motion. I'm not the one looking to change everything and take Will away from his home."

"I can't get into that," she said. "I love you, Mara. I love you both."

"I'm sorry. I shouldn't have said all that. I know this is killing you. I love you too. It gives me a lot of comfort to know you'll be with Will on Monday. Thank you. This whole thing has upended your life and that's not fair."

"Just let me know if there's anything else I can do," she said. "If Will wants to hang out this weekend, I've got some time. Bree and I would love to take him to the art museum or something."

"Thanks," I said. "I miss you two. Can I count on you to pick him up from school on Monday?"

"Of course," she said. "But Mara, what are you going to tell him?"

I paused. "I haven't figured that out yet."

She stayed silent. There was nothing more to say. We said goodbye and I found myself staring at nothing for far too long.

So much felt out of my control. Will's life. My life. Justice for Neveah.

A quick text to Sam added on more layers of uncertainty. The forensics lab was a day behind. He didn't expect any word on my phone until tomorrow afternoon at the earliest. I was supposed to just sit and cool my heels. When I asked him whether he'd told Gus about my spotting Margolis and Claire Sizemore together, I got those three blinking gray dots for several minutes.

I shoved the phone in my purse and tore out of the house, not at all sure where I would go.

I drove around for a while. Past Will's school. Past the courthouse. Past the Sheriff's Department. Past the cemetery. I thought about leaving flowers on Neveah's grave again. Instead, I ended up driving to the place where she'd been most alive.

I sat in the parking lot of Maumee Valley Montessori. I had no clear plan of attack. I just knew I needed to be here. The kids came out for recess. Someone new led them one by one. She was young. Pretty. But she wasn't Neveah Ward.

A quiet tap on my window startled me. Aimee Petersen smiled and waved. I'd met her a few times when I came to talk to Neveah. She was another teacher's aide under Louella's employ.

"You okay?" she asked.

I opened the door and stepped outside, winging it. "Yes. Sorry. I got distracted."

"Are you looking for Louella?"

"What? Uh. Yes."

"Sorry," Aimee said. "She's out today. Emergency root canal. Is there something I can help you with? Do you want to come inside? I was going to call you, actually. Neveah left a lot of stuff inside and Louella hasn't been able to bring herself to do anything about it."

"You were going to call me?" I asked.

"I don't know who else to call. None of the numbers Neveah left were any good. Her dad just doesn't seem like the right person to know what to do with any of it. To be honest? In the last few months before she died, Neveah was as close to you as anybody. Louella, bless her heart. But her heart's the problem. There's so much of Neveah left here. It's unsettling for the kids and for the rest of us who loved her. It's all just sitting in a box, tossed to the side."

I found myself following Aimee into the school. She brought me to Louella's office. The last time I was here, I'd watched Neveah through the two-way mirror, reading *Stone Soup* to a group of enraptured four-year-olds.

"It's just this one box," Aimee said. "Nev had other stuff. School supplies. Stuffed animals and puppets she brought in. Louella said she thought Neveah would like it if we just kept that for the kids."

"She's probably right," I said. "That does sound like something Neveah would want."

Aimee set the box on Louella's desk. I leaned over and peered in. It contained personal items. A lunch bag, insulated cups, an allergy inhaler, a lanyard with her ID photo. There were also more notes and textbooks like I'd found at her rental house.

"She used to do homework here sometimes," Aimee explained. "I think you knew she'd started taking classes again just before the trial started. She kept her Chromebook here. That's gone."

"The police have all of that," I said. "They searched it for evidence after ..."

"Right," Aimee cut me off.

"Anyway, I just couldn't bring myself to throw this stuff in the incinerator like Louella asked me to. She cries whenever anyone brings it up. But we had to clear this stuff out of Neveah's locker so someone else could use it."

"Aimee!" A shout from the classroom drew Aimee's attention. Another one of the teacher's aides had her hands full with a class coming back in from lunch.

"I'll be right back," Aimee said.

I waved her off and went back to the box of Neveah's personal effects. Aimee was right. It was mostly junk now. Neveah had been taking a Human Growth and Development class. Another in grant writing. She took detailed notes in her tight, looping handwriting.

I understood Aimee's reticence, but five minutes in, and I knew I'd recommend the incinerator.

I pulled out a thin file folder at the bottom of the box. This one was different. It wasn't related to Neveah's school work. It was her personnel file here at M.V.M. Louella must have cleared out everything she had related to Neveah.

I sat at Louella's desk and opened the file. Louella kept meticulous notes on Neveah's performance. There were glowing reports by Louella. She also had outside evaluators coming in as part of the school's accreditation process. Neveah earned high marks from them.

Such a waste. So much promise. At the back of the file, I found Neveah's resume and application to M.V.M. She'd applied for a position here just three weeks after the rape. I remembered meeting with her for the first time right after she'd been hired here. She was still so shell-shocked and traumatized. And yet, she'd excelled here.

Louella had marked the resume with a big, red stamp. "Hired."

The last set of pages were Neveah's references. She'd listed two professors. One had been the one whose class she'd been taking the night of the rape. Ronald Perry. She'd taken three political science courses from him before switching to early childhood development. He gave her straight As.

Lastly, Neveah had two letters of recommendation in her file. One came from her former high school English teacher. Neveah was a strong, conscientious student. Years ago, Neveah had served as this teacher's nanny one summer. Her aptitude for working with children had been evident back then. Her teacher wrote she'd been a natural fit. If only she'd pursued that path from the beginning. Would everything have turned out differently? Would Denny Sizemore ever even have met her?

I picked up the final letter with tears in my eyes. I shouldn't have come here. It was just too sad. I had enough of my own problems to worry about without trying to chase the ghost of Neveah Ward.

The signature on the bottom of the letter stopped me cold. I blinked. Did a double take.

"As my personal assistant for a number of years, Neveah has proven herself extremely capable at whatever tasks she's been asked to perform. She is one of the most reliable employees who has ever worked for me and I cannot recommend her highly enough."

It was signed by Web Margolis. Beneath his signature, Louella had written her own note. "Immediate hire."

"You okay in here?" Aimee asked, startling me. I folded the letter and slid it into my purse.

"All set," I said.

"Any idea what I should do with all of that?" she asked.

I closed the box. "Just burn it," I said. "There's nothing left to save."

Aimee frowned, but nodded. I wasn't telling her anything she didn't already know.

"I'm afraid I have to get going," I said. "Thanks for showing me this."

I brushed past Aimee and fished for my phone. I didn't know Gus's number off the top of my head. All of that was stored on my regular phone. So I called the Sheriff Department's main switchboard and asked to be transferred.

"Gus," I said. "Whatever you're doing, clear it. I'm heading over. I have something you need to see."

I didn't give him a chance to argue. I clicked off the call and drove into town as fast as I could.

33

Gus and Sam were out on a call when I got to the Sheriff's Department. Sheriff Clancy let me into Sam's office to wait. It gave me a solid forty-five minutes to fire up my laptop and find what I needed. Heart racing, I scribbled down notes until my fingers went stiff. I didn't even hear Gus and Sam finally walk in. I jumped out of my chair when Sam shut the door behind him.

"Everything okay?" Gus asked. "We got here as quickly as we could. We were on scene at another homicide out on Fullman Street. Drug deal gone wrong."

"Sit," I told them. I'd taken over most of Sam's desk. The men looked at each other, then me, then did what I asked.

I pulled out the pages from Neveah's personnel file. I'd availed myself of the copy machine down the hall and handed sheets to each of them.

"What am I looking at?" Sam asked.

"Read the signature at the bottom of the letter. This is who got Neveah Ward her job at M.V.M. And he lied about how he knew her. He said she worked for him."

"Web Margolis," Gus read. He rested the papers on his knee and looked up at me. "It doesn't surprise me. She called in a favor after she withdrew from school. She was out of money."

"We never asked her how she got the job," I said. "Why didn't we ask her?"

"What does it matter?" Sam asked. "She went to work for Louella after the rape. It had no bearing on the investigation."

They were three steps behind me. I needed them to catch up. I heard myself. Rapid fire speech. I couldn't sit down. They thought I was crazy. Unhinged. Too close to it.

"Gus," I said. "Louella Holmes signed the bottom of this letter. She stamped it. Dated it. She was the only one making hiring decisions for the school. The only one who ever interviewed new hires."

"I get that, but ..."

"No!" I cut him off. "You don't get it. Don't you see? You interviewed Louella. I interviewed Louella multiple times."

"Right," Sam said. "But Louella wasn't a witness in this case. Neveah didn't start working for her until after the rape. She didn't know Louella until after the rape."

"She lied! They both lied. Web lied to Louella about how he knew Neveah. And Louella lied to you about how she came to hire Neveah," I said, feeling like my head was about to pop off.

"You just said you never asked Neveah how she got the job," Gus said. "Neither did I. It wasn't relevant."

"No, not Neveah. Gus. Louella lied. I was there when you questioned her in the hospital after Neveah died. Remember? You showed her a picture of Margolis. She said she didn't know him. Said she'd never seen him before."

"Maybe it slipped her mind," Gus said. "She was pretty upset when we spoke. She'd just gotten the news Neveah died."

"Gus, you asked her if she knew Web Margolis and she lied. She acted like she had no idea who he was. We thought it was nothing. There were no calls to Web to or from Neveah's phone. Her landlords said they hadn't seen Margolis anywhere around in the months before Neveah died."

"Mara," Gus said. "Margolis was cleared. We've been over this. He was out of the country when Neveah died. Where are you going with this?"

I went back to the stack of papers on the desk. Thumbing through, I handed Gus and Sam another matching set.

"I did some digging," I said. "Maumee Valley Montessori is a community-based, private non-profit. She runs completely on donations. I found the list of her major donors going back the last five years. Look who's on it."

They read together.

"Mar-Bradley Logistics," I said. "That's Web's company. Look! He's responsible for almost a hundred thousand dollars in donations over the last five years. I found this too."

I handed them a copy of the photograph I found from the local paper three years ago. It was a benefit held for M.V.M.

She stood in the center of a group of her major donors at a ribbon cutting for the new ADA-compliant playground.

"Third row, fourth from the left," I said. "That's Web Margolis. He was at the event. He contributed ten thousand dollars to the playground project alone."

"Why the hell would she lie about it?" Sam asked. "You found all this out in what, an hour?"

"Just about," I said.

"So why the hell didn't that son of a bitch tell me all this when I interviewed him?" Gus said.

"You didn't ask," I said. "That's not a criticism. Like you said, Louella didn't hire her until after the rape. He had an alibi the day Neveah died. He told you he helped Neveah out when he could. You didn't ask for specifics about anything that took place after Sizemore raped her. Why would you?"

"Mara," Sam said. "You're right about all of this. But so what? Web Margolis hasn't committed any crimes related to Neveah Ward."

"No," I said. "But something doesn't add up. Why would Louella Holmes lie about all of this? Why tell you she didn't know Web?"

"She was pretty upset the day I interviewed her," Gus said. "As I recall, she could barely get through it."

"Right," I said. "Because she was grieving for Neveah. It was a shock. They were close. That was all understandable at the time. But what if that wasn't all that was upsetting her? What if she was scared you'd start poking into her business?"

They were still giving me that look. Like they were simply humoring me by listening to all of this.

"You have to re-interview her," I said. "You have to bring Louella in and find out why she lied about her relationship with Web Margolis."

"I don't like that she lied either," Gus said. "But again, Margolis isn't a suspect in any crime. His contributions to M.V.M. were legal. Her acceptance of his contributions was legal. She's running a Montessori school, not a brothel."

"Gus, please," I said. "This wasn't just something that slipped her mind. She was afraid. For some reason, she didn't want you to connect her to Web Margolis or the fact that Margolis connected her with Neveah. Maybe it's nothing. Maybe you're right. She was just traumatized and panicked at the moment. But we have to talk to her again. I told Sam, I saw Web Margolis with Claire Sizemore yesterday. They were intimate. Not in a romantic way necessarily, but their body language told me they're more than just acquainted. We need to know what's going on."

"What's Kenya's take on all of this?" Gus asked.

There was a knock on Sam's door. Another detective poked her head in. Her eyes darted to me, then back to Sam. "Hey, Lieutenant, can I borrow you for a couple of minutes? Sorry to interrupt."

Sam gripped the chair arms and pushed himself up. "I'll be back. Don't do anything nutty for the next few minutes. We'll figure this all out."

He closed the door behind him.

"What do you think happened?" Gus asked. "You've got a theory. Let's hear it."

"I don't know," I said. "But I'm trying to follow the money. Take a look at this donor list. Is there anyone else that raises any red flags for you?"

Gus looked back down at the list I'd given them. Some of the biggest names in the state had contributed to M.V.M. over the years.

He stared at it, eyes narrowed, hunched over.

"Anything?" I asked.

"I don't know," he said. "This name here. The Brunell Corporation. It's familiar. Google it for me, would you?"

I did. "It's incorporated in Delaware," I said. "That's not surprising. It's listed as a wholly owned subsidiary of another corporation, Daltmon Media. When I pull that up, there's a list of another of their wholly owned subsidiaries. PeachWorks."

Gus's head snapped up. "PeachWorks? Are you sure?"

"Yeah," I said, sliding the screen around so he could see.

"Brunell is owned by Daltmon Media. Daltmon Media also owns PeachWorks," he said. "You're sure about that?"

"Well ... yeah," I said again. "Gus, what is it?"

"We keep a LEO profile," Gus said. He grabbed his cell phone and punched something in.

"What now?"

"LEO," he said. "It's code for Law Enforcement Officers. We keep a dummy profile on a bunch of different apps and websites to monitor for criminal activity. Look."

He turned his phone so I could see the screen. As he did, the MOCA dating app started to load. Just below the progress bar at the bottom, I saw what had caught his attention. The PeachWorks Company logo.

"PeachWorks owns MOCA," I said.

"And the company that owns PeachWorks gives money to Louella Holmes's school," I said. "To the tune of at least a quarter of a million dollars over the last five years. Gus ..."

"Yeah," he said. "I know. I need to have another conversation with Louella Holmes."

"Gus," I said. "Hurry."

He nodded. He took his phone back.

"I was just there," I said. "At M.V.M. That's where I saw the personnel file. Louella wasn't there today. One of her aides said she was out with a root canal. You'll have to try her at home. Do you know where she lives?"

"I can find out in about two seconds."

"I want to go with you," I said. "I want to hear what she has to say."

"No way," he said. "Right now, you're a civilian on this."

"She trusts me," I said. "If you march up her driveway, she might get suspicious. We want her at ease. Let her think this is just some benign follow-up visit. She already knows the investigation into Neveah's death is officially closed."

Gus let out a low grumbling noise. But I knew he was about to say yes. Or would have. Sam walked back into his office, his expression grim.

"Good," he said. "I'm glad you're still here. You too, Gus. You should hear this."

Sam was holding a set of papers in one hand. In the other, he held my phone.

"You got the forensics back?" I asked, my throat going dry.

He nodded. "Mara," he said. "Someone's been tracking you."

"What?"

"What?" Gus chimed in.

"Tracking me?" I asked. "Tracking what?"

Sam straightened and met my eyes. "Everything, Mara. Absolutely everything."

34

"When did you get this phone?" Sam asked. I sank back down into the chair opposite his desk. Sam sat perched at the edge of the desk, his face stern. I wasn't his friend now. Nor his colleague. I was a potential crime victim.

"Last year," I said. "It's been almost exactly a year."

"Who else has access to it?" he asked.

"It's either in my purse or briefcase. But it sits on a charger in the kitchen or my nightstand. Or on my desk at work. I mean, it's my phone. I always have it."

"Do you have a housekeeper?" Gus asked.

"No," I said.

"What about Kat?" Sam asked. "Jason's sister. Mara, she stays with you sometimes, right?"

"You think Kat tampered with my phone? She wouldn't."

"She's Jason's sister," Gus said. "Who knows what she'd do?"

"I know," I said. "Kat's not some mole for Jason."

"Would she know your passcode?" Sam asked. "Would anyone?"

"No," I said. "I've never shared my passcode with anyone. Not even Jason. And I change it every few months. Sam, what's on here? What exactly did you find?"

"A tracking app was installed on your phone sometime in the last year. We're not able to pin down exactly when yet. Still working on that part. It's hidden so you wouldn't see an icon or anything. The thing just operates in the background."

"Where would someone get something like that?" I asked.

"They're readily available," Sam said. "A quick google search is all it takes. There are dozens of them. Though this one is pretty high end. It's tracking more than just your location. There's a feature on it that can record you."

"When I'm on a call?" I asked. Icy tendrils of panic snaked their way through my core. Someone had been listening to my phone conversations. For as long as a year.

"Yes," Sam said.

I tried to let it sink in. It was too much. Too big.

"Jason," I said quietly. "You think this was Jason?"

"Maybe," Sam said. "Let's not get ahead of ourselves though. He isn't the only person who would stand to gain something from recording your private conversations."

"Neveah," I said. "I told you. Nobody knew when I was planning to put her on the stand."

"You said from the beginning the way you found her felt like a message," Gus said. He started to pace. Fists balled. "They knew. Those sons of bitches knew you were on your way to pick her up. You were the last phone call she had."

"We don't know that for sure either," Sam said. "But if it's something to do with cases you're working on, then you've maybe got someone in your office who had access to your phone. It wouldn't take much. Even thirty seconds before your lock screen triggers. Someone could have picked it up and installed this without knowing your passcode."

"Adam," I whispered. "Remember Adam Skinner?"

"The creepy intern?" Gus asked. "The one you had working with you on the Emmons case last year?"

"He tried getting overfamiliar," I said. "Then he more or less threatened me with a phony sexual harassment claim. It went nowhere. Kenya fired him. But yes, if you're looking for someone in my office with a potential ax to grind against me, he'd be one. But no one's seen or heard from him in months. He's gone. Out of Maumee County somewhere."

"Still," Sam said. "We need to have a conversation with him. Gus, consider yourself assigned to this case."

"Good," he said. "Mara, I need to talk to everyone. Including Jason and your ex-sister-in-law."

"Lord," I said. "I get it. I do. It's just the timing couldn't be worse. Jason's going to accuse me of drumming this all up. I'm supposed to produce Will to Judge Small's chambers on Monday afternoon. He's supposed to give testimony about who he wants to live with."

I started to shiver, but not from the cold. Rage like I'd never felt began to bubble up.

Jason.

Was he capable of this? Would he have violated my privacy in this way to serve his own ends?

"Doyle Stratton, remember I told you Jason's lawyer knew about the rock through my window," I said. "You were the person I called first, Sam. I explained to you on the phone exactly what happened. Jason shouldn't have known about that when I went to court the next day. It wasn't public. But he knew."

Sam met my eyes. "I'm sorry," he said. "If this was Jason, we're going to find out. That's a promise."

I shook my head. "He's not stupid enough to leave his fingerprints on this if it was him. You won't be able to connect it to him. I know it. I didn't know him well enough to think he was capable of something like this. But he's cunning. Ruthless. I just never thought he'd direct any of that to hurt me. No. If this is Jason, we'll never find a direct path to him."

As I said it, I knew in the deepest part of my heart it was true. But I knew something else too. No matter what happened, I was not bringing Will to court on Monday.

35

The next day, with Will contentedly working on a new *Titanic* puzzle in his room, I called Jeanie on my brand-new phone and filled her in on the tracking device Sam found on my old phone.

"He's sure?" she asked. "Someone's been recording every phone call?"

"He's sure the app had the capability of doing that, yes. They're going to want to question Jason. I'm telling you right now, I will not subject Will to Judge Small's questioning on Monday. Not until this is resolved."

"Then he'll hold you in contempt," she said. "You run the risk of Small deciding to grant Jason's custody motion outright."

"Not if I can prove Jason was behind bugging me."

"I can't believe I'm saying this," she said. "But you better hope it was Jason behind it. The minute Stratton gets wind of this, first he's going to vehemently deny his client had anything to do with it. Second, he's going to use it as further proof that your home isn't a safe environment for Will. This has the potential of backfiring in a very big way."

"What would you have me do?" I shouted. "I'm not giving Will up. I'm not letting Jason anywhere near him until I find out whether he's behind this. I don't care if I have to pack a bag and disappear for a while with him. I will protect my son."

"Just ... just calm down. It won't come to that. I just need some time to think and to come up with a plan. And you need to quit telling me you're ready to break the law. I need a promise from you, Mara. You're not going to violate any court orders for the next thirty-six hours. Okay?"

When I didn't immediately answer, Jeanie yelled. "Okay?"

"Fine," I said through tight lips. "Thirty-six hours though. If the rules don't apply to Jason, they don't apply to me either. I know what's best for Will."

"You know, this would be a lot easier if Jason were a shitty dad on top of the rest of it."

"Not something I want to wish for, Jeanie," I said.

"I know. Just let me go do my job. I'll figure something out. In the meantime, be careful, okay? This phone bugging thing is dangerous stuff."

There was a knock on the door. I walked to the kitchen and tapped the panel on my brand-new alarm. Sam recommended an upgrade to it after the rock incident. I had cameras installed all the way up to the road.

"I'll talk to you later, Jeanie," I said. "And if I haven't said it before or enough, thank you."

"Yeah, yeah," she said, brushing me off. Then she ended the call. On the monitor, Sam stood on my front porch, smiling for the camera.

"Please tell me you have good news," I said, swinging the door wide to let him in. Sam was still in uniform. My eyes went to the Nine he kept holstered on his right side.

"Nothing new on the tracker app," he said. "Forensics lab is working on getting me their official, full report. We'll go from there when I get it. In the meantime, we tracked down Adam Skinner, your ex-intern. He's living in Fort Myers Beach, Florida and working as a bartender."

"Was he questioned?" I asked.

"Not yet," Sam said. "The phone forensics guys think they might be able to give me a better window of time for when that tracker was put on your phone. They need twenty-four hours."

"You didn't have to come all this way to tell me that," I said. "Thank you though."

It was then I realized Sam was doing more than paying me a courtesy visit. He stood in the kitchen, his eyes darting over the room. He was casing the joint.

"What is it?" I asked.

"I don't want you to freak out, but I'd like to send a crew out here to do a bug sweep. If someone went to the trouble to bug your phone ..."

"You think they've bugged my house?" I felt sick. Dizzy. I gripped the side of the nearest kitchen chair.

"I don't think so," Sam said. "But I want to be sure. Is Will here now?"

"He's up in his room," I said. "Sam, this can't happen with him here. He's too smart. He'll know exactly what your guys are looking for."

"So we'll do it when you have him out of the house. Can you take him out for ice cream or something? If you can give me two hours tomorrow afternoon, I can give you peace of mind."

"Of course," I said. " I know it's a Saturday but can they do it today? I'm taking Will to a friend's house in an hour. He'll be gone until probably four o'clock."

"Perfect," Sam said. "I'll make it happen. And it's just a precaution. Don't worry."

Sam's phone rang. As he pulled it out, I saw his caller ID. It was Gus.

"What do you have?" Sam asked. He narrowed his eyes and turned away from me. He spoke softly into the phone so I couldn't hear.

I waited a few agonizing moments for him before Sam turned around and came back to me.

"What's going on?" I asked.

"Well," Sam said. "Web Margolis is in the wind. He left town on his private jet the day before yesterday. His assistant either doesn't know or isn't saying where he's gone or when he'll be back."

"Great," I said.

"But," Sam continued. "Gus has talked to Louella Holmes. She's agreed to come back down and answer a few questions. He wants you to listen in. Can you make it?"

"Of course," I said.

I went to the stairs and called up to Will. "Buddy! Change of plans. I've got an appointment so I need to take you to Ben's now. Can you be ready in five?"

"I'm ready now," he yelled down, sounding excited.

I looked at Sam. "Just let me get our coats."

"I'll drive you both," Sam said.

"In your cop car?" Will asked, beaming as he bounded down the stairs. "Can we use the sirens? Just sayin'."

Sam smiled. "Well, hey, there, kiddo. No sirens. But if you hurry up and put your shoes on, I'll let you work the lights."

36

The first time Gus Ritter interviewed Louella Holmes, he'd done so informally outside David Pham's lab. This time, she sat in the cold, stark, cement-walled interrogation room at the Maumee County Sheriff's Department.

Gus made her wait. It was all part of his interrogation technique. The three of us, Sam, Gus, and I, stood behind the one-way mirror watching as Louella fidgeted in her seat.

"Does she smoke?" Sam asked.

"Not that I've seen," I said. "I can't say I've ever smelled it on her. She does have that look though."

Louella couldn't quite figure out what to do with her hands. She kept folding them and unfolding them at the table. She looked up at the camera in the ceiling, checked her purse. Her phone. She'd get no cell reception in the room.

"Be careful, Gus," I said.

He nodded, checked the clock on the wall, then went in.

Louella sat straighter in her seat and put on a smile as Gus walked in. He held a yellow notepad and left his suit coat off. He smoothed his tie as he sat in front of her.

"Sorry to mess up your day by having you come down here," he said. "I'm just trying to close out all my files on a few things. I'll get you out of here in a jiffy."

"I'm happy to help," she said. "But I've told you and Mrs. Brent everything I know on Neveah. I understand she came to my office. I wish I'd been there to greet her."

"This whole thing has been rough on her too," Gus said. "She got pretty close to Neveah during the rape trial."

"She was easy to get close to," Louella said. "Such a sweet girl. Such a waste."

"Mrs. Holmes," he said. "You didn't have any luck with her father, did you? We've been trying to get a hold of him to pick up the last of Neveah's personal effects. He's been dodging my calls."

"Neveah didn't really want anything to do with him," she said.

"Have you had any luck hiring someone to replace her?" Gus asked. He put the notepad down and took a more casual posture in his chair.

"He's good," I whispered to Sam. Sam nodded.

"Watch this," he said.

"Oh, I haven't even been able to think about that yet," Louella said, her words coming more quick and easy. "I don't suppose I'll ever find anyone as good as Neveah. I mean, I will.

Eventually. It's just so hard. Even the thought of it makes me sad."

"I bet," he said. "She was a real find for you."

Louella nodded. "One of my best hires."

"Lucky you found her," Gus said.

"Yes."

Gus paused. His eyes darted to the wall, making contact with Sam.

"What made you take a chance on her?" Gus asked. He was doing a version of what I would have done on cross-examination if I had her in court. Get her to recommit to the lie.

Louella laid her fingers flat on the table. "You just get a gut feeling about people," she said. "I bet it's like that for you, too. You know. When you work with a rookie. You can tell when people have good instincts. You know it when you see it."

"Sure," he said. "Mara said that too. She said when she witnessed Neveah working with the kids, she was great with them. It's such a shame. How are they handling her death? Your students?"

"Neveah worked with the younger ones. The pre-schoolers. They ask about her from time to time. But I'm not sure many of them really understand the concept of death. They just know she's gone."

"They're resilient," Gus said. "And that was the first time Neveah ever worked with little kids?"

"Oh, I think she babysat. We talked about that at her interview. But that's a world of difference from teaching. I think Neveah would have been a good one."

"She was going back to school to ultimately get a teaching certificate?"

"Right. Detective, what is it that you need from me to close out your files?"

"Oh," Gus said. "Sorry. Right. You said you took a chance on Neveah because of your gut feeling. So she wasn't recommended to you by anyone?"

It was subtle. Just a tiny flickering of her eyelids. But Louella kept her smile in place.

"She had references," Louella said.

"References. Do you recall who those references were? Again, I'm trying to make sure there's no stone I've left unturned in Neveah's circle."

"I don't ... I don't recall," Louella said.

"You don't recall how Neveah thought to apply for a job at M.V.M.?"

"It's been a while," she said.

"Well, it was last year though, right? Wasn't she the last new person you've hired?"

"I guess," Louella said. "Why are you asking me all of this? What difference does it make?"

"Well, I mean, she wasn't interested in teaching or working with kids before she came to you is all. She wanted to go into politics. That was the whole deal why she was taking a class that Denny Sizemore guest lectured. I'm just trying to get a clear sense of how she came to you. You think it was out of the blue?"

"I don't know," she said. Louella pushed her chair back. "I really wish I had more for you. This has been very difficult for me. I took that girl under my wing. I trusted her. You ruled her death an accidental overdose. I had no idea she was using. It meant she was lying to me. Around kids. I really don't have anything more to say."

"You ever seen him?" Gus asked. He slid a picture of Web Margolis across the table. Louella was halfway to standing. She glanced at the photo. Would she lie yet again?

"I don't know. I need to get back."

"Do you know who that is, Louella?" Gus asked.

"She's lying," I whispered to Sam. "She's lying right now!"

"Maybe he's familiar."

"Maybe. You ever see him with Neveah Ward?"

"I never really saw Neveah outside work. Not until that trial started."

"Sit down, Mrs. Holmes," Gus said. "We're not done. I asked you if you know this man."

She sat down and stared hard at Gus.

"How did Neveah Ward come to ask for a job with you, Louella?"

"I don't remember," she said.

"You don't remember." Gus pulled another photo out of the stack in front of him. It was a picture of Neveah. She was dead. She was lying on David Pham's table. Bluish skin, her eyes frozen open.

"Take that away!" Louella cried. "My God. What's the matter with you?"

Gus took another sheet of paper out. It was the recommendation letter I'd pilfered from Neveah's personnel file. He slid it to her and tapped the signature line.

"You gonna tell me you've never seen this document before?"

Louella held her purse in front of her chest like a shield.

"Tell me about Web Margolis," Gus said. "Tell me how you didn't know him. You know your donor records aren't hard to find, Louella."

"A lot of people donate to the school. I'm very fortunate."

"You knew Web Margolis. You knew him well enough to fast-track a recommendation he made to you to hire Neveah Ward."

Nothing. She just stared at him.

"You didn't run a background check on Neveah, did you? You didn't run a drug test. There was no record of it at all in this file."

"I trust my instincts," she said.

"I talked to Aimee Peterson. She was hired two years ago. She told me she had a background check before she started working for you. Why didn't you run one on Neveah?"

"That's good," I whispered to Sam. "That's really good. I didn't even think to ask that."

"I have to go," Louella said. Tears filled her eyes. She trembled.

"Look at this," Gus said, shoving the autopsy photo of Neveah back under Louella's nose. "This is what they did to her. Take a good, hard look. This is what they do to people who don't play the game. Is that what you're afraid of?"

"You can't do this," she said. "I'm not under arrest."

"You're right," he said. "You're free to go if you'd like. But how long do you think it's going to be before another girl stops playing by the rules? Neveah loved you. She said you were like a mother to her. She trusted you, Louella."

"Stop. Just stop it. I did everything I could for that girl!"

"You sure you were doing it for Neveah? Or were you doing it for whoever pays your bills?"

"It's not like that!"

"What's it like? You lied about knowing Web Margolis. Why?"

"I haven't done anything wrong," she said.

"Why did you lie about knowing Web Margolis? He sent Neveah to you. Why you? I'm going to find out. Like you said. You have a long list of donors. I plan on hauling every single one of them in here. What else do you do for men like Web Margolis?"

Louella didn't answer. Her face filled with contempt.

"She was in trouble," Gus said. "Real trouble. Neveah trusted you. She thought you were someone she could confide in. She thought you were different. Now look where she is."

"No," Louella cried. "No. I wasn't part of that. I tried to take care of Neveah. Tried to help her build something with her life. She was good. She was great."

"Web Margolis told you to hire her after Denny Sizemore raped her. And when Web asked you to do something, you did it, isn't that right?"

Her lip quivered. Louella Holmes folded into herself. "No," she whispered. "No, no, no, no."

"What else has Web Margolis asked you to do?"

Her head snapped up. "I didn't kill that girl. Is that what you think?"

"I think you know a hell of a lot more than you've been telling me and Mara Brent. And I think what you know might have saved Neveah's life."

"No," she said. "I don't know anything. I've never known anything. That's not what this is."

"So what is it?"

"I have to make a phone call," she said.

"You're not under arrest. Not yet, anyway. But you might be."

"For what?"

"Obstruction of justice comes to mind." Gus was bluffing. He was right. So was I. There was something Louella was hiding. And it was eating her alive.

"I didn't know, okay? I didn't know they would do this. I didn't know they would hurt that girl."

"Who are they, Louella? Web Margolis?"

Her eyes widened.

"She's dead," Gus said. "Did they put a needle in her arm? Is that what happened?"

"I don't know!" she shouted. Gus tapped the image of Neveah again.

"Look at her," Gus said. "Really look at her!"

Tears streamed down Louella's face.

"Did you know this was going to happen?" he asked.

"I told you. I didn't know. I didn't know. I didn't know! I told her to be careful. I told her. I warned her."

Gus sat back. My breath caught. She knew. My God. She knew.

"What did you warn her about, Louella?"

"You can't. You don't know."

"So tell me. I know you didn't want this to happen. I know you tried to protect Neveah. She trusted you. But she didn't listen to you, did she?"

"No," Louella cried. "You're the ones she trusted. She was so certain. I tried to tell her to leave town. I was so scared for her."

"You wanted her to drop the rape case. Recant. But she wouldn't, would she?"

Louella just shook her head. Sobbing, she pulled the picture of Neveah closer. She picked it up and held it to her breast. She rocked back and forth.

"You can help her now," Gus said. "You can't save her, but you can help me make sure Neveah's story gets out. She would want that. You know she'd want that."

"You don't know what you're asking me. You need to let me call one of the mechanics."

The last word. She said it so softly I almost couldn't make it out. The mechanics.

"The mechanics?" Sam and I said it together.

A flicker went through Gus's eyes as I knew he was asking himself the very same question.

"What?" Gus said.

"I need a good mechanic," Louella said through gritted teeth, whispering the word mechanic. Whatever she meant, she thought Gus would understand.

"Let me in there," I said. "Right now."

"No way," Sam said.

"That's a code if ever there was one. Tell her the mechanics can't help her. Tell her she has to write down who they are."

Sam nodded, following my train of thought. "Wait here."

Sam went through the side door. Louella jumped when she saw him. I prayed my gut instinct was right.

"Gus," Sam said. "Can you give us a minute?"

Gus looked bewildered, but played along. He slipped through the door and came to join me.

"A mechanic won't help you this time," Sam told Louella. "Not this time. They've packed up the shop and gone home, Louella. We're on our own."

Her mouth dropped. "You're lying."

"I'm not," he said. "You have to help yourself now. You knew it was always going to come to this. You knew it when they killed Neveah, didn't you?"

She collapsed on the table, burying her face in her hands. "Yes. I knew it. I should have left. I couldn't. How could I leave my children?"

Sam took the pad of paper and slid it across the table to Louella. "Write down as many names as you can remember," he said. "We'll start there. You know Mara Brent. You trust her. So do I. If you come clean now. Right now. Before anyone else knows you're here, it's not too late. You can do something for Neveah now, even if you couldn't when she was still alive."

With tears streaming down her face, Louella nodded. "They promised I'd never be implicated. They promised the school was safe."

"My God," I whispered.

"You better get in there," Gus said. "She needs to see your face."

I walked through the door.

"I think you better tell us who the mechanics are, Louella," I said.

"Then you'll help me?" she asked. "You can cut me a deal?"

"First the names," I said. Neveah's initial statement to Gus thundered in my ears. I'd read the transcript a hundred times. A throwaway line. Something Denny said to her when he kicked her out of his car, bleeding. I'd thought nothing of it. *She'd* thought nothing of it. She thought it actually had something to do with her broken-down car.

Now, I knew it meant everything. He'd told her, "Cheer up, honey. I know the name of a good mechanic."

With her hands trembling, Louella Holmes started to write.

37

"Kat," I said. "I know I don't have the right to ask this. But can you stay with Will tonight? Something's come up at work and I might be here a while. He's over at his friend Ben's house. If you can't, I understand, I'll ..."

"Of course!" Kat said, her voice almost breaking. "Whatever you need. Whatever Will needs. Bree and I were headed to Luigi's. I can pick him up. Would you mind if I had him stay over?"

I squeezed my eyes shut. My love for her flooded my heart. "He would love that," I said. "Thank you. Kat ... I don't know what we'd do without you."

"You will never have to find out," she said. "I'll call Ben's mom and let her know I'm going to be picking him up today instead of you."

"Tell him I'll call him in a few hours," I said. "Kat, he's going to be so happy."

"Good," she said. "Me too. I'll talk to you in a little while, Mara."

I hung up and clutched my phone to my chest. "Can you come back in here?" Sam poked his head out of the interrogation room. "Louella's ready to talk."

I nodded, slipped my phone in my briefcase, and went back in to join them. Louella had written two words in large block lettering at the top of the yellow pad we'd given her.

"The Mechanics."

Gus sat with a casual posture, one leg crossed over the other.

"Tell me how it works," he asked. "From beginning to end, Louella."

"I need immunity," she said. "If you can't offer me protection, then I can't tell you anything."

"I can't offer you anything until I know what you have, Louella," I said. "Who are the mechanics?"

"We already have you for obstruction," Gus said. "You lied to me about your involvement with Web Margolis. Neveah Ward is dead and you know who was involved. Now's the time to help yourself."

She dabbed at her eyes. A few minutes ago, Louella had signed a Miranda waiver. I'd made sure of it. Gus had a small voice recorder pointed at her in the center of the table.

"I don't know them all," she said. "Only a few. Web Margolis, obviously. You have to believe me, all I ever wanted to do was run the school. The rest of it? I just didn't think there would be any harm. They promised me this would never touch me."

"Who promised you?" Gus asked.

"They would fix things," she said. "It was small stuff at first. Local issues. I couldn't get the zoning variance to run the school. Dale Kramer was the mayor back then. I went to him. He said he would help me. That he'd put me in touch with the right people. That's just how it worked back then. If you wanted something done in town, you paid the right people. My cousin Robbie Holmes sat on the planning commission. I came up with the money. He was going to make sure the zoning board did right by me. Only ... they didn't just want money."

"What did they want?"

Louella shredded the tissue in her hands. "It was more and more every time. I needed money to make the playground handicap accessible. To build a ramp. You have no idea what it takes to run a school like I do. There are grants, sure, but it's never enough. And I want M.V.M. to be affordable for all families in Maumee County."

"You've taken in hundreds of thousands of dollars, millions over the past decade," I said. "You've never been short on donors."

"What did they get for their money, Louella?" Sam asked.

"I never asked," she said.

"The playground," Gus said. "That didn't cost hundreds of thousands of dollars. What happened to the rest?"

She stared at the wall.

"You were laundering their money," I said. "Your donors were Ohio power players. Big business. Well-connected people. What did their money buy?"

"I was never involved in that," she said. "I gave them a private meeting space. That's about as hands on as I ever got."

"The mechanics," Gus said. "Who were they?"

"Fixers," she said. "I don't know all they did."

"But you know some," Gus said.

"I know some. A few years ago, Dale Kramer got pulled over out of state for drunk driving. It was when he was running for state senate. I don't know what they did. Who got bribed, but there was a meeting in the event room in the north wing of the school. The Kramer family made a fifty-thousand-dollar donation when we needed a new roof and upgraded electrical. My accountant took care of all of that."

"His name," Gus said.

She wrote it down.

"There were two sets of books," she admitted.

"The one you filed with the IRS, the other was for payoffs to the mechanics, is that it?"

She nodded, tears streaming down her face.

"What do you know about what happened to Neveah?"

She took a breath. "I got a call from Web Margolis. It was a couple of days after Neveah reported Denny Sizemore had raped her. The story broke in the news. I couldn't believe it. Denny was ... Denny has always been protected. The things he's done to Claire."

"Who was protecting him?" Gus asked.

"I can't tell you a specific name. But I'd get a check. I would give it to the accountant. Then there would be a request for a meeting. They had master keys to the building. That was one of the terms. I wasn't supposed to ask questions. So I didn't. But there was a doctor they would bring in. I saw it once. I came back to my office late one night. I didn't know anyone would be there. Oh, the screams. I thought they were killing Claire Sizemore. They had her in one of the classrooms. She had broken fingers and this doctor, um ... Turner, his name was Turner. He was from out of town somewhere. Sandusky, I think. I don't know what they had on him to get him to do that. But he set that poor woman's bones and they only gave her rum to numb the pain. Another time, it was stitches. See, she could never go to a hospital. They'd have to report Denny for domestic violence if she did that."

"What about Neveah?" I asked.

"Web told me he needed me to hire her. He said I should just keep an eye on her. Let him know if she said anything about her involvement with Sizemore. She never did. Not to me. She was a good girl. But I knew."

"What did you know?" Gus asked.

"I knew they were never going to let her testify against Denny. They were watching her. Web thought working for me would appease her. And they thought I'd be able to persuade her to come to her senses. I tried. I tried to tell her."

"What did you tell her?" I asked, my stomach churning.

"I told her she had to play their game. That I was worried about what would happen if she crossed the wrong people.

But she wasn't afraid. She was never afraid! She thought once everyone heard her story in court, there'd be nothing Denny could do to her. I'm so sorry. I started to think she was right. She said they had his DNA. That there was no way he could deny what happened. I wanted her to be right. I really did."

"Do you know who killed her?" Sam asked.

She shook her head. "I don't know his name. Two nights before Neveah died, a big check came in. That's when I knew. There have only been two other times I got a donation that big. Both times, a day or two after, I'd read something in the news and then I'd know."

"What did you know?"

"Do you remember when Judge Booker down in Athens County wrapped his car around a telephone pole? It was just before he was going to trial on a major drug dealer. The new judge threw out the case. Then the other time, this star witness in the fraud case against Leeman Construction turned up dead of a drug overdose. They brought this thug in from Cleveland. Both times. He met with them in the basement the night of our annual Christmas party."

"Do you have a name? A description?"

"I could pick him out of a line-up," she said. "You can't mistake the guy for anyone else. He's maybe six foot five and has a tattoo of an eagle on his right forearm."

"Who's they?" Gus asked.

"The mechanics," Louella said, exasperated. "Denny's one. Dale Kramer. I told you that. There's the accountant, his name is George Murphy. Doctor Turner from Sandusky.

There are a few more. I'll write down what I can. But you have to promise. You have to protect me."

"Can I speak to the two of you out in the hall?" I said to Sam and Gus.

Without a word, they followed me out. I felt like my head was going to pop off.

"My God," I said. "This is bigger than my powers. She's talking about potential federal crimes. We'll need someone from the U.S. Attorney's office down here."

"We can't let her leave," Sam said. "Someone is going to figure out where she is. We brought her in through the front door. Christ. A civilian clerk, a maintenance man. Somebody's seen her. If we let her go home, she's going to be dead by morning."

"And we don't offer witness protection at the county level," I said. "The best you can do is keep her here. I need to make a call."

"You need to make several," Sam said. "I need to get a hold of somebody I trust at the FBI."

"Get a warrant for Murphy the accountant," I said. "Get him into custody as fast as you can or he's going to disappear. If he can corroborate any of this ..."

I looked through the window. Now that Louella Holmes had unburdened herself, she was smiling at me. Smiling.

I wanted to wrap my arms around her neck and squeeze the life out of her. For Neveah.

38

"You're sure?" Sam asked me. It was hours later, after dark on Saturday night.

"I'm sure," I said. "I want to see it. I need to see it."

He wasn't happy. I knew everything I'd asked him went against protocol.

"You're going to sit in this van," Sam said, tight-lipped. "I don't care what you see or hear. You don't move. If Deputy Craig tells you to do something, you do it. You don't come out until I come and get you. Got it?"

"Got it," I said. Deputy Sergeant Craig was Belinda Craig. She'd been with the Maumee County Sheriff's Department for twenty-four years. One of the most senior field ops officers, I knew Sam trusted her with my life.

"Don't worry about us," Belinda said. "You just make sure they get in and out quickly. I got a bad feeling about this guy."

Once Louella started talking, she couldn't stop. She warned Gus and Sam that George Murphy wasn't going to go quietly.

He leaned into the mild-mannered accountant role by day. In his private life, he was the most serious of doom-preppers. She said he bragged about it all the time.

Sam closed the van door. Belinda had a headset on. She'd hear everything that happened but from three blocks away and translate it for me.

My heart thundered behind my ribs. This should be easy. Routine. The SWAT team had quietly cleared a block radius around George Murphy's two-story house on McLain Street. Another block over, this would be Chatham Township.

"They're moving in," Belinda said. "First team's got eyes on the front door. Three more guys in back."

I said a prayer.

"What if he sees them coming?" I asked.

She put a finger up to her lips.

"Decoy's knocking on the front door now," she said. The team had decided to send in an officer dressed as a delivery guy. If they could just get Murphy to come to the door, this would end quickly.

"He's not answering," Belinda said. "But they see movement inside the house."

I collapsed my hands together and pressed them to my forehead. If someone got hurt. If someone else died ...

"He's coming to the door," Belinda said.

Then she said nothing for the most agonizing thirty seconds of my life.

"No," Belinda said, her tone sharp. "No. Dammit. He's moved further into the house."

"They have to identify themselves," I said.

"They just did," she said. "Hold on. Shit. He's trying to run to the back of the house."

"If they kill him ..."

"They're going in," she said. "Hang on, Mara."

I waited. I prayed. I heard shots fired. I sat up and Belinda grabbed my arm.

"Stay put," she said. "Just stay put. The suspect is secured. They've got him in custody. They're doing a sweep of the house. It's going to take a while."

My heart started beating again. Belinda took off her headset just as someone pounded on the van door. She opened it. Sam stood there, sweat pouring down his face. He was out of breath.

"We've got him," he said. "He tried to put up a fight. He's got a pretty sophisticated computer room so they're being very careful. It's likely he's got it booby-trapped."

"We can't lose that evidence," I said.

"We won't. Come on."

He held a hand out for me. I stepped out of the car. I followed Sam around the corner just as George Murphy was led out of his front door in handcuffs. Unshaven, wearing a dingy tee shirt with a rip at the collar. I realized that might have happened during the arrest.

He saw me. He froze. He knew who I was.

"Mara," Sam said.

It was so hard to keep my prosecutor hat on. I wanted to be Neveah's friend.

"We're all clear," someone shouted from the front door. I recognized him as one of the computer forensics detectives and relief flooded through me.

"Come on," Sam said. "You can ride back to the station with me. I just got a text from Special Agent Monroe out of the FBI field office in Toledo. I caught him out of town. But he'll be here in a few hours."

"Do you trust him?" I asked.

"I do."

George Murphy came down the sidewalk toward us. He was sheet white and terrified. He dug his heels into the pavement, as if that might slow them down. Tears streamed down his face and he whimpered.

"Good lord," Sam said. "He's a mess."

When Murphy came near me, he stopped dead. Frozen. Behind him, three deputies came out carrying plastic totes.

"He's got reams and reams of paperwork and ledgers in a basement office. It was hidden behind the staircase. That's where our guys fished him out."

"Hopefully, it'll have high value," I said. He was staring at me. Bloodshot eyes. Where a moment ago, I'd seen terror. Now, George Murphy's mouth curved into a smile.

Oh yes. He definitely knew who I was.

"Mara, come on," Sam said. He saw the look on Murphy's face.

"Wait," I said. I walked up to him. Blocked his path.

"You've read him his rights?" I said to one of the deputies.

"Yes, ma'am," he answered.

"Did you know?" I asked. "Did you arrange it?"

"Mara!" Sam said. He grabbed me by the elbow.

All traces of fear left Murphy. If anything, he seemed relieved at the sight of me. It unsettled me deeply. He kept his eyes locked on mine. Then, Murphy actually winked at me.

"Mara!" Sam shouted. The deputies pushed Murphy forward and got him in a patrol car. He'd have a long night ahead of him.

"Has he asked for a lawyer yet?" I said to Sam, feeling rage churning in my heart.

"I want you to go home," he said. "Get some sleep. If Murphy does or says anything you need to know about, I'll call you."

I turned to him, gearing up to protest.

"Go home, Mara," he said. "It's safe for you there. The bug sweep came back clean. I've got this. And you need to be there when Will wakes up."

Will. God. It was well past time. I should have been home. After midnight. Sunday morning. Tomorrow, I was supposed to bring him to court.

"Okay," I said. "But I'll be back at the station by seven. And you promise me. If there's anything."

"I promise," Sam said.

I believed him. As I turned to leave, George Murphy met my eyes from the back of the patrol car.

He was smiling at me. He mouthed two words. I could have been wrong. Maybe I was just too keyed up to think straight. But it looked like he'd just said, "You're next."

39

Will was too snuggled up in Bree and Kat's guest room to move him. I watched him for a moment though. The angelic rise and fall of his chest as he clung to the plush Sherpa blanket Bree found for him. Rollie, her new Aussiepoo, slept at the foot of the bed, snoring. The puppy gave me a tongue-curling yawn as I leaned over and kissed my son on the forehead.

"Can you even stand the cuteness of it?" Kat whispered as I walked with her back to the kitchen. Bree had poured me a glass of red wine.

"Bless you," I said as I took it from her. She'd just got home herself after a double shift at the hospital. She was still in pink scrubs with her wheat-blonde hair pulled back. Kat came behind her, rubbing her shoulders.

"Rollie's in love with him," Bree said.

"It's mutual," Kat said. "It was a real love fest earlier. Lots of hugs and kisses. Will's training him to walk on a leash properly."

"I'm glad," I said. "Except he's going to start begging me for a dog."

"He doesn't have to," Bree said. "He talked himself into a job offer. I'm working afternoons for the next few months. Will's going to come over after school and walk Rollie for me. Six bucks a pop for thirty dollars a week. If ... um ... if that's okay with you."

I laughed. "He came up with the plan on his own?"

"Sure did," Bree said, sipping her wine. "My original offer was four bucks a day. His counter was seven and we settled in the middle. I told him I'd pay him a ten-dollar-a-week bonus if he picked up the lawn brownies too. He said he'd think about it. Just sayin'."

I laughed. "Thank you. That'll be great for him."

"It's great for me too," Bree said. "Rollie? That dog poops like it's his job. Ten bucks is a bargain."

The wine hit. Bree and Kat must have read something on my face.

"Mara," Kat said. "Stay here tonight. We've got a whole other guest room that never gets used. We can all go out for breakfast in the morning. Will loves the blueberry pancakes they make at Polly's Diner over on Eighth Street. That way, you can have another glass of wine."

I was about to protest. Say it was too much and I didn't want to put them out. Bree reached across the table and touched my hand.

"We're all family, Mara," she said. It was then I noticed the diamond ring on her finger. My heart lifted. I grabbed her hand and brought the ring into the light.

"Seriously? When? How?"

"Kat proposed last week," Bree said. "It's a story."

"We haven't set a date yet," Kat said. She put her own hand out and I saw the matching diamond on her finger. It was beautiful.

"We're waiting until after things ... settle," Bree said.

Things. I almost asked her what things. But I knew. We were a family. Yes. A dysfunctional one at the moment, thanks to Jason and me.

"You've put your life on hold enough for us, Kat," I said. "You two should set the date that makes you happy."

"We will," Bree said, smiling up at Kat.

"Does Will know?" I said.

Kat shook her head. "Not yet. Soon. When things are ..."

"Stop," I said. "You're doing it again. You deserve to be happy and to share your news."

"We will," Bree said. "Promise."

I was happy. But exhausted. Bree and Kat could read it on my face. The second time they asked me to use their guest room that night, I said yes.

It was good. Perfect, actually. This was a happy home filled with love and laughter. I could forget about Jason. I could forget about Neveah Ward. Just for a few hours.

40

Pancakes with Kat, Bree, and Will filled my soul. He talked a mile a minute.

"We're going to go to the Field Museum in Chicago and see Sue," he said. "She's a replica of the largest, most intact T-Rex ever found."

Will rattled off a whirlwind of dino statistics after that. Bree did little figure eights with her head, trying to keep up with him.

"Chin up," Kat whispered to her. "We're taking it as a positive trend. He's starting to move away from disaster obsessions."

"There is one theory that the K-Pg extinction actually killed most of the dinosaurs in one day. Can you imagine the destruction? The carnage?"

I hid my laugh behind the hand as I held my fork.

"Soot and ash!" Will said as he raced to keep up with Bree after we paid the bill. "They all suffocated, is what this guy on Radiolab said. Just sayin'. I can send you a link."

"I'll listen on my way to work," she promised.

I hugged Kat at the car. "Thank you," she said. "Just ... thank you."

"He doesn't know about tomorrow," she said, and I knew it wasn't a question.

"I'm working up to it," I said. "Give him a couple of hours for the sugar rush from the blueberry syrup to wear off. Then I'm going to talk to him."

"I'll be there, Mara," she said. "Just like I promised. I'll pick him up from school. He'll get through it. We'll all get through it."

There was nothing left I could say. I hugged Kat one more time. I hugged Bree. Then I piled Will into the car and drove him home.

"Will," I said as we pulled into the garage. "I'm going to need to talk to you about something in a little while, okay?"

He already knew something. The moment we left the restaurant, Will became pensive, staring out the window. Gone was the happy dinosaur chatter.

He knew.

"I didn't take a bath last night," he said. "Can I do that now? Can I take two today?"

"Sure," I said. Baths were how Will reset after he'd been overstimulated. "Just make sure you wipe up the floor and keep the curtain inside the tub."

"I know that," he said. "I'm not a baby, Mom."

"Okay, kiddo," I said. He opened the car door. I was just about to get out myself when another car pulled into the driveway behind me.

Sam. He was driving a county-owned vehicle.

"I'm taking a bath," Will said, cocking his head to the side. It was unlike him. Sam was one of his favorite people. But my son's emotional IQ was off the charts. He saw something in Sam's posture as he got out of his car.

"Hey, buddy," Sam said, raising a hand to wave to him.

"I'll be upstairs," Will said. Then he disappeared inside the house.

I got out of the car and went to Sam's.

"I've been waiting down the road for you," he said.

"We spent the night at Kat's," I said. "You didn't call."

"Mara," he said. "There's something I need to tell you. Special Agent Monroe will be here in about an hour. There's not a lot of time to get through this. But there's enough."

"Sam?" I said, my pulse quickening.

"Will he be okay inside by himself for a little?" Sam asked.

I looked back at the house. "What? Yes."

"Good," he said. "We can talk in my car."

In his car. Away from the security cameras. Out of Will's earshot.

"What's going on?"

I sat in the passenger seat of Sam's cruiser. He shut the door and turned on the ignition. Soft, classical music played through the speakers. Bach. Violin Concerto in D Minor.

After today, I would never be able to hear that piece again without thinking about what Sam Cruz told me over the next ten minutes.

"George Murphy wants to cut a deal," he said. "He gave us everything, Mara."

"Okay?"

"Those ledgers we pulled out of his house? They're his failsafe. Names, dates, locations, bank account numbers for offshore accounts. It's all there. He's naming names. He's corroborated everything Louella Holmes suspected. The mechanics is a vast network of corporate bigwigs like Web Margolis but also state, local, national politicians. A few judges too. And ... there was a records clerk in our office too. She's the one who sold information about Gus saying crap about Sizemore at the Brass Monkey."

"To Simon Pettis," I said. "He was tapped into these mechanics?"

"Yes," Sam said. "Sizemore and Pettis were part of it. Sizemore has been paying bribes for years to get dirt on anyone who runs against him. Murphy can connect the dots to Neveah. You were right. Sizemore hired a hitman to fill her with a lethal dose of fentanyl the morning she was going to testify against him."

"Oh God," I said.

"We've got the name of the contract killer. He's connected to the Russian mob. He's based in Detroit. We can get him."

"How much?" I asked. "How much was Neveah's life worth to Sizemore?"

Sam let out a breath. "Fifty grand."

I felt myself blinking rapidly.

"Why? Why take it that far?"

"Murphy says that was Pettis's strategy after he was brought on board. Sizemore made a faulty assumption about her. She wasn't just some random student he spotted in a class. He had a copy of Professor Perry's class list in advance. Her name was memorable. He knew she was dating Margolis and that she had a profile on MOCA. Murphy says Sizemore thought that made her safe."

"Safe? As in, a good candidate for rape?"

"That she'd know to keep quiet if things got out of hand. Or that the mechanics would take care of it afterwards. These guys were using MOCA to traffic girls for years. Like I said, Sizemore thought she was safe for him. Anyway, that's why he didn't bother taking her inside Chatham Township. He didn't think it would matter."

"But she didn't play by the rules," I whispered. "She reported the rape to the Maumee County Sheriffs. To Gus."

"Yeah," Sam said. "These guys ... the mechanics. Gus isn't in their pocket. Things were set in motion before anyone could do something about it. Before they could silence her. As soon as that rape kit went into the system, they had to let it play out."

"They waited," I said. "God. Sam. They waited until the trial started. Until the jury was sworn in and I called my first witnesses. Pettis knew that was the only way double jeopardy would attach. Once that happened and then Saul shot down Pettis's attempt to get Neveah's sexual history in, that girl had an expiration date."

"Yes," Sam said. "Murphy put it on paper. He was in the meeting with Pettis and Sizemore."

"My God," I said. "You've looped Agent Monroe in? The feds can make a RICO case out of this."

"Not yet," he said. "He doesn't know the specifics of what we have."

There was a brown paper bag on the seat between us. Sam pulled out a thick green ledger.

"What is this?" I asked. But I knew. "Sam? You took this from Murphy? You've broken the chain of custody."

"Mara," he said. "Two of the names in there. Members of the mechanics."

I couldn't breathe.

"Len Grantham, Jason's campaign manager ... and Jason, himself."

No. No. No.

"It goes back to when Jason was working for the Attorney General's office. He sold information on Sizemore's opponents. There was also a woman Jason was seeing. Several, actually. One of them tried to blackmail him a few years ago. Before you found out about the one affair. Grantham paid the mechanics to make her back off. She was a recovering drug addict. Six years sober. They put a needle in her arm too. Didn't kill her, but it was enough to make her spiral into a relapse. Enough to keep her under control."

My whole body shook.

"It's all here," Sam said. "I'm sorry."

"This isn't happening," I said. "This can't be happening."

"He used you," Sam said. "When you were assigned to prosecute Sizemore, the mechanics went to Jason. It turns out he'd paid someone to bug your phone sometime last year. The mechanics called Jason to get access to the data."

"Who?" I asked. "Who did he pay to put that tracker on my phone?"

Sam swallowed. "Adam Skinner. Your former intern."

My vision swam. I needed air.

"Murphy says they knew Jason had the tracker on your phone. They leaned on him to share what he had after you were assigned to the case against Sizemore. Jason cut a deal with them. He gave them access as long as he was able to keep using what he needed from it against you in the custody fight."

I picked up the ledger. "It's in here?"

"Yes," he said.

"Why?" I asked. "Why did you bring this to me? Why here?"

Sam stared at me. "Because Jason's involvement is all there."

I ran my hand over the hard green cover. I couldn't open it.

"Sam?"

"It's your call," he said. "The minute the FBI gets a hold of that, Jason's looking at federal charges. Big ones, Mara. Will might not see him outside of a prison yard until he's well into adulthood. If then."

I dropped the ledger and gripped the dashboard.

"If that ledger doesn't get into Agent Monroe's or anyone else's hands, then ..."

"Don't," I said. "Don't say it."

I fumbled for the door handle. "Will's inside," I said. "I have to ..."

"I have an hour," he said. "Then Monroe gets here. I'll hold on to it that long. You need to tell me what you want me to do."

"Why?" I looked at him. "Why would you do this? Risk your career to tell me this?"

A muscle twitched in Sam's jaw. "Because he's Will's father in spite of everything else."

I nodded, wiping a finger under my eye. I would not, could not cry now. I could not fall apart.

"I'll be at the station waiting for Monroe," he said. "You still have that burner phone we gave you?"

"Yes."

"You text me on it within the hour. Yes or no. Yes, this ledger disappears and nobody knows it ever existed but us. No, and it goes back in with the rest of the evidence I hand over to the FBI. Nobody will ever know we had this conversation. Then you take the battery out of that phone and burn it."

I closed the car door and walked into the house. Will was already out of the tub. He sat in his robe, hair wet, thumbing through an issue of the *Smithsonian* magazine.

I sat beside him. He had soap behind his ear. I grabbed a hand towel and wiped it away.

"I love you," I said.

Will nodded but didn't lift his eyes from the magazine.

One hour. One hour to decide how the rest of my son's life would play out.

"We had fun today," I said.

"Yeah," he said. "Kat and Bree are getting married."

"You knew that?"

"Sure," he said. "You can just tell."

"Are you happy about that?"

He nodded. "Can I call her Aunt Bree?"

"Well, I suppose you should ask her. But I bet she'd like it."

"Uh huh," he said. He turned a page.

"Will, you know how much Dad and I love you. Even if sometimes we can't get along with each other."

"I know that," he said, turning another page.

"Will, baby, I need you to look at me. I need to know you're hearing what I'm saying."

Will put a hand flat on the magazine. He looked at me, eyes solemn. Wise in ways I could not comprehend.

"Something's going to happen, isn't it?" he asked me.

I blew out a breath and smiled.

"Yes," I said. "Yes, baby. It is."

41

Maumee County Domestic Relations Court
Monday
4:00 P.M.

I sat on the bench down the hall from Judge Small's courtroom. I wasn't even supposed to be in the building. Jeanie wanted me to wait back at the house. I could just make out her shape behind the beveled glass to Judge Small's chambers. Small stood near her as a looming black shape in robes.

Lord, the judge would scare Will to death. The man looked too much like Darth Vader with all that billowy black fabric. Will's court-appointed guardian ad litem and the county social worker were in there with Judge Small. Waiting.

The elevator opened. Jason stepped out. He'd just brought Doyle Stratton today. Jason too, was supposed to wait outside the courthouse. I knew he wouldn't. He was Congressman Jason Brent, after all. The rules did not apply.

"Mara," he said, seeing me sitting there.

"Congressman," Doyle said. "If you could ..."

"I'd like to speak to Will's father," I said. "Privately."

I rose when I spoke, locking my gaze with Jason. I was calm. Centered. Every moment of my life with Jason replayed in my mind.

"I'll advise against that," Doyle said. "You're not even supposed to be here."

"Neither are you," I said to Jason, not Doyle. "I need five minutes, Jason."

He tilted his head slightly to the side. I noted the hint of a smile.

"Of course," he said. "Doyle, it's all right."

"Judge Small's jury room is open," I said. "We can go in there. I've already cleared it with his bailiff."

Jason nodded and made a courtly gesture, sweeping his arm to the side. The perfect gentleman. He held the door for me. I caught him winking at Doyle as he closed the door behind him.

He thought he had this under control. Me ... under control. I had come to my senses at last. His King Solomon strategy had worked.

I set my briefcase on the table and pulled out a red file folder. I laid it between us and sat down, folding my hands.

I'd done this a thousand times. Sat across from murderers, thieves, rapists, drug kingpins. And now, I sat across from

Jason Brent. The man I'd once fallen in love with. Planned a life with. Loved. Hated. Had a son with.

"What's going on?" Jason said; just a glimmer of doubt crossed his eyes.

"Later today, a man is going to be charged with Neveah Ward's murder," I said.

Jason narrowed his eyes. "That's ... wow. I thought the locals were saying she died of a drug overdose."

"She did," I said. "That was her cause of death, yes. But it wasn't the *manner* of her death. A man named Leo Roscoe put a needle in her arm against her will. That's an alias, of course. His real name is Rostovich, I'm told. He goes by many other names, too."

Jason gave me a blank nod. "Well, that's good. For you, I mean. I know how connected you were to Neveah. I'm sure that's given you a sense of relief."

I opened the red file and pulled out a grainy photo of Leo Roscoe and slid it across to Jason. He barely glanced at it. Nothing. He gave me nothing. Not a flicker of fear. He was cool. Calm.

"Mr. Roscoe was a paid hitman," I said. "The police believe he's responsible for several other high-profile contract killings across three states."

"Quite a break," Jason said. "It ought to be a boon for your career. Or Kenya's anyway."

"Jason," I said. "Will isn't moving to D.C. with you. You are not winning custody of him."

He sat back and smirked. "I think we're done here. We're going to let Judge Small decide after he's spoken with my son."

"Will isn't here," I said. "He won't be speaking to Judge Small or any other judge about matters involving his parents. Ever."

Jason's eyes narrowed. "You're under a court order to bring him here."

"You never asked me how we found out about Leo Roscoe," I said.

"I don't care," he snapped. "Where is my son?"

"He's home," I said. "My home. Where he belongs. And where he'll stay."

I pulled another stack of papers out of the red file. Sam made me copies of George Murphy's ledger pages and I slid them across the table. Jason looked at them. It took a moment, but he absorbed everything on them. He knew what they meant. It was all there. The dates. The payments. The meetings.

Still, his face betrayed nothing.

"The mechanics," I said. "Fixers, right?"

"What the hell is this?" Jason sneered.

"Our future together," I said.

"Blackmail?" he said. "You're trying to blackmail me? This is bogus. I don't have any idea what this is."

"What this is is enough evidence to put you away for ten to twenty years. You and your boy Len Grantham. Federal prison, Jason."

He still didn't glance down at the papers. But he knew. I wasn't bluffing. His stone-cold expression was all the admission I needed. He knew what those papers would reveal.

"You bitch," he said. "This is your price? Will? I'm his father. My future is your future. His future. You want me to drop the custody case for this?"

I took a beat. Then another.

"It's good that Doyle is here," I said. "He'll tell you not to say anything else. I'm going to advise you the same thing. Right here. Right now. Don't say another word. I'm sure I'll be called to testify against you."

"What?"

"I thought about it, Jason. Because you are Will's dad. He might hate me for this someday. Before he understands it. If he ever understands it. I don't. But the thing is, if I played that card. Blackmail? If I buried the evidence against you, then I'd become one of you. Just another fixer. And someday, some way, somebody's going to find out what I did. And then Will would lose me, too."

"You can go to hell," he said.

"I loved you once," I said. "I really did. And I know you love Will as much as you can love anything. I want that to be enough for his sake. But right now, you need to get ready. Because when you walk out of this courthouse, there will be three U.S. Marshals outside waiting to take you into custody."

"You really hate me that much?" he asked. "You're willing to ruin Will's life? And then what? Trade me in for the coroner? For Pham? That's fitting. You should end up with someone like him. You suck the life out of everyone who tries to get close to you."

I'd never told Jason that David Pham asked me out. Another blow to my chest. He knew because of the tap on my cell phone. I kept my back straight and gathered my things.

When I opened the door, Doyle Stratton burst in and rushed to Jason's side. Jeanie was standing out in the hallway. She had already filled Doyle in on what was about to happen.

"Come on," she said. "We'll scoot out the service exit. Let that bastard make the front page of the paper all by himself."

Jason was screaming at me as I shut the door on him and walked away.

42

One week later ...

A late spring breeze lifted my hair as I walked up the hill to Neveah Ward's grave. The headstone Louella Holmes ordered had finally been placed. She'd chosen looping lilacs engraved in rose-colored stone. I slipped the bouquet I'd brought into the permanent vase beside it.

A shadow passed behind me. "I'm sorry," I said. "I wish I could have protected you better. But maybe you can rest easier now."

I wasn't sure if I could.

I heard someone coming behind me. I turned and shielded my eyes from the setting sun.

"Thought I might find you here," Sam said. "Sizemore and Pettis were arrested about an hour ago. They're bringing charges against Margolis and six others with ties to the mechanics organization within the next few weeks. Murphy and Louella Holmes got their immunity deals. They've turned over everything they have. I thought you'd want to know."

"Thanks," I said. I noticed he held a small bouquet of wildflowers.

"Most of it's going to be tried in Federal Court, but Pettis and Sizemore are facing conspiracy to commit murder charges here in Ohio. Kenya's probably going to want to agree to a change of venue."

"Yes," I said. "Half of our office will probably be called as witnesses." A numb calm came over me. Pettis and Sizemore could face life in prison. Life.

"Another girl came forward," Sam said. "She said Sizemore raped her at a convention in Columbus two years ago. There will be more. This guy's got a pattern. He's going to be held accountable. He's going to pay, Mara."

I hoped wherever she was, Neveah knew. What she'd done mattered. It wasn't in vain.

What I'd done mattered too. Jason's arrest made national news. They'd taken him quietly outside the courthouse. But someone had cell phone footage anyway. The image of him being led away from me in handcuffs would stay with me forever. And with Will.

I sat on the stone bench and stared up the hill. Sam sat beside me. Steady. Strong. My friend.

"Thank you," I said.

"For what?" he asked. "This was you. If you hadn't been such a pain in everyone's ass, this case never would have broken."

"No," I said. "Thank you for giving me the choice about Jason. For Will. I know what that might have cost you."

He stared straight ahead. The wind started to pick up. The sun had nearly disappeared, leaving behind a pink band across the horizon.

"There's a storm coming in," he said. "The weather nerds are calling for two inches of rain."

"Do you think I made the right one?" I asked. "The right choice?"

He looked at me. A curious light played at the corners of his eyes. His lips curved but it wasn't quite a smile.

"What is it?" I asked.

Before he could answer, my phone buzzed with an incoming call. I pulled it out of my back pocket and read the caller ID.

David Pham. Sam saw it too. "I owe him a rain check," I said as the first sprinkling drops fell on my arms. "And here it comes."

"Mara," Sam said. "I was wrong about something."

"What's that?" My phone kept ringing.

"I don't know if you're ready for me, but I don't think I care. And I very much don't want you to answer that phone call."

I looked back down at my screen. In another few seconds, it would go to voicemail.

"My life," I said. "It's about to get even more complicated, Sam. Jason will be indicted. The trial will be big, awful, and messy. I have to figure out how I'm going to make Will understand all of this. And then there's ..."

"Mara, I said I don't think I care," he said, giving me a sheepish smile.

My phone beeped one last time as the call went to voicemail.

"Come on," Sam said. "You can feel the charge in the air. We shouldn't be out in the open like this. I'll walk you out."

We stood. I started to walk with him, then stopped. He turned to face me.

"Sam," I said. "I meant what I said. It's going to get hard. Very hard. For Will. He will always come first for me. Always."

His smile faltered, but he met my eyes. "I know."

"I don't know what's going to happen. If Kat will end up hating me. If she'll even survive losing Jason to prison. Or how Will can handle any of it. But Sam, I don't know if I can do this alone," I said.

He came to me and took my hand. "You won't have to, Mara. That's a promise. And the answer is yes. You did the right thing. And when it's time, you'll make the right choice again."

There was that mysterious light in his eyes. But his hands were warm in mine. Together, we walked back up the hill.

UP NEXT, VOW OF JUSTICE. JUST WHEN CONGRESSMAN Brent's sensational criminal trial gets under way, there's a break in Waynetown's most notorious cold case murder. With

her world crumbling around her, it's up to Mara to bring a killer to justice for good. https://www.robinjamesbooks.com/mara6

UP NEXT FOR MARA BRENT...

Catch more of Mara Brent with her sixth book, Vow of Justice.

https://www.robinjamesbooks.com/mara6

DID YOU KNOW?

All of Robin's books are also available in Audiobook format. Click here to find your favorite! https://www.robinjamesbooks.com/foraudio

NEWSLETTER SIGN UP

Sign up to get notified about Robin James's latest book releases, discounts, and author news. You'll also get *Crown of Thorne* an exclusive FREE ebook bonus prologue to the Cass Leary Legal Thriller Series just for joining.

Click to Sign Up

https://www.robinjamesbooks.com/marabrentsignup/

ABOUT THE AUTHOR

Robin James is an attorney and former law professor. She's worked on a wide range of civil, criminal and family law cases in her twenty-year legal career. She also spent over a decade as supervising attorney for a Michigan legal clinic assisting thousands of people who could not otherwise afford access to justice.

Robin now lives on a lake in southern Michigan with her husband, two children, and one lazy dog. Her favorite, pure Michigan writing spot is stretched out on the back of a pontoon watching the faster boats go by.

Sign up for Robin James's Legal Thriller Newsletter to get all the latest updates on her new releases and get a free digital bonus prologue to Cass Leary Legal Thriller series. http://www.robinjamesbooks.com/newsletter/

ALSO BY ROBIN JAMES

Mara Brent Legal Thriller Series

Time of Justice

Price of Justice

Hand of Justice

Mark of Justice

Path of Justice

Vow of Justice

With more to come...

Cass Leary Legal Thriller Series

Burden of Truth

Silent Witness

Devil's Bargain

Stolen Justice

Blood Evidence

Imminent Harm

First Degree

Mercy Kill

Guilty Acts

Cold Evidence

With more to come...

AUDIOBOOKS BY ROBIN JAMES

MARA BRENT SERIES

Time of Justice

Price of Justice

Hand of Justice

Mark of Justice

Path of Justice

CASS LEARY SERIES

Burden of Truth

Silent Witness

Devil's Bargain

Stolen Justice

Blood Evidence

Imminent Harm

First Degree

Mercy Kill

Guilty Acts

Made in the USA
Las Vegas, NV
08 May 2022

48616550R00204